LOVE LIES BLEEDING

LOVE LIES BLEEDING

Geraldine Evans

Severn House Large Print
London and New York

This first large print edition published in Great Britain 2007 by
SEVERN HOUSE LARGE PRINT BOOKS LTD of
9-15 High Street, Sutton, Surrey, SM1 1DF.
First world regular print edition published 2005 by
Severn House Publishers, London and New York.
This first large print edition published in the USA 2007 by
SEVERN HOUSE PUBLISHERS INC., of
595 Madison Avenue, New York, NY 10022.

British Library Cataloguing in Publication Data

Evans, Geraldine
   Love lies bleeding. - Large print ed.
   1. Rafferty, Joseph (Fictitious character) - Fiction
   2. Llewellyn, Sergeant (Fictitious character) - Fiction
   3. Police - Great Britain - Fiction 4. Detective and
   mystery stories 5. Large type books
   I. Title
   823.9'14[F]

   ISBN-13: 978-0-7278-7598-3

Printed and bound in Great Britain by
MPG Books Ltd, Bodmin, Cornwall.

To George, with love

Prologue

'Look at that daft mare.'

DI Joe Rafferty's chin narrowly missed connecting with the reception counter as Constable Bill Beard grabbed his head-propping arm and inadvertently pulled it from under him.

At the best of times, Beard, the station's self-appointed grey-sage, treated the younger officers who had attained superior rank with an over-familiar *lèse-majesté*. But this, thought Rafferty indignantly, even for Beard, was a *lèse* too far.

But he had hardly got the first word of his protest out before Beard waved his complaint aside much as he might swat away a particularly annoying probationer, pointed the podgy forefinger of his other hand across the reception desk of the police station's entrance and voiced the inviting suggestion, 'Fancy being out of your head at nine in the morning.'

Cajoled away from his annoyance by Beard's proposal, Rafferty murmured, 'Mm,' and expectantly awaited the pleasant chink of bottle against glass.

Chance would be a fine thing, he realised moments later as chinks came there none. Instead, the unpleasant *clunk* of a cold Monday morning on sober duty impinged on his unwilling psyche.

Breathing out on a disappointed sigh, his gaze followed Beard's pointing digit and he peered, squint-eyed, through the rain-lashed glass. He picked out the fate-favoured young woman who had attracted Beard's interest just as she stepped off the opposite pavement.

Bill was right – the young woman's gait *did* seem uncertain. Her road sense was even more so, he realised with a wince moments later, as the furious blast of a horn followed the screech of brakes. Without looking, she had lurched into the road in front of a white van. Fortunately, she had stepped off the pavement just a couple of seconds after the lights at the pelican crossing changed to green, so the van hadn't had a chance to pick up speed.

As with many drunks, she appeared to have a guardian angel on twenty-four-hour standby, for the van juddered to a halt on bouncing springs just inches from her body. The driver, an unshaven youth of around nineteen, lowered the grimy side window. Through the gap, he thrust a face that shock had turned a paler shade of white than his grubby van and directed a tirade of abuse after her.

But the young woman continued on her unsteady path across the road, accompanied by the screech of more brakes from the oncoming traffic on the other side, seemingly as oblivious to these as she was to the van driver's curses and to the fact that she had narrowly avoided a close encounter of the deadly kind.

Though a tiny part of him admired her disregard for the conventions that one shouldn't be the worse for drink before the hour had even hit double figures, Rafferty acknowledged that Bill's phrase 'daft mare' hit the spot. Although it was pouring with rain all she wore was a thin multi-coloured summer dress and a crimson, crocheted cardigan of more style than substance, which she clutched across her dress with a taut fist. She had no umbrella and the torrential downpour had plastered her hair to her skull.

Bill gave the long-suffering sigh of the endlessly put-upon. 'What do you bet but she's another one of those sad souls from the psychiatric hospital? Get 'em in my reception regular, I do. One old dear is always begging for a shilling, as if decimalisation had passed her by entirely.'

Rafferty, having endured plenty of stints on reception in his younger, uniformed days, knew better than to accept the bet. Instead, he was about to rush out, do his shining-knight act and rescue the clearly oblivious damsel from further death-defying acts as she continued on her unsteady, if determined, path across the road. But before he had taken two steps, she reached the pavement on this side without further near-misses.

Rafferty realised he had been holding his breath. He exhaled with relief even as he wondered whether Bill's guess as to her current abode was correct.

The asylum had been built in the middle of open countryside half a mile or so beyond the market town of Elmhurst, in keeping with the Victorians' belief that insanity should be kept at a decent distance from respectable normal citizens.

But gradually the town had crept up to the hospital's gates, a process hastened in recent years as the large, once self-sufficient asylum sold off large plots of its land to developers and sent most of its patients out to receive the dubious benefits of 'care in the community'.

As Beard had said, it was a regular occurrence to see the remaining patients wandering aimlessly in the town. Often, as if drawn by some unseen cord, they made their way to the police station, perhaps believing that its reassuring blue lantern would offer them sanctuary from life itself.

Experience had brought a shoulder-shrugging detachment to Beard and he confided matter-of-factly, 'I have another regular – young girl she is – about the same age as that one. Early twenties, I'd guess, or thereabouts, who carries a doll around with her everywhere she goes. God knows what brought that about. I could understand it if she was an old un, as it was the normal thing back in their youth that their babies would be taken from them if their bun in the oven was put in at the wrong regulo, but—'

Bill broke off, grabbed Rafferty's arm again and said with weary triumph as the girl reached the door to the police station, 'There, what did I tell you? She *is* coming in here.'

As the slender young woman tried to push the heavy door, she must have realised it needed both hands and all her weight to open it, for she released her firm grip on the cardigan. No longer tightly clutched, the cardigan fell open. Even through the drenching it had received, the bloodstains on her thin summer dress were clearly visible. The entire upper area of the bodice was so stained with blood that the dress's pattern was entirely obliterated.

Rafferty's mouth fell open. Believing she must have suffered some dreadful injury, he again stepped forward to offer assistance. But the comment Bill snorted in his ear

11

made him pause.

'Bet you this one's come in to report she's just murdered her husband.'

Rafferty hesitated. After almost thirty years in the force Beard had seen everything there was to see. Nothing fazed him; certainly not damsels in distress, even if they were as beautiful as Rafferty now saw this one was.

Forestalled by Beard's comment and the belated realisation that anyone with chest injuries that had bled so profusely would hardly still be walking around, he waited, his previously sleepy pulse now racing as the dazed-looking young woman, her shoes click-clacking irregularly in tune with her unsteady steps, crossed the black and white mock-marble flooring.

It seemed to the waiting Rafferty to take her an age to reach the desk. While he waited, he studied her appreciatively. For, in spite of being drenched by the chill rain of an unseasonably cold August morning, the weather had been unable to damage the beauty of her delicately boned face and deadly pale but flawless skin. Slender as a fairy's wand that could be blown over by the merest puff of wind, she swayed slightly before their mesmerised gaze as she fixed the uniformed Beard with large, grey eyes luminous with a tragedy curtained only by swooping dark lashes.

Rafferty, overcome by her beauty, took a

gallant's step forward and offered a hand to assist her. To his chagrin, she didn't seem to see it, or him. As if her life depended upon it, her gaze remained firmly fixed on the re-assuringly uniformed bulk of the older man.

Finally, she reached the desk. With both hands, she clutched the varnish-worn wood in a death grip, again ignored Rafferty, and with a yearning desperation in her face gazed across the desk that separated her from Beard and in a voice that cracked with hor-ror, whispered, 'I think I've just murdered my husband.'

Rafferty had time to notice only Bill's ex-halation of satisfaction at being proved right twice in one morning, before she collapsed at his feet.

One

'And that's all this young woman said?'

At Llewellyn's bemused question, Rafferty nodded. 'Yep, Dafyd,' he confirmed. 'That's all.'

Unsurprisingly, his logically minded Welsh DS found his recounting of that morning's incident in the daily life of police station reception folk somewhat bizarre.

The university-educated Llewellyn, who had read his way through all the most infamous murder trials in the annals of British justice and injustice, and who had presumably assumed, on joining the police service, that he was going to pit his wits against some of the most cunning killers on the planet, even now still found it hard to accept that, in the main, murderers were not very bright and thus easily caught.

This latest one, at least, although being more willing than most to confess to her crime, prompted a piquant curiosity that was out of the ordinary murder run. Because, after collapsing unconscious at Rafferty's feet, the hastily summoned police

15

surgeon-cum-pathologist, Sam Dally, had taken charge, carted her off in an ambulance and imposed an embargo on her being questioned at all.

Not, from what Dally said, that she was in a position to provide answers. According to their tame – or not so tame – medic, although now conscious the young woman who had made such a dramatic entrance was as out of it as one of the undead.

'Surely she said *something* else before she collapsed?' Llewellyn persevered with his touching belief – in spite of plentiful experience proving the contrary – that other people were not unreasonably perverse, but behaved as logically as he did himself. 'Who confesses to murder and then says nothing more?'

With a perverse satisfaction of his own, Rafferty replied, '*Her* for a start.'

Admittedly Llewellyn was right, in that, once embarked on a confession, murderers generally didn't want to stop till they had poured it all out.

'Illogical, I know. But seeing as Sam says she's in this deep-trance state – now, what was it he called it?' he wondered aloud to himself. 'Catalonia would it be? No. That can't be right.'

'Catatonia?' Llewellyn suggested, in a tone so dry, Rafferty's forehead creased as he suspected the better-educated Llewellyn of

16

mocking his ignorance.

But whether he was or not, the Welshman's poker face didn't betray him and Rafferty conceded, 'Yeah, could be. It has a familiar ring to it. Anyway,' he added, 'Dally reckons our murdering zombie lady's retreated from reality. Hasn't said another word since she collapsed, not even the usual demand for a solicitor, which, given her confession, is unusual, seeing as the guilty ones invariably scream far more loudly for a brief than the innocent ever do. We don't even know who she is as she had no handbag or purse with her. Seems she just "did the mortal deed" – if deed she did – left her home and the husband, and came here wearing just what she stood up in.

'Dr Dally, who was here at the time about some other matter, took one look at her and insisted she was carted off to hospital. He said he'd be surprised if she didn't develop a fever or something after the drenching she received. Of course, Dally being Dally, the knower of all things, he was happy to tell me his prediction was proved right when I rang the hospital. Apparently, she's running a high temperature and not responding to their questions. No way we could interview her.'

Llewellyn's Welsh-dark eyes gazed contemplatively at Rafferty. 'So, what now?'

Rafferty pulled a face as, reluctantly, he

dragged a pile of files towards him. 'As this young woman's still in a world of her own, I suppose we wait until Dally says otherwise. What else can we do?'

'But if she *has* attacked her husband and he's bleeding to death in their home, waiting is hardly an option,' Llewellyn pointed out.

'And neither is sneaking into the hospital and snatching a picture of her in her sickbed so we can give it to the media and ask the public: "Do you know this woman?" The human-rights lot would have a field day if we did.'

That was an argument guaranteed to put a stop to Llewellyn's questions. Dafyd Llewellyn, although a man of strong morals and high principles, was a firm believer in human rights; even those of young women who claimed to have committed the ultimate sin.

'Anyway,' Rafferty added, 'I very much doubt he's still bleeding. If I'm any judge, from the amount of blood on her dress, her husband is already long beyond our help.'

Rafferty gazed at the pile of files he had just dragged towards himself. He sighed as he opened the first of these and took in the thickness of its contents. More bureaucratic bumph from Region, he thought. When did they think he was going to get any *real* police work done?

More than willing to abandon, even if only temporarily, the close-typed script of yet more politically correct gobbledegook, he looked up at Llewellyn and said, 'But on the plus side, at least we know *one* thing about her – that she's *not* from the psychiatric hospital, which Bill Beard thought favourite. I rang them, and all their patients are present and correct. I've had Jonathon Lilley ringing around the others in the area, NHS and private. None of their patients is missing, either. If she wasn't lying in the hospital, doing this zombie impression and with her bloody clothes bagged and tagged, I'd wonder if me and Beard didn't have a mutual hallucination and conjured up this self-confessed husband killer to liven up a slow morning.'

He leaned back in his chair – at least it put a distance between himself and the paperwork – and said, 'Anyway, *you're* meant to be the clever one.' Still smarting from the suspicion that Llewellyn had got one over on him with the catatonia thing, he added slyly, 'If you're so bright, *you* tell me how we should proceed.'

Llewellyn looked thoughtfully at him for several seconds. Then he too sighed, pulled half a dozen of the files from Rafferty's pile, walked across the room to the desk in the corner and sat down before he said, 'I suppose you're right. We wait.'

When Rafferty arrived home that evening,

he and Abra, his girlfriend, decided to have a quiet night in. During dinner he told her about the dramatic confession made by their visitor that morning.

'Poor woman,' said Abra, instantly all sympathy, much to Rafferty's chagrin. 'She must have been desperate,' Abra continued. 'I suppose she was worn down by some brute of a husband. Probably been beating her up for years.'

It sounded as if Abra thought *all* men were beasts. It was another unwanted reminder that she was still nursing a grievance against him over their difficult time back in June when she resented what she regarded as his lack of support. He was only too aware that she thought he had let her down. With hindsight, he agreed with her.

Rafferty, although his conscience pricked, felt honour-bound to spring to the defence of the male of the species.

'Well no, I doubt it – or rather, I suppose he might have been beating her up, but the timescale's unlikely. She can't be any older than her early twenties. Something of a stunner, too,' he murmured half to himself in appreciative, if unwise, remembrance. 'It's hard to believe any man would want to re-arrange a face as beautiful as that. I felt rather sorry for her, actually.'

Abra's gaze narrowed at this and Rafferty realised his admiration of the young woman might have been better kept to himself. Why was it, he wondered, that women always hated it when you praised the good looks of other females?

'Sounds like she's brought out the Sir Galahad in you,' she commented with a sharp little edge to her voice as, with a clatter, she began to stack their plates. 'I'd watch that tendency, Joe. It could be compromising in a policeman.'

Rafferty immediately tried to downplay the young woman's attractions. With what he thought a nicely judged throwaway air, he commented, 'She's a bit on the thin side for me.' As he realised his words were insufficient to soothe the little green god after the words of praise that had gone before, he gave them some support. 'Anyway, there's not much chance of me being compromised just yet as Sam Dally had her removed to hospital after she collapsed and promptly pronounced her incommunicado.

'Though I can't say I'm surprised she collapsed after making her announcement. Probably one of these bulimics or anorexics we hear so much about now, as she was pretty much a bag of bones. No man wants a stick insect for a partner.'

'Mm. Strange they were bones you seemed to like well enough a minute ago.'

As his self-defensive measures hadn't worked, Rafferty decided teasing might work better. 'Not jealous are we?' he asked. 'Just a little bit?'

'Should I be?' Abra countered.

'Of course not. What could you possibly have to be jealous about? I've only just met the woman and then she totally ignored me, preferring the more mature charms of Bill Beard.'

Abra gave another indeterminate little 'Mm' before adding, 'If she doesn't ignore you next time you see her, maybe you should let Dafyd do the questioning? It might be safer. After all, eating-disorder thin Lizzies learn plenty of devious tricks to make sure they get their own way and stay thin. And you already sound a little too susceptible to her slender attractions to me.'

With that, she stalked off to the kitchen, whence Rafferty soon heard several more crashes and bangs.

'Me and my big mouth,' he muttered to himself as he decided it might be politic to offer to load the dishwasher and make the tea.

In the end they only had to wait three days before they were able to see the young woman who had made such a dramatic entrance; Rafferty had hoped for longer, as it was clear he still had some way to go to get back in Abra's good books after his thoughtless behaviour back in June. He could do without another murder case right now, with all the extra hours and accusations of neglect likely to spring from it, which he remembered with such painful clarity from his marriage to Angie, his late wife – particularly as Abra had clearly elected to take a dislike to their suspect...

He supposed he ought to be thankful the young woman had confessed. It would make his life simpler – in theory at least. But in practice, once one of the legal types that bedevilled his life had got hold of her, she'd retract. Most of them did.

But he had to admit he was curious about the girl. And when the hospital rang to say that she had started to respond to their attempts to communicate with her, he wasted no time in finding Llewellyn and hurrying them both off to see what she had to say for herself.

When they arrived at the hospital, they were directed to the first floor. They found their mysterious young woman secluded in a side ward. As previously arranged by Rafferty, she had a bedside guard round the clock, just in case she decided to disappear for real rather than into another catatonic trance.

As Constable Lizzie Green rose at their entrance, Rafferty nodded and told her to wait outside.

Against the much-laundered white pillow,

the young woman's skin looked even more washed out than it had at her collapse. In spite of having been *non compos mentis* for much of the last seventy-two hours, she had deep mauve shadows under her eyes and looked exhausted and as fragile as a porcelain figurine that might shatter into a thousand pieces at any moment.

As he looked at this frail and ethereal creature who had claimed to have committed murder, Rafferty was beginning to think he and Beard *had* shared a mutual hallucination. In a moment he'd wake up and find it had all been a dream. But as the young woman lying so still in the bed failed to dissolve before his eyes, he pulled up a chair and sat down.

'I'm Detective Inspector Rafferty,' he began before he introduced Sergeant Llewellyn. 'Perhaps you could tell us *your* name?'

To Rafferty's surprise, as he had half expected her previous state of catatonia to have affected her memory, she answered without hesitation.

'My name's Felicity Raine.'

'Mrs?'

This time she hesitated. Her lack of readiness to claim the title was unsurprising, if the 'Mr' half of the marital pairing really *had* died at her hands. But then she nodded and said, 'Yes. But, of course, you already know that.'

That 'of course' indicated that she had clear recall of the events of three days earlier and that he had been one of the witnesses to her claim to having murdered her husband. But although she was talking, she was clearly still barely in this world. Her voice was slow and uncertain, as if she had only recently learned to speak.

'And your address, Mrs Raine?'

She provided this information in the same slow, flat monotone with which she had provided her other details. It was almost as if she was experiencing the world through some kind of protective mist that made it seem shadowy and not quite real. Of course, that might just be due to the shock she must be experiencing if she *had* just killed her husband, whether deliberately or otherwise.

As soon as she had told them her name and the address she shared with her presumed-dead husband, Rafferty gave the nod to Llewellyn and his sergeant hurried off, clutching his mobile, to arrange the uniforms to check the address out for the bloody corpse of her partner. On his way out, he sent Lizzie Green back in to act as a witness in case Mrs Raine decided to blurt out a repeat of her previous confession.

After giving her the statutory caution, Rafferty asked gently, 'Do you remember coming into the police station three days ago?'

Felicity Raine, her expression troubled, nodded.

'And what about what you said when you got there? Do you remember that?'

Again she nodded.

'And was it true? *Did* you murder your husband?'

There was that hesitation again, Rafferty noted. She looked confused and her answer, when it came, was spoken in tones even more dazed than before, as if she couldn't, herself, quite believe what she was saying or take in the enormity of what she had done.

'I suppose I must have done. Yes.'

She gazed at Rafferty from troubled eyes and said, 'It's odd and you'll think me dreadfully callous, I'm sure, but I can't *remember* killing him. Isn't that strange?'

Her long slender fingers clutched each other, as, in an anguished voice, she all but pleaded for an answer from Rafferty. 'How can I have forgotten? You'd expect the memory of such an act to be a vivid one. But I can't remember it at all. All I remember is finding myself stretched out on top of Ray, both of us covered in blood.'

She shook her head. 'I suppose I must have shut my mind off. Afterwards.' She shuddered then, as she added in a whisper so faint that Rafferty had to strain to hear what she said, 'The doctor said I was suffering from shock. Delayed shock. No doubt, memory of it will come back to me in time.'

'Can you tell me why you killed him? How?'

'As to the why—' She broke off and stared sadly at him from the large, luminous grey eyes that Rafferty remembered so well. 'Raymond – my husband – and I had been arguing a lot lately,' she said in a voice so low that again Rafferty had to lean close to the bed to hear her. 'Nothing I did seemed to please him.'

When she said nothing further for a moment, he thought she had relapsed into her previous state of fugue. She stared beyond him as if she no longer saw him and had already forgotten the second half of his question.

He prompted her before she disappeared back into the nether world. He wanted to hear it from her own lips; it was the only way, he thought, that he would be able to dispel his doubts. 'And *how* did you kill him?'

'A knife. With a knife.' She shuddered again. Her eyes rounded in horror as she added, 'There was so much blood. It was all over him, all over me. How could I do that when I loved him so much?'

Rafferty shook his head. He had no answers for her.

She looked down, as if she expected still to be wearing her bloodstained dress, and frowned at finding herself in a hospital gown.

'My clothes,' she began fretfully.

'Don't worry about them for now. We've got them safe.'

'I see. Thank you. It's just – just that my husband gave me that dress for my last birthday. I don't want anything to happen to it.'

As Rafferty watched, the expression in her eyes turned from tragic to appalled, as it hit her that this was one dress she would never want to wear again.

After that, a silence fell between them, broken only by Llewellyn's return. As he entered the small hospital room, his gaze met Rafferty's and he gave a brief nod.

Llewellyn's confirmation that Felicity Raine's husband was dead made her claim that she had killed him the more believable. But as he gazed at her delicate face and the figure so slender it barely left a trace under the dark blue duvet, Rafferty was again conscious of a glimmer of doubt. For, in spite of the bloodied state of her when she had turned up at the police station, in spite of her own anguished confession, her slender figure made it difficult for him to conjure up a picture of her knifing anyone, much less the husband she professed to love. Apart from anything else, it was so unusual for a woman to use a knife as the means to kill that the number of such cases made up a tiny percentage of female killings.

She seemed to have retreated into herself again, Rafferty noticed. He wasn't too worried about it, though. For now, he was content with just the bare facts. They could get the rest later.

He followed Llewellyn out to the corridor. 'So, let's hear it,' he invited.

'It's just as she told you,' Llewellyn replied, grim-faced. 'According to Hanks, when he and Tim Smales broke in they found Mr Raine sprawled out on his back on the living-room floor, covered in blood. The knife was still in his chest.'

Rafferty frowned. 'She attacked him from the *front*?'

Llewellyn nodded.

Rafferty took a moment or two to absorb the information, then he asked, 'Little chap, was he?'

'No. Actually, I asked Hanks the same question and he said he was tall and muscular.'

Rafferty frowned at this discovery. He gazed through the window of the small side room to the patient in the bed. This case was rapidly becoming more bizarre, more surreal with each succeeding discovery, he thought. It seemed this was a thought that Llewellyn shared. He too let his gaze settle on Felicity Raine and his next words echoed Rafferty's thoughts.

'To look at her, you wouldn't think she would have the strength to kill him. Mrs Raine is slender, seven and a half stone if that, and can be no more than five foot three or four.'

Rafferty nodded. 'And looking as if butter wouldn't melt.' In the face of the evidence, he pushed his doubts aside, hardened his heart and said firmly, 'But melt it did.'

He instructed Lizzie Green to stay with Mrs Raine and set off towards the stairs. 'I suppose we'd better go and find out when she's likely to be released into our custody. If she *has* killed her husband, I want no one to be able to claim later that she wasn't fit for questioning.'

Two

The home of Felicity and Raymond Raine was situated in a quiet country lane lined with the wild flowers of an English summer: as they got out of the car, Rafferty recognised the deep red blooms of great burnet, the pretty pink of campion and the dense white clusters of meadowsweet. Its strong perfume rose up to greet him as he brushed past.

It was a large, attractive old house of higgledy-piggledy construction. With its 'double pile' design and several gables as well as the small-paned windows, Rafferty guessed it dated back to the sixteenth century. Sometime, long ago, before such things had to be passed by planning committees, a previous owner had built two side extensions off the main house which only added to its picture-book prettiness as they rambled off in a picturesque fashion, as if keen to demonstrate their independence from the main structure. The currently whitewashed walls even had the requisite strongly perfumed old-fashioned roses climbing up trelliswork either side of the stable door, which was currently propped open to ease the many comings and goings of the police team.

After PC Smales noted their arrival on his clipboard, Rafferty and Llewellyn climbed into their protective gear, slipped under the crime-scene tape and entered the house.

With the fragrant scents of the roses and meadowsweet still lingering in his nostrils Rafferty gasped as, in their place, an altogether stronger smell invaded his senses. The flower perfumes couldn't compete with the pungent, sickly-sweet aroma of three-day-old death. And after the beauty of the outside, the scene that met their eyes as they entered the living room was like a take from a horror movie. Although aware that this wasn't make-believe, part of Rafferty was still waiting for some invisible director to shout, 'Cut!'

As Llewellyn had said, Raymond Raine lay sprawled on his back on the now-bloodied dove-grey carpet. The knife sticking out of his chest looked like one commonly used in kitchens. It was large, with a black handle decorated with an ornate pattern in brasswork.

The fact that he was lying on the floor some distance from either of the large settees caused Rafferty to shake his head as again he wondered that the petite Felicity Raine had managed to overpower such a well-built man. Now if he had been asleep on the settee ... Unless she had drugged him first? But the post-mortem would tell them if that was the case.

~ The room was tastefully furnished in a pleasing mix of modern and antique furniture. A beautifully carved chest that Rafferty guessed was Elizabethan stood under the casement window. The plain, white-painted walls of the room made the dark wood appear to glow even more darkly. Rafferty just had time to make these brief observations before Dr Sam Dally arrived.

'God,' he complained, as if offended that the daily grind should force such sights upon his delicate sensibilities, 'the place looks like an abattoir.' He sniffed. 'Smells like it, too. And even if they *do* say the female is more deadly than the male, it's hard to believe that little slip of a thing did this.'

'Not you too, Sam,' Rafferty complained. Although as Abra had rightly suspected, part of him felt sorry for Felicity Raine, who seemed more confused than evil, he was coming round to the belief that she *had* murdered her husband. They had her confession and all the circumstantial evidence backed it up. It was seldom they had such a straightforward case and Rafferty was determined not to let his own pity or Llewellyn's and Dally's remarks influence him. Like most men, they would be susceptible to a pretty face.

Besides, Rafferty reminded himself, you have the pretty face of Abra at home. He wanted to keep her sweet and, to encourage her to be sweeter than she was currently being, he had organised a special evening for them both, so was relieved not to have a difficult murder case to solve right now. He certainly wasn't about to look this particular confession gift horse in the mouth, or any other part of its anatomy.

As Dally set about his examination of the dead man, Rafferty and Llewellyn, side by side and with an unspoken but obviously shared destination, left the living room and its bloody cadaver and went into the hall in search of the kitchen.

As Rafferty had already observed, the Raines' home was detached and spacious. It consisted of the roomy lounge they had already seen; as well as a formal dining room nearly as large, with a long, dark table that could seat ten; a breakfast room at the back, on the sunny side of the house, its used dishes from the morning of Raine's death still on the table; and a smaller study across the hall from the dining room, which facts Rafferty's quick door-opening and closing revealed as he searched for the kitchen.

The fourth door Rafferty tried led down a short passage to the kitchen. Another door off to the left led into the breakfast room, he saw as he poked his head through.

He glanced round the kitchen. Instantly, his gaze lit on the knife block. It was sitting on one of the expensive-looking solid-oak kitchen units that lined the walls. There was one knife missing, he noted; the rest of the set matched the largest one that was currently protruding from Raymond Raine's chest. The decorative brasswork on the kitchen knives was visible above the wooden block and was the same pattern as on the murder weapon.

Rafferty called out to Adrian Appleby, the head of the Scene of Crime team, and told him to get the knife block and its contents photographed *in situ* and then bagged up.

Appleby nodded and shouted through to Lance Edwards, the police photographer.

While Lance began to take some shots of the knives Rafferty gazed out of the kitchen window. Beyond the large, plant-filled and obviously modern addition of the Victorian-style conservatory that led off the kitchen and breakfast room, he could see the well-stocked garden, its end lapped by the waters of the River Tiffey.

Apart from the hushed conversations of his colleagues in the kitchen and living room, all he could hear was the sound of birdsong through the open window. And as he absorbed the glories of nature to counterbalance the pictures in his head, a grey heron, with a beguiling grace given its long legs, landed on the opposite bank of the river. Rafferty held his breath for a moment's delight in the midst of horror, before marvelling that murder – and such a murder – had occurred at this tranquil spot; the setting looked like a veritable Garden of Eden. But clearly it was an Eden no longer. The snake had done its work well.

Across the river, the heron raised its slender head. It stood motionless for some moments as if taking stock. Perhaps it had caught the taint of blood and death wafted towards it on the light breeze, for it immediately took wing, flapping its way into flight in a leisurely manner as it uttered a deep, harsh *krau*. Airborne, it tucked its legs behind it as elegantly as a ballerina before vanishing as suddenly as it had appeared.

Rafferty, reminded by the bird's sudden flight that he too ought to get moving, touched Llewellyn's arm and said, 'Let's make a start getting the team organised. If Mrs Raine does retract her confession, we'll need letters, bank statements, et cetera, anything that might provide evidence as to the state of the Raines' marriage. Oh, and see if you can find an address book with the family and friends listed. But you know the drill.'

Llewellyn nodded and made for the kitchen door.

Rafferty called after him before he disappeared. 'I'll be with Sam' – no doubt, he groaned to himself, given the state of the body, he would be regaled with a selection of Sam Dally's more black-humoured observations. 'I'll see you out front when we've both done here.' He paused. 'By the way, I meant to ask if you noticed that cottage we passed, twenty yards closer to the main road?'

Llewellyn nodded.

'I shall want to have a word with the occupants as a matter of urgency. They may be able to tell us something useful. With the two houses isolated together in the lane, maybe the close proximity encouraged a greater intimacy than most modern-day neighbours manage.'

Llewellyn nodded again and disappeared.

Rafferty strolled slowly back through the house before thrusting his head through the doorway into the living room, where Sam Dally had just finished his examination of Mr Raine's body.

'Don't be shy, Rafferty.' Sam, although he had his back towards the door, seemed to have a sixth sense where teasing Rafferty was concerned. 'Come away in. There's no need to hover in the doorway like some green probationer.'

Rafferty grimaced at Sam's sly comment and came further into the room. To outface the team's concealed grins at Dally's comment, he asked, 'So what do you reckon as to the time of death? Does the approximate time tally with what Felicity Raine said?'

Sam's chins gave a turkey-wobble as he nodded. 'He's certainly been dead over seventy-two hours.' Dally sat back on his heels and glanced over his shoulder at Rafferty, who, in spite of Sam's invitation, still hovered in the doorway. 'Rigor's come and gone and bacterial action's given the trunk the usual greenish tint, but it has yet to reach the extremities.'

Too much information, Rafferty thought, but he knew better than to speak his thought out loud. He often wished Sam would just give him the approximate time of death without going into all the gory details. But that, of course, wasn't Sam's style.

'The skin hasn't started to get that characteristic marbling effect which comes any time between four and seven days after death.' Sam intoned further macabre details that made Rafferty's stomach churn. 'So, yes, we're in the right time frame.'

'Glad we've got that so comprehensively established,' Rafferty commented in a dry little aside for the benefit of the listening scene-of-crime officers.

'You know me, Rafferty. I like to be thorough.' Sam's plump, pink face split in a smile that made him look even more like a mischievous cherub than usual.

'What about the knife wound? Just the one

38

thrust, was it?'

Dally nodded. 'A single thrust, straight through the heart. His killer was either lucky or skilful, as the knife missed the ribs and breastbone. Practically like plunging it through butter.'

Rafferty shuddered at Sam's description. A description rendered even more vivid by the way he rolled his 'r's in a determined Scottish burr. To Rafferty, the words brought an unwanted clarity to the knowledge of how easy it was for a man to pass from this life to the next...

Dally heaved himself to his feet. 'I'm done,' he said. 'Doubtless I'll see you at the post-mortem.'

'Doubtless.' Rafferty's lips thinned at this. He braced himself as he wondered with what stomach-turning forensic nitty-gritty Sam would insist on regaling him with at this later corpse-cutting.

Sam left, followed shortly after – once the coroner's officer had sanctioned its removal – by the body of Raymond Raine. Rafferty followed both of them out and stood in the front garden. Thankful to be away from the abattoir stench inside, he filled his nostrils with the fresh, rose-fragrant air, taking in lungful after lungful in an attempt to rid them of the other aromas.

Llewellyn was hard on his heels. He confirmed the troops had received their orders.

'OK. Let's get along to the neighbours and see what they can tell us.'

Summer had that morning elected to return, and in place of the chill rain that had heralded the beginning of the case, today the sun was warm on their backs as they walked the short distance down the pretty lane with its sweet, wild-flower edging to the cottage belonging to the Raines' only neighbour.

This cottage, detached like the Raines' house, was much smaller and plainer in design. It was on the opposite side of the lane to the one they had just left and lacked the lapping music of the river at its garden edge. Which was probably just as well, Rafferty thought, as he heard the piping voices of young children from the back garden; youngsters and rivers were never a happy mix.

The woman who answered the door to their knock appeared flushed and breathless. She looked to be in her late forties or early fifties and was dressed in clothes suitable for garden romps with the grandchildren, in practical, worn, dark green slacks and a light green T-shirt which was well daubed with what looked like the drips from red ice-lollies. It was thin and had the well-washed look of a top that had encountered similar stains many times.

'What's happened?' she asked as soon as Rafferty had introduced himself and Llewellyn. 'I heard all the police cars, but I couldn't come out as I've got my grandchildren staying. I've kept them in the back garden as I didn't want them frightened, much less asking questions that I suspect – from all the police activity in the lane – that I'd rather not answer. When I saw all the cars go past I knew it had to be the Raines' house you were going to. The lane's a dead-end,' she explained. 'There's only the two houses in it.'

She studied them carefully for several seconds before, in a half-whisper, as if reluctant to voice the question and hear the answer, she said, 'Please don't tell me he's killed her this time.'

Rafferty and Llewellyn exchanged glances at this.

'A violent man, Mr Raine?' Rafferty queried. Felicity had made no such claim either before her confession or since.

Mrs Elaine Enderby, as she now introduced herself, nodded. 'But surely you've discovered that for yourselves by now,' she commented. 'I always suspected he knocked her about, though Felicity denied it even when she sported a black eye. I did warn her that hiring that good-looking young chap to do her garden and odd jobs would be like a red rag to Raymond. Though that's probably the worst thing I could have said to her.

'After that, in order to keep up the pretence that Raymond *didn't* knock her about,

41

I think she felt she had no choice *but* to take him on.'

'I see. Can you tell us this gardener's name?' If he spent much time at the house he might have witnessed the Raines' marriage at first hand.

'It's Nick Miller. And way too handsome for his own or anyone else's good. He has a string of female clients. And for some of them, the rumour is he does more than look after their requirements in the gardening department, if you get my drift. Yes, Nick Miller could be said to keep very busy.'

Very much getting her drift, Rafferty was quick to ask, 'Spend much time at the Raines' house, did he?'

'Every Wednesday morning and Thursday afternoon. Though God knows what he spends his time doing while he's there – the garden's mostly lawn.' Elaine Enderby smiled and pulled a face. 'Sorry. My tongue's run away with me. I don't want you to get the impression that Felicity is one of the customers who require the "extras" he provides. It's more a case that with all the attention he receives for his gigolo antics, he's beginning to think gardening's beneath him, so he spreads it out in a leisurely fashion while he sits admiring his muscles in the potting shed.

'But anyway, never mind him. You were telling me about Felicity – how you do side-track a person, young man. I hope she's not

42

badly injured?'

Amused to be addressed as 'young man', when October would see him hit forty, Rafferty shook his head. His mind moved on to consider the implications of what Mrs Enderby had told them. If Raymond Raine *had* been violent towards his wife, it could mean mitigation; maybe the murder charge would be reduced to manslaughter if that could be proved.

'But come away in and we can talk,' Mrs Enderby invited. 'We'll have to sit in the kitchen so I can keep an eye on the children.'

Loud, childish laughter flew on a light breeze through the open back door and window and she told them, 'I filled the paddling pool as an inducement to them to stay in the back garden. But where water's concerned, I always like to keep an eye and ear cocked for mischief.'

Mrs Enderby's kitchen was as different to that of the Raines as it was possible to be. Here there were no expensive solid wooden units nor dangerous sharp knives on show. Instead, there were large pine dressers – old family pieces, perhaps, as they were mellow with age – cluttered with practical, unbreakable, childproof jugs in sturdy blue and white enamel, side-by-side with pretty but mismatched plates and mugs.

There was a good-sized rectangular pine table with six chairs just under the window.

Most of the table was covered by pictures, presumably painted earlier by the children.

Fondly, Mrs Enderby pointed to a picture of a green, stick-like figure with what looked like antennae rising from its head and said with a smile, 'That's me. Martian lady.'

Rafferty smiled back. He glanced briefly out of the kitchen window. It seemed Mrs Enderby's practicality extended to the garden, for it was filled with vegetables: runner beans lush with leaf growth and bean pods climbed up wigwams of bamboo canes, their bright orange flowers swaying gently in the light breeze. The children's play area was safely fenced off so they couldn't damage the vegetables which filled most of the plot.

As they settled at the table, Rafferty commented, 'You said you thought Mr Raine was violent towards his wife. What else can you tell us about them?'

'But you haven't told me what's happened yet,' Mrs Enderby pointed out. 'I asked you if Felicity was all right, but you barely answered me. So what's happened to her?'

Rafferty didn't see any reason not to tell her. Apart from the fact that news of the murder would soon filter out via the media, who had no doubt already been tipped off by one of their regular sources at the police station, Elaine Enderby seemed the kind of gossipy witness who could provide him with further valuable information. 'I'm afraid there's been murder done,' he began. 'Mrs Raine—'

Both her hands flew to her mouth. Above it, her eyes rounded with horror and she exclaimed, 'There, what did I say? I always worried he'd kill her in the end.'

'It's not *Mrs* Raine who's dead,' Rafferty quickly corrected her assumption. 'The body we found in their living room was that of Mr Raine.'

Elaine Enderby took her hands away from her mouth, which had rounded in an 'o' that matched that of her eyes. 'No,' she said flatly. 'I don't believe it.' She gazed at him from troubled blue eyes before curiosity got the better of her and she asked, 'What did she do? Poison him?'

Rafferty said, 'No. Mr Raine wasn't poisoned.' He didn't say any more and Mrs Enderby didn't question him further.

After some seconds' silence, she told them firmly, 'If Felicity killed him, he must have driven her to it.' She paused, as if suddenly remembering something she thought could be important. 'Unless – unless that man I've seen hanging about the lane did it. He appeared furtive enough. Maybe he's someone with a grudge against Raymond. Felicity let slip once that he could turn on a sixpence if he didn't get his own way. But when she realised what she'd said, she immediately clammed up and changed the subject. I couldn't get any more out of her.' This failure clearly still rankled.

Although interested to learn of Raine's less than placid temperament, for now Rafferty was more interested in the other thing that Elaine Enderby told him and he asked, with an unintended sharpness, 'What man was this?'

Mrs Enderby shrugged. 'I don't know who he was. But my husband and I saw him on several occasions last week, just sitting in a car parked behind the trees opposite Fliss's house. You know, where the lane widens?'

Rafferty nodded. As Mrs Enderby had said, the lane was a lot wider at that point and there was room behind the trees for someone to park up and conceal themselves behind their lush summer growth, if they were intent on being inconspicuous.

'You know, it's strange, given what you've just told me, but my husband and I haven't seen the man at all this week.' She glanced questioningly at Rafferty and asked, 'Do you think—?' before she broke off and said matter-of-factly, 'But I don't suppose you're interested in my speculations.' She gave a brief, strained smile. 'I'll stick to what I *do* know. And that is that Jim – my husband – went out on Friday evening and asked the man what he was doing there, but he didn't get any coherent answer. The man just muttered something Jim couldn't catch and drove off. Jim said this man looked the worse for wear and smelled strongly of drink. But although he drove off when my husband challenged him, he was back again on both the Saturday and Sunday. He was still there when it got dark. Whatever he was up to, he was certainly a determined sort to sit there for hours on end.'

And to sit there on the night prior to the murder, Rafferty added silently, before Mrs Enderby continued:

'As I said, my husband noticed him again when he drove home from his club night on Sunday evening. He was going to tackle him again once he put the car away, but I persuaded him against it. I was worried the man might turn violent if he was challenged a second time, particularly if he'd been drinking. I went round to Fliss's house several times to mention it and ask her if she'd seen him as I couldn't be sure that she had and I wanted to warn her. But the house was empty each time I called. My husband and I only noticed this man because the approach from our house up the lane gives a different angle to that from Fliss's house. Anyway, as I failed to catch Felicity, I ended up shoving a note under her door.'

Mrs Enderby's face shadowed. 'Maybe we should have called the police then? I did think about it, but...' Her voice trailed away. 'I had made my mind up to ring you this morning, but then, all the police cars and activity put the thought from my mind. Well, that and the necessity of keeping my grandchildren distracted from all the upset. Perhaps if I'd rung you this morning, as I'd intended, Raymond wouldn't be dead.'

Given that Felicity Raine's confession was now over three days old, Elaine Enderby's failure to ring them this morning made no difference, as Rafferty reassured her before he asked, 'This man – what else can you tell us about him? He could be a vital witness so I need to trace him. Could you give me a description?'

Mrs Enderby hesitated. 'Let me see ... He wasn't old, no more than mid–late thirties. He had thinning, dark hair. As I said, he seemed rather dishevelled: unshaven and with a creased white shirt that looked as if he'd worn it for days.'

'What about the car?' Llewellyn put in.

'That's easy. It's the same make as mine. A blue Renault Clio. I've even remembered part of the registration number. It was FLS. It stuck in my mind because it reminded me of Fliss's name.'

Rafferty thanked her while Llewellyn jotted all this information in his notebook. Given the information Mrs Enderby had supplied, he didn't think this man should be too difficult to trace.

'Did you know Mr and Mrs Raine well?' he

asked. 'Only, anything you are able to tell us about them and their relationship could be helpful.'

'I knew Fliss more than him. She spent quite a bit of time here. I think she regarded my house as a refuge and me as some sort of stand-in mother. Though Fliss never talked about her family – I got the impression she was alone in the world. I've always found Felicity a very private person. There was something about her that made you keep such curious questions to yourself. I think she deliberately kept other people at arm's length because she was worried about what she might inadvertently let slip about her abusive marriage. Anyway, as I said, with no mother of her own in evidence and with a mother-in-law who was far from motherly, Felicity seems to have volunteered me for the job. Apart from her husband, I think I'm the person Felicity is closest to.'

'Obviously, we need to contact Mr Raine's family,' Rafferty said. 'If you know the address of his parents, it might speed things up.'

'Stephanie Raine, Raymond's mother, lives in that large, detached Georgian house on the corner of Watling Street, not far from the swimming pool. I was driving past with Fliss one day and she happened to point it out to me.'

Rafferty nodded. He knew the house. It

was a perfect period piece. He lusted after ownership each time he passed it.

'It's no more than five minutes' drive away, which most women would regard as too close for comfort when it came to their mothers-in-law. It certainly was for Felicity: Stephanie Raine – she's a widow, by the way, and a pretty glamorous one – was in Felicity and Raymond's house pretty much every day, far more often than a sensible mother-in-law would judge to be wise. She even had her own key to the front door. Felicity must often have become fed up with it and with the way she fussed over Raymond, always kissing him and touching him. She wouldn't let him alone. Inappropriate, I'd call it.'

Elaine Enderby said that Stephanie Raine had been in her son and daughter-in-law's house nearly every day, yet clearly she had been conspicuous by her absence since her son's death, now nearly half a week past. She couldn't have shown her face, for if she had she would have found her son's body lying dead in the living room. But for it being August and the height of the holiday season, Rafferty would have found her failure to visit more than a little curious, but given the holiday aspect he didn't, for the moment at least, attach any significance to her failure to put in an appearance.

'What did Felicity feel about her mother-in-law's behaviour?' Rafferty asked. 'And what about Raymond himself? How did he feel about it?'

'I never noticed Raymond object. His mother's possessive behaviour seemed to amuse him more than anything – one of those male ego things, I suppose. As for Fliss, she rarely referred to it. She's never been one to talk about feelings much. Though I certainly got the impression that Stephanie was jealous of Fliss. I heard them out in the garden a few times during the summer when I was passing in the lane with the dogs and Stephanie could be sugary-sweet towards Fliss, but the sugar always had a *double entendre* taint to it. Taken one way, what she said could be complimentary, but taken another, it could be insulting. I always got the impression that Ray's mother put on an act in front of him and that she behaved in an entirely different manner when she and Fliss were alone.'

'And do you know if Mrs Raine Junior was aware of her mother-in-law's true feelings towards her? And if so, did she confide in her husband?'

'Oh, Fliss was aware of them, all right. She might be a pretty blonde, but that doesn't mean she's stupid. As to whether she confided in Ray...' Mrs Enderby shrugged. 'Somehow, I doubt it. Felicity wasn't the confiding type. I often got the impression from Fliss that she felt part of a *ménage à trois* with her

51

husband and mother-in-law. As I said, Stephanie Raine was always very possessive of Raymond.

'But that's often the way with only-children, boys particularly, isn't it? Though she doesn't look old enough to be the mother of a man of Raymond's age. But she's not poor. Felicity told me that her father-in-law had left Stephanie pretty comfortable financially, so no doubt she's had the occasional nip and tuck to keep the years at bay.'

After another ten minutes they had learned as much as Mrs Enderby could tell them about the Raines. Pausing to give Mrs Enderby a card and to remind her to contact them if she thought of anything else, they left the calm of her kitchen and walked back to the murder scene. But before they reached the house, Rafferty veered off in the direction of the trees that Elaine Enderby had mentioned.

The soil here was still damp from the heavy rain earlier in the week; it was shaded by the trees and would receive little drying sunlight. Tyre marks were clearly visible. He pointed them out to Llewellyn.

'Get one of the team from the house to take shots and casts of these tracks,' he instructed. His gaze rested on one of the trees as out of the corner of his eye he noticed some damage to the trunk. He walked over and hunkered down. 'Looks like blue paint here,' he told Llewellyn. 'I'll want more shots and samples of the paint; and this pile of cigarette butts our waiting mystery man presumably smoked will need to be bagged, too. If by some miracle Felicity Raine should turn out to be innocent, this man could be a suspect. It's clear he had a keen interest in either one or both of the Raines. I'd certainly like to question him as soon as possible, even if only to eliminate him from the inquiry.'

While he waited for Llewellyn to return with one of the SOCOs in tow, he wondered at his own pleasure at securing a glimmer of hope for Felicity Raine. Was he, too, guilty of letting a pretty face interfere with his judgement?

Perhaps he was, but – although she had readily admitted to killing her husband, the fact that she couldn't remember doing so left that tiny element of doubt to niggle away at him.

Maybe she was right and she would recall the deed itself in due course. But if she didn't, he wanted to be sure in his own mind that she *had* killed him, rather than been set up to take the rap by some third party.

He'd be happier when they traced the man Mrs Enderby had noticed sitting in his car in the lane outside the Raines' home. He must have had a compelling reason for such determined watchfulness. Perhaps this mysterious, waiting stranger had had murder in mind?

Llewellyn returned then, trailing one of the SOCOs and Lance Edwards the photographer, and Rafferty put aside his speculation.

Time would reveal this man's identity. Maybe, when they had that, they would learn the reason for his presence outside the Raines' home and whether he had a motive for murder. He just hoped they found him sooner rather than later.

Three

Rafferty called the station and arranged for Mary Carmody, his sensible thirty-something DS, to accompany him to the home of Mrs Raine Senior to break the news of her son's violent death. He left Llewellyn to supervise the routine work at the scene.

Only five minutes later, as Elaine Enderby had promised, they drew up outside another large, detached property. Unlike her son's picturesque, rambling riverside home, Stephanie Raine's was a conventional Georgian property with no lumps of stone meandering in a haphazard manner off from the main structure. Here all was formality and the clean lines that were Rafferty's preferred building style. The conservative simplicity of the house gave him a perhaps unreasonable hope that when she learned of Raymond's death, Stephanie Raine's reaction would be as conservative as her home and that her grief would be contained and borne with a dignity that would make his and Mary Carmody's task less harrowing than was sometimes the case.

The oak front door was huge and pitted with scars as if it had been under siege in the past. It didn't really go with the house, but its heavy iron furniture was, like the house, clearly designed to impress. Perhaps a previous scion of the Raine family had liberated it from the local medieval priory during the Tudor years of religious plunder.

Rafferty's loud knock on the stout oak door must have reverberated within with a resonance impossible to ignore, for it was quickly opened by a young woman who, to judge from her charming accent and eccentric English, he took to be a French *au pair*.

His confidence ebbed a little at this discovery; he had hoped, after they had broken the news of her son's murder, that in her grief Stephanie Raine would receive the support of some middle-aged housekeeper with a body and heart as stout and native-bred as the oak door that guarded the entrance.

Slowly, so the young woman didn't misunderstand him, Rafferty explained who they were and that they needed to speak to Mrs Raine. 'I'm afraid we have come to break some bad news to her. Is she at home?'

The young woman's eyes rounded in curiosity at this. But before she had a chance to do more than nod to confirm that Mrs Raine was at home, an irritable, disembodied voice floated down the curved staircase.

'Who is it, Michelle?' this voice demanded.

'How many times must I tell you not to leave my friends standing on the doorstep?'

As Rafferty looked up, the owner of the voice reached the first-floor-landing banister and peered over.

Rafferty gained an impression of blond beauty of a certain age, and recalled that Elaine Enderby had described Stephanie Raine as glamorous. She was still in her night attire – *en déshabillé* was the expression he remembered Llewellyn had used to describe a similarly diaphanous cream silk négligée.

'I don't know you,' this vision informed him. 'What do you want? If you're selling something—'

'*Ce sont les gendarmes, Stephanie,*' Michelle told her in a loud stage whisper. 'They are come to crack open the bad news.'

There was a brief silence before Stephanie Raine, her voice suddenly shrill, demanded, 'Bad news? What bad news?'

She didn't wait for an answer, but hurried down the stairs as quickly as her mule-heeled slippers and trailing négligée allowed.

She was a striking woman, Rafferty noted as she reached them, even if she wasn't quite the vision of loveliness she had seemed to be at a distance. But for a woman who was of an age to be mother to Raymond, who looked to be in his early thirties, she appeared remarkably radiant, with a becoming blush to her cheeks. He looked for a sagging jaw or lined forehead and found none, and concluded that Elaine Enderby must be correct in her suspicion that Stephanie Raine had treated herself to some timely nips and tucks.

Mary Carmody persuaded Mrs Raine into the drawing room, which opened on to the formal entrance hall, and gently led her to a chair.

'What is it?' she asked as she waved away the hovering, touchy-feely Michelle and addressed herself to Rafferty. 'For God's sake, tell me what's happened!'

'I'm afraid the bad news concerns your son,' he told her. 'He—'

'My son?' she queried as if she was unable to take in what she was hearing. 'But—'

'Yes. I'm afraid Mr Raine has been involved in an incident. A violent incident at his home,' Rafferty began.

'But he's all right? Ray's OK?'

When her questions brought only an uncomfortable silence, she stridently demanded, 'Tell me, for God's sake. Don't sit there like stuffed dummies.'

Rafferty cleared the frog from his throat, took a deep breath and said in a rush, 'I'm afraid your son's dead, Mrs Raine. He died in a violent assault at his home on Monday morning.'

'No!' Something like a wail issued from

Stephanie Raine's throat. She gripped the arms of her chair and stared at him with suddenly tear-washed eyes.

Just behind Stephanie, Michelle's hands flew to her mouth and she let off a stream of shocked exclamations.

'*Mon Dieu.* But how can this be? Monsieur Raymond, 'e was 'ere only the day after yesterday.' She frowned at this obviously inaccurate statement. '*Non,*' she said, clearly annoyed that her limited grasp of English had so deteriorated in the face of the shock of Rafferty's news. She apologised and said, 'My English, which I have such pride taken, she vanish. Of course, it was not the day after yesterday. *Quel idiot!* It is not possible *avec Madame en lit* – in bed – with the influenza. Raymond 'e 'as the fear of contagion so 'e would not visit.'

Michelle's words at least told Rafferty why Stephanie Raine had not in the last few days made what Elaine Enderby had claimed were daily visits to her son's home.

Stephanie, perhaps affronted that her *au pair*'s words implied her son had been a weakling, gathered herself together sufficiently to rebut the slur. 'It's not that at all. Ray runs the family business. He can't – couldn't–' her voice broke on the word – 'afford to be ill. Now, please be quiet, Michelle. Your twittering isn't helpful.' She pointed to a chair some ten feet distant and said, 'Go and sit over there. I can't bear you hovering over me all the time.'

Mrs Raine turned back to Rafferty. As she wiped the tears from her cheeks, she sat up straight and tried to compose herself. 'So what happened? Was he attacked during a burglary?'

'We have no reason to think so. In fact he—'

'Just a minute,' Mrs Raine instructed as she stared at him with a frown.

Rafferty, who had geared himself up to the difficult explanation that Felicity Raine had confessed to killing her husband, stumbled to a halt. He wondered what was coming next. Apart from her instant correction of Michelle, Stephanie Raine had so far reacted little to their news.

But now, as if she had taken a few seconds to absorb what he had said, she repeated, 'You said Ray died on Monday morning?'

Rafferty nodded.

'But, but today's Thursday.' Mrs Raine's gaze narrowed and the shrill note returned to her voice. 'You mean you've taken over three days to come and tell me that Ray's dead?' She stared at him as if she couldn't believe her ears.

Rafferty sensed that understandable fury was about to replace her grief. He quickly broke in and explained the reason for the delay before Stephanie Raine had a chance to get over her shock and unleash the rage.

'He was only found an hour or so ago, Mrs Raine. We came as soon as we learned your identity and your address.'

'But why didn't Felicity – his wife' – she almost spat the word – 'tell you my address? Come to that, why hasn't she even contacted me? Surely—?'

'Mrs Felicity Raine has been in hospital.' Rafferty was brief in his explanation while he quickly considered how much it would be wise to divulge at this time.

'In hospital?' she repeated. 'Was she also attacked, then?'

Reluctantly, wondering what deluge he would set about his head, Rafferty said, 'No. Felicity Raine wasn't attacked. But she's in a state of shock and it was thought best to hospitalise her.' Rafferty paused, again uncertain how best to proceed. How *did* one break the news that a woman's only son was dead and probably, given Felicity Raine's ready confession, killed at the hand of his wife?

In the end, he decided to keep it plain and simple. Time enough later, he thought, for fuller explanations. Now, he cleared his throat and told her as plainly as he could, 'I'm afraid there's more bad new, Mrs Raine. Your daughter-in-law has confessed to murdering her husband.'

'What?' Stephanie Raine leapt to her feet,

belying her invalid status. Her eyes seemed to spark with a malevolent fury at this news. 'You're saying that that little bitch killed Ray? Yet you're letting her loll around in a hospital bed pretending shock as if she's a grief-stricken widow rather than a vicious murderer? I can't believe I'm hearing this. Why isn't she locked up in a cell where she belongs?'

Whatever reaction he had expected, it wasn't this loud demand for instant punishment that echoed round the large elegant drawing room. Stephanie Raine, the veins standing out on her neck, was now far from being the vision of beauty Rafferty had been deceived into seeing from the twenty-foot distance of the first-floor landing.

She hadn't paused to ask how Felicity had explained her deed, or even if she might have had cause to attack Raymond. Her first instinct had been to curse the younger woman.

'Your daughter-in-law is confused and distraught, Mrs Raine,' Rafferty began. 'For all we know to the contrary at the moment, Mr Raine's death might just be a terrible accident and your daughter-in-law may have confessed from a sense of guilt. But until we're sure she knows what she's saying—'

Stephanie waved away his explanation. 'How did she kill him? Where?'

'Your son was found in the living room with a kitchen knife in his chest. It would have been a quick death,' he added in an attempt at consolation, an attempt that clearly failed.

Stephanie spluttered with hysterical laughter and said, 'It sounds an unlikely *accident* to me. What was she doing in the living room with a kitchen knife? God, but you men can be such fools. I suppose she used her well-practised, doe-eyed innocent act to fool you? Wait till I get my hands on her.' Stephanie Raine's scarlet-painted and astonishingly long fingernails curled as if in anticipation of tearing her daughter-in-law limb from limb.

From her words, Rafferty thought it unlikely he would need too many guesses as to her likely reaction should they manage to gain the mitigating proof that Raymond Raine had been a wife beater. But perhaps he was being unfair to her; *he* had never had a close family member killed in such a violent manner. Unsure how best to deal with this hate-filled outpouring, Rafferty attempted to apply reason.

'Please, Mrs Raine. I know you've just had a bad shock, but try to calm yourself or—'

'Calm myself? *Calm* myself?' she repeated in a voice that rose to equal her apparent astonishment at what she was hearing. 'You sit there being stoical in the face of someone else's grief, and tell me to calm myself? Are you mad? Or just stupid? Have you any idea what it's like having you tell me I now have to bury Ray when only fifteen months ago I danced at his wedding?'

She turned, snatched up a framed photograph that rested on a small side table nearby and thrust it under his nose. 'Take a look. Such a happy day – or so everyone thought.'

Rafferty took the picture. Felicity really was the radiant bride, her face aglow with happiness, her blond hair crowned with a ring of tiny white rosebuds that secured a little wisp of a veil beneath. Her dress was a floaty, calf-length creation with a demure, sweetheart neckline which revealed the glint of gold and diamond at her throat.

He was startled when the picture was plucked from his hand. Stephanie stared broodingly at the photo for several seconds, her expression unreadable, then, with a laugh as bitter as aloes, she turned it and slammed it face-down on the table with sufficient force to crack the glass.

'Strange to think how smoothly everything went on the day; maybe it was an omen that the rest wouldn't be as smooth. No expense was spared. Ray insisted that Felicity must have the best of everything. He paid a fortune for his bridal gift – that gold and diamond necklace she wore on the day.' Stephanie made a disgusted sound in the back of her throat. 'And yet, only a few weeks ago, when I asked her why she doesn't wear it any more, she told me she'd lost it. It seems she took as little care of Ray's gift as she did of Ray.' Suddenly she slumped back into her chair, her face deathly pale, as if only now that she had vented her spleen against Felicity was she able to truly take in the enormity of her loss.

Rafferty turned and spoke to Michelle, who through this exchange had been seated open-mouthed, her gaze moving from one to the other as if she was an absorbed spectator at some international tennis tournament. Quietly, he suggested she call Stephanie Raine's doctor.

At this instruction, the *au pair* lost her English entirely. Her face fell, she turned to Stephanie and said, '*Qu'est ce que c'est est le nom de vôtre docteur, Stephanie? Je ne lui connais pas.*'

Stephanie roused herself sufficiently to tell Michelle in a long-suffering voice, 'For goodness' sake, girl. He's in my phone book on the hall table. Under "doctor". But I don't need – or want – a doctor,' she shouted after the disappearing Michelle.

Rafferty, keen to pass Stephanie Raine over to another authority so he could get back to the crime scene, said quietly in Mary Carmody's ear, 'Go with her and ring the doctor yourself. Just make sure he gets here, and quickly.'

Carmody nodded and followed Michelle

out of the room.

Fortunately, Mrs Raine's doctor arrived shortly after. He evidently had greater skill – or maybe just greater practice – at calming hysteria, for within five minutes of his arrival he had persuaded Stephanie to take a sedative and go back to bed.

Unwilling to leave the scared *au pair* to cope with further hysteria once the doctor had departed and the sedative had worn off, Rafferty told Mary Carmody to remain behind until one of Mrs Raine's remaining family could be found and asked to stay with her. Quietly, he instructed her to question Michelle and learn what she could about the Raines' marriage and what might have prompted Felicity to stab her husband. Although the husbandly violence that Elaine Enderby had suspected might well be the cause, it was possible that there was another reason for it entirely, one they as yet knew nothing about.

Shortly after, Rafferty headed back to the scene of the crime, anxious to see what the team had managed to discover during his absence. He found Llewellyn in Raymond Raine's study.

Expectantly, he asked, 'What have you got, Dafyd?'

'Remarkably little, unfortunately,' Llewellyn revealed. 'Though I have turned up a Mr Michael Raine from an address book I found in the desk drawer. I spoke with him by phone to confirm his identity and break the news. He told me he's the late Mr Raine's first cousin. He volunteered to formally identify Mr Raine. So, to save Mrs Raine Senior further distress, I agreed on your behalf and sent Lizzie Green and Hanks to accompany him to the mortuary.

'Anyway, there's no doubt about the dead man being Raymond Raine. Michael Raine told me he and his late cousin ran their own fashion business, a family affair. Maybe you've heard of it?'

Although from the stylishly suited Llewellyn's tone Rafferty guessed his sergeant thought this unlikely, Rafferty *had* heard of the Raine fashion empire. It was simply that he hadn't made the connection to this case.

'They were partners, I gather, though I got the distinct impression from the way Michael spoke that Raymond Raine was the boss, the one with the controlling interest. I also received the impression Mike Raine didn't like, to use the vernacular, to have to play second fiddle in this familial orchestra.'

Rafferty nodded. 'Perhaps they were *killing* cousins rather than the kissing sort. But whatever sort they turn out to be, we'll need to see this Michael Raine urgently. As he presumably knew the Raines in both a personal and business capacity, he should be in a position to tell us a lot.'

He glanced around the expensively furnished room and said, 'Raine was clearly a wealthy man; his money could well be a factor in his death. Have you managed to find the name of his solicitor yet?'

Llewellyn shook his head. 'I asked his cousin, but he was unable to tell me. And for someone who seems to have been an important businessman, Mr Raine seems to have had a marked aversion to paperwork of a more personal nature.'

'What do you mean?'

Llewellyn gestured at the two desks and the four-drawer filing cabinet against the wall. 'I've looked through them all, and have found little but household accounts, nothing of a more intimate nature.'

'Perhaps he keeps such stuff at the business premises?'

'Not according to the cousin. He told me Raymond always liked to keep private matters private.'

Given the lavish house and the apparently wealthy lifestyle of the dead man, Rafferty had already considered the possibility that inheritance might well have been a factor in his death. He was keen to discover as much as he could about the murdered man, yet, as Llewellyn continued his explanation that not only the study but also the rest of the house had been systematically searched for revealing paperwork and they had found little of importance, it seemed that learning more about the late Mr Raine might take longer than he had expected.

Certainly, as Llewellyn now confirmed, they had found no trace of the will that Rafferty had hoped the team would turn up. But that was no doubt stored at the solicitors whose identity they had still to discover. It was strange that a man of Raine's obvious wealth who must, surely, have retained the services of a solicitor to see to his affairs didn't keep such information in an easily accessible place. It was even more surprising that his cousin and business partner claimed not to know the solicitor's identity.

Rafferty wished he'd asked Stephanie Raine for this information when he had the chance. But it was too late for that now. Stephanie Raine, sedated by her doctor, was not, for the time being at least, in a position to advise him of anything.

'What about Raine's wife? Surely Felicity Raine can tell us?'

'She says not.'

Felicity Raine was still at the hospital. Rafferty had been told she would be released into police custody as soon as her temperature reduced.

'When I spoke to her she said that Raymond had never confided in her about money or legal matters and she had no idea as to the identity of his solicitor as she had never thought to ask. Or so she said,' Llewellyn added.

'Damn the man,' Rafferty muttered, an imprecation swiftly followed by the silent apology his conscience demanded for the sin of maligning the dead. But he had fully expected Llewellyn and the rest of the team to turn up more in the way of answers than they had so far managed. He had certainly expected to be in a position to speak to the late Mr Raine's solicitors and learn more about his financial situation. Yet Raine had, for reasons best known to himself, elected to turn what should have been a simple matter into one far from simple.

In spite of his doubts about Felicity Raine's guilt, even Rafferty had to agree with the implication in Llewellyn's last comment that Felicity's claim to knowing nothing about her husband's financial and legal affairs sounded disingenuous.

Given the quantity of expensive designer labels attached to the clothing that Llewellyn now told him he had found in her wardrobe, Felicity had obviously enjoyed her husband's money, the spending of it and the pleasure it could bring. Most women would also require some assurance that this enviable lifestyle would continue indefinitely and most certainly *would* ask about wills, insurance policies and the like. Though he acknowledged that that didn't mean all husbands were willing to share such information.

From the circumstantial evidence of his large, opulent home and all its expensive contents, it was clear that Raymond Raine had been a man of considerable means. This conclusion made Rafferty wonder who else – apart from his wife (which could, presumably, be taken as a given) – would profit from his death.

'What about Felicity Raine's family?' he now asked. 'What have you managed to find out about them?'

'Nothing. Felicity confirmed that Mrs Enderby was correct when she said she thought that the younger Mrs Raine had no close family. Certainly, Mrs Raine's own address book has few entries. And apart from Mrs Enderby's phone number, those of Mrs Raine Senior, the gardener Nick Miller and the Raine family business, most of the entries appear to be for hair and beauty salons and similar establishments.'

Fortunately for Rafferty's growing feelings of frustration, Llewellyn's logical mind came into its own before another half-hour had passed.

'I've been wondering about this desk,' he remarked.

The desk to which he referred was an attractive piece of furniture – a bureau rather than a desk. Rafferty guessed it was eighteenth century. It was certainly a beautiful thing; opulent. Its interior, he now saw as he raised the roll-top, was fitted with lots of little drawers, its exterior inlaid with exquisite, intricate marquetry made up of many different-coloured woods. The whole thing glowed like a multi-faceted jewel in the shaft of sunlight flooding through the window.

They had taken Mr Raine's keyring from his pocket before his body's removal to the mortuary and Llewellyn had had no problem gaining access to the two desks and the filing cabinet.

'Wondering what, exactly?' Rafferty asked.

'Whether it might not have a secret drawer; many desks of the period incorporated such a feature.'

Intrigued, Rafferty joined him. Soon they were measuring and tap-tapping for all they were worth. Even so, it took thirty minutes of painstaking effort before the bureau's secret drawer was discovered. But when revealed it proved worth the time and trouble, because within they found the identity of the late Mr Raine's solicitor.

Rafferty was relieved. Now, perhaps, they would be able to move forward in the investigation.

'Well done, Dafyd. Can you get this Jonas Singleton on the phone, tell him his client's dead and that we need to speak to him urgently?'

Llewellyn nodded and took out his mobile.

Five minutes later, with the appointment with the solicitor arranged for that evening, Llewellyn said, 'Wonder why the late Mr Raine felt it necessary to keep such information hidden so discreetly? It's not as though his solicitors would have revealed confidential information to anyone, much less potentially interested parties.'

Rafferty too was intrigued as to why Raine should have felt it necessary to hide such information. But whatever Raine's reasons, Rafferty was pleased they would now be able to speak promptly with his solicitor. It was a relief they wouldn't have to waste precious time canvassing every firm of solicitors in Elmhurst and its immediate environs. Solicitors could be a testy, stuffy lot, who made endless complaints about the workload required whenever Rafferty or one of his colleagues made a simple enquiry. As Rafferty had felt like saying on more than one occasion, if the legal eagles were to apply as much time and energy to their filing arrangements as they did to their billing systems they would have no need to complain that assisting the police was demandingly labour-intensive.

Rafferty was surprised to discover that a young man of thirty-two, as Llewellyn told him was Raymond Raine's age, should have used one of Elmhurst's more long-established firms of solicitor. He would have thought he would have preferred one of the younger, more thrusting practices which had sprung up in the town. But, as yet, he reminded himself, he knew very little about Raymond Raine – apart from the so far unproven suspicion that he abused his wife and that he was secretive. Clearly, delving into Raine's character and background was a priority. Rafferty hoped that between them the solicitor and Raine's cousin would be able to enlighten them on both counts.

Eager to move on in a case that had started with such a bang but which had then limped for lack of information, Rafferty walked across the study to where Llewellyn, industrious as ever, sat further exploring Raine's desk, and tapped him on the arm.

'Come on, Dafyd,' he said. 'We've found what we were looking for. We haven't got time for you to do your *Antiques Roadshow* impression. I want to speak to Raine's cousin before we see his solicitor.'

Llewellyn had just finished locking the desks and filing cabinet when Rafferty became aware of a disturbance coming from the front of the house. He heard Timothy Smales's voice raised in protest and hurried back out to the open front door.

'What the hell?' he muttered as he saw Smales attempting to restrain a young man of muscular physique and determined countenance. As he took in the mud-spattered blue van abandoned in the drive and the macho, heavy-duty workman's toolkit strapped at a rakish angle to his waist, Rafferty recalled Elaine Enderby's description and guessed the young man must be Nicholas Miller, the gardener/handyman.

'What's going on?' Miller demanded of Rafferty as he wrenched his right arm from Smales's grasp, almost sending the younger and slighter-built Smales flying in the process.

'Perhaps you could tell me who you are, sir?' Rafferty enquired.

'I'm Nick. Nick Miller. Mrs Raine's gardener. I don't know who your officer thought I was when he grabbed hold of me.' Miller directed an unfriendly stare at the red-faced Smales.

Given the macho, tight-T-shirted physique and the leather toolbelt that held the accoutrements of his trade and which he wore with more than a hint of swagger, Rafferty suspected that Timothy Smales had thought him someone got up for an audition for the gay band The Village People. However, he kept this suspicion to himself; somehow he thought it unlikely the macho Miller would appreciate the allusion – the gardener looked as if he took himself and his masculinity seriously and expected others to do the same.

'I'm sorry about that, sir,' Rafferty said.

'But my officer has orders to stop anyone approaching the house. As you might have noticed from the police tape across the gate, this *is* a crime scene.'

Miller hitched the belt of his low-slung toolkit higher and replied belligerently, 'I came in the back way. I didn't see any police tape.'

Rafferty frowned. His eye alighted on Smales's tomato-red countenance. Annoyed that his team had failed to discover and secure the second access point, Rafferty said to Smales, 'I'm sure Sergeant Llewellyn here must have told you to check the boundaries for other access points.'

Beside him, Llewellyn quietly confirmed it.

After tartly commenting, 'Better late than never, I suppose,' Rafferty brusquely ordered, 'Get off and put some tape up at the rear, before anyone else gains access to the scene. And while you're at it, find a spare body to guard it.'

Smales scurried off, as if grateful to have escaped a worse scolding for his carelessness.

Miller, obviously pleased to have his intrusion on a crime scene so easily vindicated, waved at the heavy police presence in the form of bodies and vehicles still littering the property, and demanded, 'So, are you going to tell me what's happened? Is Felicity – Mrs Raine – OK?'

That was a moot point, Rafferty mused, seeing as she was currently in the hospital nursing a fever and a guilty conscience and was shortly expected to be transferred from the hospital to Elmhurst's police cells.

Rafferty, thinking it the speediest course if he wanted the gardener's co-operation, gave Miller a brief explanation of events.

The young gardener's tanned and handsome face tightened at the news of Raine's death and Felicity's confession, but beyond that he betrayed little emotion. He didn't even ask any further questions, which might have been expected in the circumstances. And when asked to supply his address Miller gave it to them curtly, as if he resented having to reveal even that much about himself. Certainly, some of his swagger had fallen away.

'Today's Thursday,' Rafferty commented. 'I gather this is one of your normal days for doing the Raines' garden?'

Miller's eyebrows rose at this. 'I see someone's been talking about me.' His lips parted in a rueful grin as though this was something he had expected. And although no one likes having their name bandied about during a murder inquiry, Rafferty got the feeling that Miller wasn't particularly put out that someone had thought to mention him. Clearly he was of the school who believed it was better to be mentioned – in whatever connection –

that to be ignored.

'Obviously you won't be doing any work here today, or for the foreseeable future,' Rafferty told him.

'Yes. I *have* managed to work that out for myself,' Miller told him sharply, as though suspecting and resenting that his trade should brand him as being earthy and dim. 'But I—' He broke off, and when he resumed Rafferty got the distinct impression that Miller's 'I have a living to earn' and 'Have you any idea when Mrs Raine's likely to come home?' were not what he originally intended to say.

'Come home? You don't seem to have understood me. Mrs Raine has confessed to killing her husband. She won't be coming home.'

'Not coming home?' Miller shook his head in amazement. 'Come on. You surely can't think she really killed him? The idea's insane.'

Rafferty shrugged. 'Insane or not, the facts are that Raymond Raine is *dead*, Mr Miller. Murdered. *Somebody* killed him and Mrs Raine says it was her.

'But I really don't have the time to discuss the whys and wherefores now,' Rafferty told him firmly. 'We have your name and address and will be in contact shortly. Now, I must ask you to leave.' Rafferty fixed Miller with a determined eye and added, 'Unless there is something you can tell us that could help with the investigation?'

'No.' The gardener was quick to deny it. 'Why would I know anything about it? I don't,' Miller insisted.

'You're sure?'

Miller clearly believed his previous vehemence should be diluted. 'No. Of course I'm not sure. How can I be? Only all this' – again he waved an arm to encompass the scene – 'has knocked my thought processes askew.'

Rafferty nodded. Maybe later when he'd had time to think he would be able to tell them something helpful. Or maybe not, Rafferty thought as he caught Miller sweep an assessing glance over the house and grounds. Did the handsome young Miller of the tanned and taut torso fancy his chances of sharing Felicity Raine's inheritance, he wondered? And if so, had he thought it prudent to keep quiet about whatever he might know about the Raines' marriage and Raymond's death, in the hope of stepping into Raymond's empty shoes as far as the beautiful Felicity was concerned? Or was he simply hoping for some easy money in the form of blackmail for his continued silence, assuming Felicity did retract her confession and force them to put together a case against her? Certainly, Miller's determinedly low profile and failure to ask the usual rash of questions was curious.

Rafferty watched with narrowed eyes as Nick Miller climbed into his dirty van with the easy grace of his enviable physique, backed in the turning circle and motored slowly up the drive. He didn't look back until he had put what he presumably deemed sufficient distance between himself and the police. Then, as he waited for the police tape to be removed to allow his exit, he permitted himself one more slow sweeping glance of the Raines' extensive home before he held up one hand in what Rafferty felt was a mocking salute and drove off.

Four

The business premises of the Raines' family fashion firm looked sleek and decidedly up-market, their jaunty yellow umbrella logo prominent on the façade.

Rafferty parked in the small forecourt and he and Llewellyn entered the understated but undoubtedly expensive reception area.

Of course, the family business was fashion design so they would require premises that reflected the appropriate image: mahogany and other old-fashioned Victoriana would have no more place here than stuffed eagles or tigerskin rugs. With its décor of black, grey and silver, with accents of white and rich scarlet, and seating in black leather and chrome, it looked coolly elegant, as did the young woman seated behind the high, curved reception desk, who was clothed in similar hues to the reception area itself.

Rafferty wondered if it was a uniform or if, as the very visible front to the family fashion business, she was required to model their latest lines as part of her duties. Her trim figure and erect posture showed off the

Raines' fashion wares to advantage. It was a shame that her welcome, smiling and warm at first, should become a cool match for her surroundings as soon as Rafferty flipped open his warrant card, introduced himself and Llewellyn, and revealed the reason for their visit and that they had an appointment with Michael Raine.

'Please take a seat,' she requested as her smile turned from cool to distinctly frosty, 'and I'll tell Mr Raine you're here.'

It was clear from the receptionist's reaction not only that the rumour mill had been at work, but that she was firmly in Mike Raine's camp.

From Rafferty's point of view, this rumour-mongering and side-taking often proved, if not always helpful, at least illuminating as to the state of relationships. The receptionist's blatant hostility struck him as potentially mirroring that of Mike Raine, Raymond's cousin, the man they had come to see.

But he mustn't prejudge a man he had yet to meet, he warned himself. And it was true that a murder in the family made people react warily when the police came calling. He was dragged from his thoughts by the still-cool voice of the receptionist.

'Mr Raine is free now,' she told them. 'You may go up and he will meet you at the lift on the sixth floor.'

Rafferty smiled his thanks. It brought no

answering smile from the receptionist.

The lift was as sleek and elegant as the reception area and its female attendant; it even had a little black padded seat running round the three walled sides, with matching, but presumably thinner, black, grey and white marble slabs like those that floored the reception on the floor and the walls of the lift under the seat. Above it, some of the most flattering mirrors Rafferty had ever seen rose on three sides to the ceiling. He took the opportunity to smooth his untidy hair and straighten his tie.

The lift was subtly perfumed, soft music issued from invisible speakers – soulful jazz of some sort, Rafferty thought, though not being a jazz fan he didn't recognise the tune. Altogether it was such a comfortable mode of upward locomotion that he was rather sorry when the lift's engineering revealed itself as being at least as expensive as the lift's interior and the doors opened, seemingly just seconds after they had closed, to reveal a man who could only be Mike Raine.

It was possible to trace the features of Raymond in those of his cousin. But although the cousins shared a finely chiselled nose and full lips, where Raymond had been well built, with a powerful physique and firmly chiselled jaw, Mike must have felt destined while Raymond was alive to remain in his cousin's shadow.

Slim to an extent that looked unhealthy, Michael Raine was still a good-looking man, though compared to his cousin his good looks would, in a previous generation, have been the wanly handsome looks of the consumptive; a pale shadow indeed.

As they shook hands, Rafferty was surprised to find how firm – challenging even – was Mike Raine's handshake. It was as if he was determined to show by the force of his grip that although conscious of the 'pale-imitation' tag, he was determined to kill it – as he had killed his cousin? Rafferty pondered the thought that entered his mind as it struck him again just how much wealth was at stake here.

But time would tell if it had been Mike Raine, rather than Felicity, who was guilty of murder. For the moment, as behind his back he surreptitiously flexed his squashed fingers, he resolved to avoid any more such painful encounters.

Mike Raine led them into his office. The room was defiantly at odds with the décor in what Rafferty had seen of the rest of the building, where presumably the late Raymond Raine's taste had held sway.

Here, there was colour in plenty. And although the floor matched the scheme of the building in its black, white and grey marbling, the rest of the room's exuberant embrace of rainbow colours seemed designed to cock a snook at such knowingly superior sophistication. Strangely, the mad colour mix didn't jar the senses. The sheer exuberance of the room seemed more to encourage a childish joy at such richness, though Rafferty, who was partial to bright colours himself, wondered if that wasn't just him.

Along with the bright colour scheme, Mike Raine also favoured modern *primitif* art in bright primaries. Rafferty wondered if their interviewee had deliberately set out to annoy his cousin.

But whether he had or not, to them Mike Raine displayed a disarming openness. Rafferty watched him covertly as the young man picked up the phone and ordered coffee. His face had a boyish quality that – to judge from the dead man's photographs at least – seemed to have been entirely missing from Raymond's. It was attractive, certainly, but in a different way to the more strongly masculine-looking Raymond.

Mike Raine interrupted his thoughts as he replaced the receiver. 'You haven't said exactly why you need to speak to me, inspector. Though if you require an alibi from me' – he gave a rueful smile that showed off his boyish good looks to advantage – 'I'm afraid I am unable to provide one.'

Rafferty, always suspicious of such frank and ready admissions during a murder case, said nothing as Mike Raine's secretary entered with the coffee, set it on the desk and poured. Then he suggested with a smile, 'Perhaps you can at least tell us where you were around seven to seven thirty on Monday morning, when your cousin died?'

'Certainly. Normally I'd have been at home. But on that particular morning, I was already at work at seven.'

'And no one can verify that, you said?'

'Actually,' Raine's secretary interrupted, 'Jane on reception said to me earlier that she saw you arrive on Monday morning.'

Convenient, was Rafferty's thought. He asked, 'Was there some breakfast meeting on the premises that required such early attendance from the receptionist?'

'No,' the secretary replied. 'But I was on holiday that day and Jane, who often fills in for me and who lives opposite the firm, assumed Mike had forgotten to mention that he was having an early start and she rushed to get ready in case he wanted her to do some typing for him.'

'I see.' Rafferty gave a slow nod, smiled, thought again, How convenient, and turned back to Mr Raine: 'And what were you working on that morning that was so special, sir, that it required such an early start?'

Mike Raine frowned, and a peevish expression replaced the boyish look. 'I'd been preparing a report on the amount of business

I'd brought to the firm in the last six months. I came in that morning specially to finish it. I wanted to have it ready so that I could present it to Ray.'

'To what purpose, exactly?'

'To what purpose?' Mike sat back in his black-leather executive chair and whirled it until he was facing Rafferty square on. 'I'm afraid Ray tended to belittle my contribution. I thought if I could prove how much my efforts have increased the profits – prove it in pages of the facts and figures he relished so much – he might start to appreciate me.'

Rafferty nodded, but he suspected there might be more to Mike's desire to prove himself to his cousin than he had admitted to; maybe they would learn what it was when they saw the solicitor.

He wondered if Mike had been relieved to learn of Felicity's ready confession. Certainly, he now asked how she was coping, with every appearance of concern for her. He even asked if they believed she had killed Raymond.

'Do you?' Rafferty countered.

Mike shrugged. 'I really don't know. At first, when your officers told me what had happened, I thought it unlikely. But now I've had time to think about it, I have to say that I don't understand why she – or anyone – would confess to murder unless prompted by a guilty conscience.' He gave a long-drawn-out sigh. 'Poor Felicity.' After a moment's pause, he added, 'Poor Raymond, too, of course. I don't think they were particularly happy together. I've always been fond of Felicity. I'll do anything I can to help her. I presume she's got a solicitor to advise her?'

Rafferty nodded. The very same solicitor who had contacted him only five minutes earlier as they drove to the Raines' business premises, to tell him his client had retracted her confession. And although he'd been expecting it from the start, the disappearance of his nice, easy case was a blow.

But it was something he chose, for now, to keep from Mike Raine. If Felicity or her solicitor didn't confide in him themselves Rafferty thought it might provide him with a useful leverage later in the case. Though given the fact that Felicity *hadn't* been in a rush to consult or confide in Mike, he found himself pondering the reason why.

Before they left, they got Mike to show them Raymond's office. It was a corner office, twice the size of Mike's and very plush. Modern art lined the walls. It shared the space with photographs of models strutting their stuff on the catwalk wearing what Rafferty presumed were Raine designs, and others of glittering celebrity parties. He spotted Raymond in one of them, glass in hand, head back, laughing and looking supremely confident of his place in the world.

'I'll need to take Mr Raine's contacts book and diary,' he told Mike.

'You can't, I'm afraid. Ray always kept such details on the computer. But I can get his secretary to print them out for you.' He opened the adjoining door and went through.

Rafferty followed him, just in case Mike tried to tell Ray's secretary to delete some telling detail, and was surprised to discover that Raymond Raine's secretary was not some short-skirted dolly bird but a middle-aged woman with neat grey hair and an awe-inspiring typing speed.

But, in spite of the still-efficient typing, it was clear the woman had been crying. Her tears, for Rafferty, only served to point up the lack of tears from Raymond's cousin. As Raymond's secretary printed out the diary and contacts list, Rafferty questioned her about her boss.

'What was the late Mr Raine like to work for?'

'I always found him a good boss. He believed in rewarding loyalty and hard work. And although he could be demanding – expecting you to do overtime at a moment's notice and get work completed yesterday that you didn't receive till today – I didn't mind. I know – knew – how hard he worked himself. No one worked harder than he did. He was a dynamic man. I'll miss him.'

On an impulse, Rafferty turned to Mike and asked, 'And you, Mr Raine? Will you miss your cousin?'

For a few seconds Mike Raine's face took on as many hues as his office walls, then he gathered his dignity about him and quietly confirmed, 'Of course I'll miss him. Raymond's always been there. It'll be strange to go on without him.'

Was that a trace of sheer delight he caught in Mike's voice? Rafferty asked himself. Or was he imagining it?

As Rafferty returned to the car with Llewellyn, he asked, 'Well, what did you make of the cousin? Not exactly grief-stricken, was he? For all his claim that he would miss Raymond.'

Llewellyn, never one to rush in with an unconsidered comment, pondered for several seconds before he observed, 'Grief-stricken or not, he didn't seem overly concerned that we might consider him a suspect – strange when one considers that, not only will he now be able to step into Raymond's shoes, but also his alibi might well be more a belated concoction of Jane the receptionist than the unvarnished truth.'

'Perhaps it's just that the thought of all that power and the corner office – supposing he *does* take over from Raymond – has knocked every other consideration out of his head? But I suppose once his brain starts working again and he discovers what Felicity has clearly not told him – that she's retracted her confession – he'll realise we'll consider him a serious suspect. I suppose we can shortly expect him to start screaming for his brief.

'And talking about that retraction, Daff, I don't know about you, but I thought it odd that Felicity Raine clearly chose not to confide in him about either her confession or its retraction. Seeing as she doesn't appear to have any family of her own, you'd think turning to the cousin by marriage who claims to be fond of her would be the natural thing to do.

'And then there's that receptionist of Mike's and her suspect alibi. Does she really think we'll believe she's telling the truth about that when it's clear she'd as soon kill anyone who threatened his inheritance? The second she discovered who we were and why we wanted to see him she produced enough frost to make me feel like a brass monkey in the trouser department.'

'Mm. She was certainly not as subtle as the décor. Do you think she and Mike might be—'

'Lovers?' Rafferty finished for him, aware of Llewellyn's reluctance to openly refer to things he felt should be private. 'Could be.

And why not? Everyone else in the country seems to be at it like knives, if the papers are to be believed. Sodom and Gomorrah, Ma calls it. She'll be predicting the Second Coming next.

'But to get back to the receptionist and Mike Raine, for all we know they're both free agents, able and willing to lie for one another like any other loving couple. She was certainly protective of him. Makes you wonder if she didn't have a hand in Raymond's death, on the principle that she might have believed that removing his cousin from Mike's path and lying for him might serve to encourage his commitment. And even if she had nothing to do with it, it seems that whoever gets to inherit the filthy lucre might well turn out to have the biggest motive for his murder. That being the case, it's fortunate we managed to trace Raine's solicitor. Because I think the sooner we speak to him and see how the inheritance land lies, the better. And given that Mrs Enderby suspected Raymond abused Felicity we have to wonder if he was abusive to anyone else. If he was, he may well have stoked the need for revenge in people other than his wife.'

'Yes, but if he was this aggressive bully Mrs Enderby's portrait of him implies, doesn't it strike you as odd that he should have been killed so violently? In my experience, it's usually the case that such large, aggressive males are dispatched by subtler, more *safe* means for the perpetrator. Even given the possibility that he was drugged – could a lay person be sure how much of the drug to administer?'

Rafferty shrugged and got in the car. 'I suppose the lay person can read up on dosage amounts required, the same as the professionals. Ma's got one of those little books at home which she uses to check up on what the doctor's prescribed for her so she can challenge him if she doesn't like the sound of it or its potential side-effects. Then there's the internet, which provides the interested with more facts than they really want to know.'

Or so he understood – his screen mostly seemed to fill up with stuff totally unrelated to his original query. 'Half of the world are medical experts, now, Dafyd, or can be if they choose.'

'Or have need so to be.'

'That too.'

'Pure speculation, of course.'

'Of course. But that's what I do best, after all. Why waste such a talent?'

But speculation was not, as Rafferty admitted to himself, getting them any further forward. 'You haven't yet put forward any possible theories.' Rafferty tried to tease a response from the generally non-theorising Welshman. 'Who do *you* think did it, now that Felicity Raine has decided to widen the list of possible suspects?'

But as Llewellyn wasn't to be drawn, Rafferty checked his watch. It was nearly seven. 'Come on,' he said. 'If we don't get a move on we'll be late for our appointment with the solicitor, and seeing as Jonas Singleton has been sufficiently obliging as to remain late in his office just for us, we don't want to get his back up.'

As Llewellyn drove away from the forecourt, Rafferty thought again about Raymond Raine's secretive nature. He was curious to discover what his solicitor could tell them about him and the rest of the family. Not to mention who exactly stood to inherit the dead man's wealth.

Five

Rafferty was relieved to find that Jonas Singleton was a relatively young man. The firm of Wilkinson, Warburton, Walker & Blenkinsop was old-established and, certainly on the surface, old-fashioned in its ways. An older member of the firm – given Raymond Raine's sudden and violent death – might be more likely to shilly-shally when it came to telling them what he knew of the dead man and his affairs, particularly if it pointed the finger at another member of the family.

But as Mr Singleton readily explained to them when Rafferty asked him about it, he intended to co-operate. He wasn't the old-style family solicitor, he was quick to assure them. The power of old money was being increasingly supplanted by new money as the ambitious younger generation, male and female, with their university study behind them and the need to service large debts in front of them, determinedly set about commanding high incomes.

It wasn't unusual nowadays for the twenty-somethings to work longer and longer hours in high-profile careers, with precious little time to arrange their affairs, which, as Jonas Singleton explained, was 'where solicitors like me, who are youthful enough to be considered part of their generation, come in. Most of the firm's younger clients won't tolerate the time-consuming way of doing business favoured by the senior partners. Life's too short, they think, to have to deal with the more fuddy-duddy older elements of the firm, which was the reason I was taken on.'

Singleton held the door to the firm's reception area open and said, 'But come through to my office so we can talk.'

Once installed back behind his desk in the bright and airy office with the latest, sleekest technology on the desk, Jonas Singleton didn't waste time in further pleasantries. Time was money, his now brisk manner implied. And probably, to him and other high-earning professionals like him, it *was*, thought Rafferty, who was old enough to think about the past nostalgically and feel it a shame that in the modern world everything seemed to revolve around Mammon.

'You said you wanted to discuss my late client, Mr Raymond Raine's, financial situation, inspector. To be frank, now he's deceased, apart from the money he has in his bank and savings accounts and so on, he doesn't *have* a financial situation, as such, certainly not where the family business is concerned – or at least, not one that should detain us above a few minutes.'

Rafferty frowned as he and Llewellyn sat down in the visitor chairs. Given that, since viewing Raymond Raine's beautiful home and expensively designed business premises, he had felt certain the man's wealth would feature strongly as the reason for his murder, he wondered if he was being particularly dense and said, 'I'm sorry, I don't understand.'

'There's no reason why you should, inspector. It's rather complicated. Perhaps it would be best if I began at the beginning?'

Rafferty nodded, relieved to be reassured that he wasn't being as dense as he had feared.

Jonas Singleton explained that the late Raymond Raine's dead father, Michael, along with Michael's brother, Anthony, also dead, had started the family fashion business from a shoestring and a market stall, from which they had quickly moved onward and upward.

Anthony had studied art and fashion design at college, whereas his brother, Raymond's father, had studied for a degree in Business Studies and Economics. It had been Michael Raine who was the business brains behind the swift success of the family firm. But equally, Mr Singleton told them, it was generally acknowledged that if Anthony Raine, the father of Ray's cousin and business partner, Mike Raine, hadn't had such an innovative flair for fashion, the other's business brains wouldn't have been needed and part of the clothing revolution of the sixties would never have happened.

But it *had* happened, Rafferty reflected; nowadays, it was hard to imagine the high-street clothes shops without their cheaper versions of the latest line in the famous Raine family umbrella logo.

'But now that you know some of the background, you'll find it easier to understand my previous statement. Raymond and his first cousin, Mike Raine, don't *own* the family business. They don't even own their own homes, as they were actually purchased by the trust set up by the cousins' fathers once the early days of the family business were behind them and the profits escalated.'

'This trust – perhaps you can explain what it entails.'

'Yes, of course. I was coming to that. Raymond Raine's father, Michael, and Mike's father, Anthony, set up a joint trust for their heirs. Both of the late former partners seem to have been singularly obsessive about the importance of the family, the continuing family line and inheritance; not so surprising, I suppose, when one knows that the

Raine family, in each of the past six generations, had produced a paucity of children,
especially boys. I think the trust was set up
to encourage Raymond and Mike to do their
duty and provide heirs.'

They hadn't been noticeably successful in
Raymond's case, Rafferty thought. He had
seen no evidence that children formed part
of the Raine household. He asked Jonas
Singleton, who confirmed it.

Rafferty, still not totally grasping the
significance of what Singleton was saying,
must have looked puzzled, for the solicitor
said:

'In effect, inspector, Mike, Raymond and
Stephanie Raine, the late Anthony Raine's
widow, lived on the interest from the trust.
They couldn't touch the capital, or at least
Raymond and Michael Junior *could*, but only
once they had met certain laid-down
conditions.'

'Which were?'

'Namely, that each of the cousins would
only come into their share of the capital
when they became fathers; if either Raymond or Mike died having failed to produce
a child, then the position of the surviving
cousin improved, in so far as his share of the
interest increased substantially. In the event
that they both died without issue, then the
bulk of the inheritance would go to the
nearest male relative, which in both their

cases would currently be Andrew Armstrong, the son of Michael and Anthony's sister. He lives in Australia,' Singleton added.

Rafferty, still hopeful of a swift conclusion to the investigation, could only hope this third of the triumvirate of cousins didn't complicate matters and was able to prove he hadn't left the Antipodean shores during the last few days.

'With Raymond's death without issue, Mrs Stephanie Raine is also due for a sizeable increase in her income.'

Rafferty supposed the trust had been an attempt by Michael and Anthony Raine to control their offspring from beyond the grave, which was far from unusual, in his experience.

'So Mike and the late Raymond Raine ran the family business,' Rafferty said. Recalling Llewellyn's earlier comment about who out of the cousins seemed to be boss, he asked, 'Were they equal partners?'

'Actually, no,' said Singleton. 'Raymond had ten per cent more and, basically, had the upper hand. And given Raymond's murder, I feel I ought to explain how that came about.

'As I said, the two brothers who founded the firm each had only the one son and when the cousins took over the running of the firm from their respective deceased fathers, as none of the female members on either side of the family showed any interest in the day-to-day running of it, they had a free rein. Certainly, Stephanie, Mrs Raine Senior, has always made clear that all she is interested in is that the money keeps coming.

'And as for Mike Raine, unfortunately for him, he discovered on the close-together deaths of his father and uncle that instead of the partnership being a fifty–fifty split, in fact, Raymond had not only the larger share, but also the upper hand in the business. He left Mike in no doubt that he was going to run things *his* way.

'Raymond was in the fortunate position of being able to throw his weight about in this manner because, unbeknown to Mike, although Mike's father had originally been an equal partner with his brother, shortly before his death he had sold ten per cent of his half-share to Michael Senior, Raymond's father. Then, two months later, Michael Senior died suddenly in a car accident.

'Mike's father had been worried about the business because he was very ill and at the time Mike had been more interested in sowing his wild oats than taking his full share of responsibility for the family firm. So, sick and facing death, Anthony Raine, who had always had more understanding of design than finance, had felt he could not let the irresponsible and wild youth who was his only son loose with half the family business as a plaything. And with his nephew Raymond older by five years, responsible and already working in the business, he felt that the owner of such a strong pair of hands who had already shown considerable business grasp should not have those hands tied by an inexperienced youth, even if this youth *was* his own son.

'His father's decision in the face of imminent death was hard on Mike. Unfair too, as it turned out. Because Mike Raine, after sowing his wild oats for a few years like most young men, calmed down. The timing of his father's death was unfortunate for him to say the least. And that of his uncle even more so, because Raymond's father had told the disgruntled younger Michael that he would restore his lost percentage as soon as he proved he deserved it. But, of course, when he was ready to take his share of responsibility it was too late because Michael Senior had died in an accident shortly before. And Raymond Raine, firmly in the driving seat and with his extra percentage of the shares in the firm, wasn't about to move over for his younger cousin.'

'So how long had the cousins been running the business?' Llewellyn asked.

'Just over two years.'

'And how did Mike feel about losing out to his cousin?' Rafferty asked.

Singleton shrugged. 'About how you would expect. Understandably, Mike felt he had been cheated. I suppose it's fair to say he was somewhat embittered. He let slip the odd complaint to me about it.'

Strangely, Mike Raine hadn't felt it necessary to explain any of this to them. And now Raymond Raine was dead...

'And what about Mrs Felicity Raine, Raymond's widow? Would she receive an equivalent sum?' Rafferty asked.

'Alas no. But as your sergeant told me earlier when he rang to make this appointment, given that Mr Raine's young widow has already confessed to killing her husband, she would not in any event be permitted by the law to profit from her crime.'

Rafferty updated the solicitor on the status of this confession and suggested, 'Can we suppose for a minute that Felicity Raine *didn't* kill her husband and is proved not to have done so? What would her position be then?'

Jonas Singleton laced his fingers together and rested his long, rather horsey face upon them. 'Her position would be just the same. When Michael and Anthony Raine set up their joint trust it was shortly after they had both married for the second time. And although they were both reasonably happy in their second marriages, neither of them had more children despite the fact they had married women much younger than themselves. But—'

Rafferty frowned. 'Sorry to interrupt, but I want to get one thing clear in my mind. You're saying that Mrs Stephanie Raine isn't Raymond's mother? His *natural* mother, that is?'

'Good Lord, no. Whatever gave you that idea?'

Rafferty was thankful that Jonas Singleton didn't wait for an answer. He wasn't eager to reveal that he had failed to check his 'facts'.

'There's only around twelve years between them. And although I know young girls seem nowadays to become pregnant at an early age with a depressing regularity, I can assure you without hesitation that Stephanie Raine is not Raymond's natural mother.'

Jonas Singleton paused to collect his thoughts after Rafferty's interruption. 'Anyway, although both Michael and Anthony Raine would have liked to have more children, in the trust they set up they stated that they felt it would be unfair to penalise their second wives financially for their failure to reproduce. In effect, Michael's second wife, Stephanie, and Anthony's wife, Juliet, were forgiven for their failure. But that forgiveness for failure to breed didn't extend to the wives of the next generation. Felicity, as the only younger wife, had responsibility for reproducing the family line.'

'So neither Raymond nor Mike had children?'

'No. And Juliet, Anthony's second wife, died of cancer a year after her husband.'

'I see.' All these deaths, and now Raymond's murder, had certainly been convenient for the remaining heirs, he thought.

'As far as the late brothers' trust was concerned Felicity was expected to do her duty and provide heirs; even the birth of a child within nine months of the father's death – subject to proof of paternity – would earn her, as the mother of the next generation's beneficiary and Raymond's widow, a share in the family wealth through her child. As the beneficiary's mother, she would be able to draw substantial sums to support the child.'

'Clearly she's failed to meet the requirement that she and Raymond reproduce – so what's the drill now?'

'Not a very kind one, I'm afraid,' Singleton told them. 'Felicity Raine failed in her duty to the family line, so she gets nothing at all. Not even the house she shared with Mr Raine and presumably thought of, still thinks of, as home.'

Rafferty was shocked, not least by the solicitor's matter-of-fact manner. 'You mean, supposing she *is* found not guilty, she'll just be chucked out on the street on her release?'

'Oh, I doubt it would come to that. I think

Stephanie Raine, even though on the few occasions I've met her she didn't strike me as being a particularly sensitive person, would be prepared to behave generously to the woman whose failure ensured her own increased inheritance – as long as, that is, she *isn't* proved to have killed Raymond. If the case against her is proven, Mrs Raine Junior will be residing at Her Majesty's pleasure, so Mrs Raine Senior is unlikely to have the opportunity to throw the younger woman on to the streets, even should she wish to. And given that, should she be convicted, Felicity Raine would be housed for the foreseeable future at the taxpayers' expense, I don't see that losing her home is likely to greatly inconvenience her.'

Lawyers, thought Rafferty, they really were all heart. This control-from-beyond-the-grave trust document struck him as being more than unfair; it had, he thought, more than a touch of the Princess Diana to it in its requirement that Felicity, like the late Princess, should turn herself in to a breeding machine. He said as much.

Jonas Singleton smiled and revealed long teeth that were as horsey as the rest of him. 'I suppose you could put it that way, yes. The same will apply to his cousin Mike's wife, if and when he acquires one.'

'It seems an unnecessarily complicated business,' Rafferty commented. 'Not to say unfair. Did Felicity Raine understand her husband's position?'

Singleton shrugged. 'As to that, I have no idea. Felicity Raine has never been my client. Even if she had been, I wouldn't have divulged the details of her husband's financial affairs without his express permission. I presume Raymond explained the facts to her.'

Given that he had taken the trouble to conceal the identity of his solicitor by hiding the relevant paperwork in the secret drawer of his desk, Rafferty was willing to bet that Raymond hadn't thought such an explanation necessary. Either way, he wasn't sure whether this presumed failure on Raymond's part made Felicity more, or less, likely to be guilty of his murder.

'But anyway,' Jonas Singleton went on, 'even if Raymond failed the fatherhood requirement and missed out on the bulk of the family inheritance, Stephanie Raine wouldn't have seen him go short. I understood she was very fond of him. I imagine if Felicity manages to prove she's innocent of killing her husband that Stephanie Raine – or rather myself and the other trustees – will see she's looked after financially. But even if that wasn't so, Mike Raine would certainly help her. It is my understanding that he has always been particularly fond of the younger Mrs Raine.'

'Ah yes, Mike Raine. We spoke to him

earlier.'

Foolishly, Mike had denied knowing the identity of Raymond's solicitor. But clearly he *had* known, as they were both beneficiaries of the same trust and would have shared the services of Jonas Singleton. Just to make sure he didn't assume any more 'facts' about the case, Rafferty asked Singleton to confirm it.

'I presume, as Mike Raine is a beneficiary of this trust, that you also represent him and that he was aware you represented his late cousin?'

Jonas Singleton hesitated, as if uncertain whether to disclose this information, but then it must have struck him that his firm was about to be involved in a murder inquiry, for he clearly decided co-operation was wiser than obstruction and nodded.

His confirmation that Raymond's cousin was also his client and that Mike was, because of the trust, certainly aware that he and Raymond shared the services of the same solicitor, posed several questions. Not least why Mike Raine had chosen to lie to Llewellyn when he had spoken to him on the phone and deny he knew anything about his cousin's affairs. Why would he lie? Rafferty wondered, before Jonas Singleton interrupted his silent musing.

'Raymond's shocking death brings another complication, and not just from my point of view as one of the trustees.'

'Go on.'

'I've already told you that both Michael Raine Senior and his brother, Anthony, the founders of the family business and the fortune that sprang from it, were obsessed with starting "dynasties". So it's not altogether surprising that the family business and family fortunes were put in trust until such time as the sons of the founders should produce issue. Now, with Raymond dead, part of the family fortune – a percentage of the business nominally held in trust for Raymond Raine – will come to Mrs Stephanie Raine as Michael's widow.'

'I see.' At least he was beginning to see that a whole host of new possibilities had been opened up. And while he might still be getting his head round the trust's stipulations, he was also forming the suspicion that Stephanie Raine's grief-stricken reaction to the news of Raymond's death must surely be far from genuine. Given the terms of the trust, it struck him as unlikely that any of the potential beneficiaries would be overly concerned about the continued good health of the others, particularly as in Stephanie Raine's case she and Raymond were merely step-relatives and not the loving mother and son he had assumed them to be. With Raymond dead, both his stepmother and his cousin stood to benefit financially, while

Felicity, the self-confessed and supposed guilty party in his death, stood to lose everything. The best she could hope for was that the trustees decided to take her on as a charity case.

But as he said to Llewellyn after they had thanked Jonas Singleton and left him to lock up, at least now that he knew their real relationship, Elaine Enderby's description of Stephanie Raine's fondling affection for Raymond as 'inappropriate' struck Rafferty as even more so. Obviously she had believed that Raymond was Stephanie's son – how much more inappropriate was her effusive fondling of a grown-up *step*son?

Llewellyn nodded. 'From your description of Mrs Raine Senior's reaction when you broke the news of Raymond's death and his widow's confession, it certainly sounds as if she disliked Felicity, hated her even. But do you think her dislike of Felicity is due more to the jealousy of an older woman for a younger one's fresher beauty, or might it be a sexual jealousy?'

'What? You reckon Stephanie had the hots for Raymond?'

Llewellyn winced at this crudity and said, 'I wouldn't have expressed it quite like that myself.' Although Rafferty was beginning to suspect the possibility himself, he always had the devilish urge to force his repressed Methodist sergeant to speak of such matters

– if only to save himself from inferences that he was obsessed with the sex lives of others. 'The thought did occur to me,' Llewellyn admitted, 'even if I would have phrased it differently.'

Rafferty grinned. 'There's nothing wrong in calling a spade a spade,' he said.

'And what about Felicity Raine?' Llewellyn added as they reached the car. 'What light do these revelations cast on her and her possible motives? Did she know about the terms of the trust? Or did Raymond keep her in ignorance of its contents and the whys and wherefores of how the family fortune was to be dispersed? Certainly, the fact that Raymond took steps to keep the identity of his legal advisers secret by concealing their contact details in a hidden compartment in his desk indicates his determination to keep Felicity in ignorance of his financial affairs.

'But ... Felicity Raine is a woman,' Llewellyn observed as they got in the car and he started it up.

'You spotted that?'

Llewellyn ignored Rafferty's interruption. 'Felicity Raine is a woman,' he repeated. 'A member of a sex renowned the world over for its curiosity. It's possible that Felicity searched her husband's study and his two desks until she found the secret compartment.

'Raymond Raine was a busy man with the

family firm to run. He would presumably have spent many hours away from the marital home. His secretary told us how hard he worked. It took the two of us no more than thirty minutes to find the secret drawer. Felicity Raine, with hours of leisure time in which to pry, may well have found the secret drawer also.'

'True,' Rafferty conceded as they headed back to the station. 'Not,' he pointed out, 'that it would have advanced her knowledge of her financial future one jot, unless Raymond *had* chosen to enlighten her.'

'Not necessarily,' Llewellyn contradicted him. 'Even if she failed to locate the secret drawer in her husband's desk, there are other ways to find out how she stood financially. The wills of the deceased brothers would, like all probated wills, be open to public scrutiny. If Felicity Raine was aware of that fact, she could have applied for copies and learned the details of the trust.'

'Yes, but if she did so, she would learn that killing Raymond wouldn't make her a wealthy widow – rather the opposite, in fact, which rather takes away her motive for killing him. Remind me to ask her if she knew the terms of the wills. Oh, and you can check with the Probate Office in the morning and find out if Felicity *did* apply for copies of the late partners' wills.'

Llewellyn nodded. 'Certainly we can ask

Felicity Raine if she knew the terms, but maybe, given the deceit practised by both Stephanie and Mike Raine, it might be unwise to take what she or any other member of the Raine family says at face value.'

Rafferty nodded. As Llewellyn had said, given the ready lies of the other Raine family members, it would be extremely foolish to take what any of them said as gospel. And even though Elaine Enderby had told him that, as far as she knew, Felicity had no close family, and Felicity herself had confirmed it, Rafferty resolved to make sure of this, too, as soon as possible. He was determined not to give Llewellyn occasion to say 'I told you so' should Felicity turn out to follow her step-mother-in-law's failure to be as truthful as a murder investigation required.

Having failed to check the truth about relationships once, he was not about to make the same mistake a second time.

It had turned into a long day. Jonas Singleton had agreed to stay late in his office especially to see them. By eight o'clock, Rafferty for one was more than ready to call it a day. But as they entered the station and he saw Bill Beard beckon him and nod towards a woman sitting in the waiting area, he suspected the day was about to become even longer.

Six

Beard nodded again towards a plump woman in her mid-thirties who was currently the only occupant of the station's waiting area. Her reddened nose and eyes revealed she was upset. This redness did no more to improve her plain appearance than did her mannish tweed trouser suit and stout brown brogues.

'Name of Sandrine Agnew – *Ms*, I shouldn't wonder,' Beard added. 'Claims she's a good friend of Felicity Raine and demanded to speak to the officer in charge. Said she's got evidence—'

'*Evidence*, yes. I'm always glad of more of that. Ms Agnew, you say?'

Beard nodded.

Rafferty beckoned Llewellyn and they crossed the floor to the waiting area. 'Ms Agnew?'

The woman, who until he spoke had seemed lost in her own thoughts, looked up and nodded.

Rafferty introduced himself and Llewellyn. 'I believe you've been waiting to see me?'

She nodded again, before earnestly asking, 'I spoke to Stephanie Raine earlier. She said that you've arrested Felicity Raine for the murder of her husband? Surely it can't be true?'

She didn't wait for Rafferty to confirm or deny it, but immediately continued. 'You've made a dreadful mistake. Felicity didn't kill Raymond. She couldn't – wouldn't. Besides, you do know he beat her, don't you? Raymond really was a very violent man and if Felicity had to resort to self-defence measures—'

It was interesting that she should make the same claim as Elaine Enderby. To have two independent witnesses suggest the same thing strengthened the likelihood that their accusations were true, and also increased the chances that the charges against Felicity Raine would be reduced to manslaughter – if they even advanced as far as a trial. It was now clear that Felicity was no longer the only suspect with a good motive for murder; and whilst any financial motive she might have had for killing Raymond was now dead in the water, the same wasn't true of Stephanie and Mike Raine, who had both been less than open with them.

'I understand your concerns, Ms Agnew,' Rafferty told her. 'But as you're a friend of Mrs Raine, what would you say if I told you that on the very morning of Mr Raine's death, she gave us a confession – a voluntary confession?'

Sandrine Agnew looked suitably startled. 'What can have possessed her?' She searched Rafferty's face for clues. 'You didn't believe her, I hope?'

'At the moment, since your friend has now retracted her confession, I'm not sure what to believe,' he admitted. 'But let me assure you that my entire team will be putting in long hours in order to find the truth. If Mrs Raine is innocent of this crime we'll find out.'

Hope glistened briefly in her eyes at his words.

'Perhaps, while you're here, you could explain why you believe that Mr Raine was violent towards his wife.'

'One would have had to be wilfully blind not to notice. It was perfectly obvious that he beat her. One only had to look at Felicity's poor, bruised face to know what went on. And then I saw her several times in Casualty – I work there as a volunteer – but when I tried to speak to her, she rushed off without waiting for treatment.'

'I see. But from what you say, Mrs Raine might have attended Casualty for something else, especially as it seems she didn't actually confide in you about this matter?'

Sandrine Agnew looked put out that this was so and that she was obliged to admit it.

'Though I suppose it's understandable that Felicity suffered from misplaced loyalty. Many women do, I'm afraid. I urged Felicity to leave him. But even though she told me several times that she would, she kept putting it off. I think she was too frightened of what his reaction might be if she did so, even though I was more than happy to offer her a roof.'

Rafferty, as he studied the rather mannish Ms Agnew, got the unmistakable impression that Bill Beard's political incorrectness had been spot on and that a roof wasn't all she would like to offer Felicity.

'She wouldn't even allow me to speak about the abuse. She just changed the subject very pointedly every time I brought it up. She was in denial, of course. Wilfully so.'

She wasn't the only one, thought Rafferty. It was clear that Sandrine Agnew carried a torch for Felicity Raine. But it seemed unlikely the exquisite Felicity would have anything stronger than feelings of friendship for the plain and ungainly Sandrine Agnew.

'But I want to do anything I can that might help her. Someone has to, and from what you say it's clear that Felicity is in no state to help herself. But until I can come up with some more pro-active way of helping her, the least I can do is make an official statement about Raymond's violence. I want to be sure it's taken into account.'

'Of course. Perhaps you'd wait here while I get my sergeant to organise someone to take it?'

'Can't *you* do it? I promise it won't take very long.'

Rafferty, thinking of the evening with Abra that lay ahead, was tempted to refuse. But then he thought of Felicity Raine, who would surely, come the morrow, find herself in the cells, and changed his mind. Besides, he reminded himself, he might learn something valuable. Sandrine Agnew had claimed to be a friend rather than just a neighbour. It was possible she knew more about the Raines and the state of their marriage than Elaine Enderby.

He collected a statement form from behind the desk and led her and Llewellyn to one of the interview rooms.

Once the statement was taken care of, Rafferty asked Sandrine Agnew, 'How come you and Mrs Raine know one another?'

'We're unlikely friends, you mean? Me being so plain and Felicity so gorgeous?'

Rafferty hastened to deny that such had been in his mind.

To Sandrine Agnew's credit, she laughed. 'I've found that not everyone is as reticent in airing their opinions as you, inspector.'

Beside him, Llewellyn shifted restlessly. A tiny sigh escaped from his lips as if in protest at such a dubious judgement. But he said nothing.

'Several people haven't scrupled to say exactly what they're thinking. Anyway, as to how come we became friends, we both used to attend the same keep-fit classes and a group of us would go out afterwards to the pub and undo the good we had just done. Gradually, people fell away, as you do when it comes to keeping fit. Felicity and I did the same, but we seemed to have struck up an acquaintance more deep than merely one of commiserating with one another over our aching bodies. And although we dropped the keep-fit, we continued with the pub bit for a while, but then that too petered out. I met her again shortly after she married Raymond and even though she said nothing, I could see that something was troubling her.'

'Apart from the violence you've already mentioned, what else can you tell me about their relationship?'

'Not a lot, I'm afraid. I didn't see much of him. Felicity and I generally met elsewhere and she rarely talked about him – I suppose she was worried that if she did so she might encourage more unwelcome questions about her bruises and black eyes.'

'May I ask *you* something?' Llewellyn asked.

'Of course.'

'Do you think there's any possibility that she could have killed Raymond?'

Ms Agnew shook her head vehemently. 'No. Never. I'd stake my life on it.'

Felicity Raine certainly didn't lack for champions. Though it must be sad to know, Rafferty thought, as Sandrine Agnew surely must, that your love was hopeless.

Once Rafferty had ushered Sandrine Agnew out, with reassurances that he would do his best by her friend, he said to Llewellyn that that really *was* it for the night. 'I don't know about you, but I for one can absorb nothing more.'

By now it was eight thirty. He'd just have time to shower and change into one of the fancy Italian suits he'd treated himself to a couple of investigations ago and, with the associations they conjured up, he thought he'd never bring himself to wear. But memories fade, even black memories.

Tonight, more than anything, he felt the best thing he could do for the investigation was to relax and let his brain and thought processes mellow during a long-booked and long-looked-forward-to evening with Abra. 'We'll sit down tomorrow morning and digest what we've learned so far and then decide on our priorities.'

After they had said good-night and Rafferty had popped into the Incident Room to check on anything else that had come in, he followed Llewellyn out to the car park. Gradually, he became aware of what a beautiful evening it was. The sky was a deep, vibrant blue where it wasn't already washed with the yellow, pink and orange of a fabulous sunset.

He smiled as he pulled out his car keys. The weather was certainly an improvement on the lashing rain that had heralded Raymond Raine's murder and Felicity's confession.

In spite of the increasing questions about the case and his early but anticipated loss of Felicity Raine's confession, he felt surprisingly upbeat. Not, of course, that his happiness had anything at all to do with the case – how could it when they now faced the long haul of a murder investigation rather than the easier confession-and-guilty-as-charged route?

But for tonight at least, he mused as he climbed in the car, he intended to enjoy himself. It might be the last chance he had for some time.

He was taking Abra out for a late meal, a special meal. He had booked a table for two for nine o'clock in the romantically softly lit courtyard area of one of the town's most upmarket restaurants, hoping to encourage Abra to finally forgive him for his less than chivalric showing in June.

He was looking forward to it. And since even the weather had decided to come out on his side, he felt he had reason to be optimistic. A balmy night, soft lights, sweet music, wine and an excellent meal would, he was convinced, encourage Abra to accept that to err is human, but to forgive is divine. It wasn't as if he had meant to be obtuse and hurtful. His hopes were high that tonight would see them back to how they had been but a few months earlier, and he was determined to spare no expense on the evening.

That was why the call on his mobile just before he inserted the key in the ignition came as such a blow.

Seven

Rafferty felt a curious reluctance to answer the demanding ringtone. He always turned his mobile off prior to interviews and had only just turned it back on.

He felt an even greater reluctance when he pulled the phone from his pocket and saw that it was Abra calling. Why was she calling now? he wondered. He had told her he would be home in good time for their restaurant date and he would be. He'd promised her that morning as he'd given her a quick goodbye kiss.

It was only just after half-eight now, so he was in plenty of time. His uneasiness increased and he found himself wishing he hadn't turned the damn thing back on because some sixth sense told him he wouldn't like what she had to say.

Squashing down his uneasy thoughts, he forced out a cheerful greeting. 'Hello, my little Abracadabra. I hope you're looking forward to this evening as much as I am. It's going to be magical, I know it. Promise me you'll dress up in that houri's outfit that

Dafyd told me you threatened to wear to his wedding.'

Rafferty still couldn't understand how he had failed to spot Abra at Llewellyn's wedding or the reception afterwards. He could only put it down to the fact that, without a partner and painfully conscious of the fact, he had made sure the night was clouded by an anaesthetising alcoholic haze.

To his dismay, Abra's reply confirmed his fear that he wouldn't like what she had to say.

'Oh God, Joe. You're making me feel guilty now. Sorry, love, but you'll have to cancel the restaurant booking. I can't come. I've been trying to reach you for the last hour to tell you, but all I got each time was your voicemail.'

'Can't come?' Rafferty became aware of the little-boy anguish in his voice and he did his best to eliminate it. 'But—'

'Please, Joe. Don't go all pathetic on me. You know I can't stand it when you do that. And it's not my fault that I have to cry off tonight, so don't think I'm doing it deliberately.'

Rafferty, about to but another but, buttoned his lip instead. When he spoke again, he tried to recapture his former breeziness. 'So, what's the matter? Why can't you come?'

'It's nothing for you to worry about – just some stupid family problem of Gloria's that

I need to sort out.'

'Family problem? Dafyd said nothing about a family problem.' Llewellyn was Abra's cousin on his mother's side. 'So what is it? Don't tell me his mother's got tired of pretending to be a prim Methodist widow and has put on her dancing shoes again to star at some seedy pensioners' nightclub?'

Gloria, Llewellyn's mother, had been a dancer before becoming the unexpected bride of Dafyd's Methodist minister father, more than proving the adage that opposites attract. Since discovering this glorious news about the mother of his sergeant, who could be a tad holier-than-thou at times, Rafferty had often wondered which of the two was the more astonished at their choice of partner.

'Dafyd doesn't know,' Abra told him. 'And you're not to mention anything about this to him. I don't want you teasing him about it.'

'What?' Rafferty gasped. 'You mean his mother really has—?'

'Don't be stupid, Joe. Of course she hasn't. It's nothing like that.'

'So what is it, then?'

'I can't tell you. I promised to keep it to myself. Look, I can't talk now. I have to go. The train's in. Besides, the signal's not good—'

Abruptly, Rafferty's mobile cut off. He stared at it in frustrated bewilderment. The sudden cut-off and the unsatisfactory and mysterious conversation that had preceded it filled him with anxiety. He rang the restaurant and cancelled the booking, wondering, as he started the car and drove home, whether he would get a black mark against his name for cancelling so late.

He shrugged heroically. What did it matter? There were plenty more restaurants in town. Besides, he had more important things to worry about; one was the gnawing conviction that the family problem Abra had mentioned was pure invention and that he would find she had emptied the flat of her possessions and left him, having finally decided she couldn't forgive him for his lack of support earlier in the year.

Abra's clothes were still there at least – most of them anyway, Rafferty discovered as he flung open the wardrobe doors.

He sank on to the double bed and stared into space. What family emergency could Gloria have that required her niece, Abra's, presence, rather than that of Dafyd, her only son? And one that it was clear Llewellyn knew nothing about? What could be so urgent that it required her to cancel their special meal and go haring off into the night?

He had thought – felt – that Abra had finally started to come round. She'd been much more loving towards him lately. His belly grew warm at the memory. But now, inexplicably, she seemed to be drawing away from him again. Surely she couldn't have taken *that* much offence at his thoughtless remarks about Felicity Raine's attractions? Or had that just tipped the balance away from him?

Although he'd rung her mobile twice since the abrupt ending to their conversation, it had been switched off each time and all he had been able to do was leave messages, messages that even to his own ears sounded that note of pathos that she disliked so much. She hadn't returned either of them.

What had he done this time? he wondered miserably as – instead of the anticipated romantic meal with all the trimmings – he contemplated a lonely evening and an even lonelier night. He had always thought Abra a reasonable woman – well, he amended, as reasonable as a man with Kitty Rafferty for a mother could think any woman. He wouldn't have thought her capable of deliberately punishing him for one unguarded remark. But he was beginning to think that was what she had done.

He found himself clutching Abra's pillow and he pressed his nose against it, breathing in her scent. It was a way to feel close to her as he stared, hollow-eyed, through the window into a night from which all hint of the earlier warm sunset had vanished.

                    ★ ★ ★

By the next day, Felicity Raine had been
declared fit for further questioning and, in
spite of having retracted her confession, she
had been charged and remanded in custody.

During the interview, she was asked
whether she or her late husband had noticed
the man in the car opposite their home. She
denied it; denied also receiving the note that
Elaine Enderby had said she had pushed
under the Raines' door.

This last claim certainly seemed likely to
be true because after he had dispatched PC
Timothy Smales to their house, he'd found
this note lodged under the Raines' front
doormat.

By Saturday, having still heard nothing
from Abra, but having heard plenty from
Sam Dally during the endurance test of the
post-mortem and Sam's macabre and long-
drawn-out descriptions of the processes of
death, Rafferty was feeling increasingly
desperate. So when he heard the phone
insistently ringing in his office, he raced
along the second-floor corridor to answer it.

But his hope that it was Abra calling, the
Abra he hadn't heard from since she'd
boarded the train for Wales, was dashed as,
to his disappointment, he heard Sam Dally's
Highland burr at the other end.

He covered his disappointment as well as
he could by putting on a cheerful voice,

unwilling to have Sam sense it and bait him. 'Hi, Sam,' he said. 'I hope you've rung to tell me you've got the toxicology reports.'

'They're all present and correct. Including the results of the tests on the milk in the two bottles delivered to the Raines' on the day of the murder,' Sam confirmed. 'Unusually prescient of you, Rafferty, that you ordered tests on the food and drink the Raines consumed that day. Both bottles of milk had Mogadon in them.'

'Mogadon,' Rafferty repeated as he tried to quell the little burst of excitement that filled him – almost, but not quite, quelling the disappointment at Abra's failure to contact him. 'Are you sure?'

'Of course I'm sure,' Sam Dally replied testily. 'I've got the lab results in front of me and unlike you, my dear inspector, I *am* capable of understanding forensic reports. And while the quantity in neither bottle was sufficient to kill the average-sized person it could certainly render them unconscious, especially if, like Mr Raine, you drank an entire pint in one go. Surprisingly, given that they're both what used to be called Young and Upwardly Mobile, neither of them tested positive for illegal drugs – or other *legal* drugs, either, for that matter. Tests on the blood sample taken from Mrs Raine when she was admitted reveal a quantity of the same drug was present in her system.

'You might be interested to know,' Sam added, 'that Mogadon is a proprietary, prescription-only preparation of the Benzodiazepin drug nitrazepam used to treat insomnia – in other words, it's a powerful sleeping tablet.

'Anyway, its presence in her system could explain her earlier amnesia as that's one of the potential side-effects of the drug, though I suppose it's possible that shock could also have had an effect on her memory.'

Even as Dally mentioned the possibility, Rafferty noted the element of doubt in his voice.

'It might be an idea to check with their GP if he prescribed sleeping tablets for either of them,' Sam suggested.

Rafferty sighed inwardly as he recognised that 'helpful' note he knew so well. He could practically hear Sam salivating as he added another little job to Rafferty's growing list of things to do, which, in a murder inquiry, amounted to a veritable Everest of checks and double-checks.

At least they now had the answer to one question, and the answer had been in Felicity's favour. For when Llewellyn had contacted the Probate Office, they had told him they had received no request for copies of the wills of the deceased Raine brothers from Felicity or, for that matter, from any other family member.

They were still waiting for the Australian police to get back to them on whether Andrew Armstrong, the third Raine-family cousin, had left the country recently.

Llewellyn had been allocated the job of tracking down the man Elaine and Jim Enderby had said had sat in his car watching the Raines' house; that task was still ongoing.

Although Sam's suggestion that he check with the Raines' GP sounded a simple enough task, in reality of course, as Sam well knew, it could turn out to be extremely time-consuming. Because if the Raines' GP replied in the negative to the question of whether he had supplied either of the couple with the drug, they would have to ask the same question of the GPs of all Felicity and Raymond Raine's friends, relations and casual acquaintances. No wonder the sly old dog was gloating...

'No prescription drugs were found in the Raines' house,' Rafferty told Sam. He had specifically asked the team to check. 'Though, now I think of it, that's unusual. Most people have the remnants of prescription medication littering their bathroom cabinets for months, if not years.'

'True. But maybe the Raines were just healthier than you, Rafferty. Not to mention neater, younger and, like yours truly, better-looking.'

'We can't all have your rich endowment of life's bounties, Sam.'

'Also true. But the late Mr Raine could certainly have given me a run for my money in the health and beauty stakes. He was one of the finest physical specimens I've had on my table for a long while. Makes you realise how many people let themselves go.'

This from the plump Dally, Rafferty marvelled. 'Tell me, Sam, were the quantities of the drug found in Mrs Raine's blood roughly the same as found in her husband?'

'Well no. Obviously not. If you ever listened, Rafferty, you might have heard me tell you that the husband downed a pint of milk. Mrs Raine had nothing like as much in her system, but of course she's half his weight and size so a smaller quantity would be all that was needed to render her comatose. I presume she watched her weight like most young women and wouldn't dream of drinking a pint of milk all at once like her husband.'

Dally went on, in his ever-helpful fashion, 'It seems to me that – if neither of the Raines was prescribed the drug by their doctor – if you trace which of their friends, relations or casual acquaintances took the drug, you could be well on your way to finding out whether Mrs Raine – or any of your other suspects for that matter – had access to it.'

'Yeah. Thanks, Sam.' Why didn't I think

of that? Rafferty asked himself in silent response to Sam Dally's statement of the bleeding obvious. He was thoughtful as he thanked Sam for his earlier information and hung up.

From Felicity's now retracted confession, to the earlier – as he had supposed – open-and-shut nature of the case, to the previous dearth of other potential suspects, everything was now the opposite of what it had first seemed.

Raymond Raine's death had been convenient for both Mike Raine and Stephanie, yet, as he'd already noted, the only member of the Raine family who had clearly been *in*convenienced (and worse) was Felicity.

And if someone else had administered the drug to both the Raines, the question why arose. So they could murder Raymond Raine and make it look as if Felicity had killed him?

Certainly, the only fingerprints found on the knife that had killed Raymond were Felicity's. Her prints – and those of Raymond and the milkman – were the only ones on the milk bottles delivered on the morning of Raine's murder and subsequently laced with Mogadon.

Of course that didn't preclude the possibility that some third party had gained access to the house after drugging the milk and had then worn gloves to stab the drug-comatose Raymond and position an unconscious Felicity so incriminatingly on top of her husband's corpse with her hand – even more incriminatingly – wrapped around the handle of the knife.

Rafferty didn't know whether his conjecture was correct. Still, he thought, taken with what Jonas Singleton had told them was her lack of a financial inducement to commit murder, it brought another element of doubt in the case against her.

It would certainly be a curious thing for Felicity to deliberately take a sleeping pill before murdering her much stronger husband. Why would she take something liable to render her drowsy at a time when she would need all her wits about her? But this was one question to which he felt confident Llewellyn would be able to provide the answer. He thought he could probably guess what it would be, too.

As by now Felicity Raine had appeared before the magistrates and been remanded in custody – and with Llewellyn still busy on the Renault Clio front – Rafferty was accompanied on the prison visit by DS Mary Carmody, who had finally been freed from her support of Stephanie Raine and Michelle, the *au pair*, by the arrival of one of Stephanie's cousins.

'So what did you find out?' Rafferty asked

her after she had reported to his office to tell him of her discoveries.

'Michelle Ginôt shares Mrs Enderby's belief that Raymond Raine beat his wife, although she said that when she suggested this to Stephanie, she ridiculed the idea. Actually, Stephanie Raine called me up to her bedroom and told me that because Michelle and Felicity had become very friendly, what the *au pair* said in her support of Felicity couldn't be relied upon.'

'And what Stephanie Raine says in detraction *can*?' Rafferty murmured to himself.

'Sir?'

'Nothing. Go on.'

'Michelle didn't deny that she and Felicity had become friends. Certainly, while I was there, Michelle admitted they had shared a few girls' nights in her flat over the garage. Michelle told me she liked to cook and that she and Felicity had shared several dinners there.'

'And what do you think? Do you think it likely Michelle would lie about Raymond being abusive, for Felicity's sake?'

Mary Carmody hesitated before she admitted, 'I don't know. It's difficult to know who to believe as they both seem to have their own axes to grind – Stephanie out of hatred of Felicity and Michelle out of friendship for a woman she believes has been grievously wronged.'

Rafferty nodded. There again, in Michelle's support, they had the same tale from Elaine Enderby and Sandrine Agnew. But while the information Carmody had provided was interesting, it did little to provide a useful pointer to the identity of the murderer.

He rose from his seat and said, 'You can go home and get a few hours' rest afterwards, but first, as Llewellyn's still tied up on another strand of the investigation, I'll need you to accompany me to the prison for another chat with Felicity Raine.'

Rafferty was keen to ask Felicity if she had any recollection of taking the drug Sam Dally had told him about.

But when they arrived at the prison and Felicity was brought to them, it immediately became apparent that she was as unable to answer that question as she was unable to recall the physical act of killing her husband.

'I don't *know* where I got the sleeping tablets from,' she told him in a voice made wretched by unhappiness and frustration. 'I don't even remember taking them, but I suppose I must have done as you say that the blood test revealed the drug's presence in my body.'

She frowned before she slowly revealed, 'My mother-in-law takes sleeping tablets, but I can't remember what sort. Maybe I helped myself to some from her bathroom cabinet?'

She gave a helpless shrug. 'I must have done so, mustn't I? I just wish I could remember that and the ... the ... well, you know.' With a catch in her voice, she said, 'I'm beginning to wonder if I'm going mad. How can I not remember killing Raymond? It doesn't make any kind of sense. Poor Ray.'

She sighed as her eyes filled with tears. She immediately apologised for them. 'You must think them veritable crocodile tears. It's stupid, I know, but I don't even know whether I'm crying for myself or Raymond.' She gave a rueful, watery smile. 'Perhaps my tears are for both of us; that our marriage should end like this, with Raymond dead and me as chief suspect. My solicitor told me I was foolish to make a confession given the circumstances.'

A confession she had since retracted, thanks to the good offices of that same solicitor.

Having managed no logical progression on why *Felicity* should have taken sleeping tablets, Rafferty decided, when he got back to his office, to approach the question of the sleeping tablets from the opposing view-point: why would someone choose to give the drug to both the Raines? So they could murder Mr Raine and arrange things so that it looked like Felicity Raine had killed him, as he had earlier thought a possibility?

137

Unless he was to ignore his growing doubts and return to the belief that Felicity was guilty as charged, he could think of no logical alternative.

But as Llewellyn often implied – more than implied – that his logic was mostly of the *il*logical sort, he was keen to put the question to Llewellyn and see what he could come up with.

Fortunately, by the time Rafferty got back, Llewellyn had returned to the station between his various Renault Clio pursuits. And he, of course, had no difficulty in coming up with an eminently logical explanation.

'I presume you've considered the possibility that Mrs Raine administered the drugs to her husband and *subsequently* swallowed a small quantity herself in an attempt to fool us into believing her to be no more than an innocent dupe of some third party?'

'Of course,' Rafferty was quick to agree. What his clever sergeant was implying, Rafferty told himself, was that Mrs Raine was attempting to encourage *him*, beguiled by her beauty as was Llewellyn's implicit implication, to leap to the wrong conclusions.

He hoped he wasn't that gullible. He also hoped – believed – that he wasn't yet ready to dismiss any possibility, as he waspishly informed Llewellyn.

Llewellyn's brown eyes regarded him steadily for several seconds without comment, before he continued on his analytical way. 'She could have acquired the drug from some casual acquaintance or via the internet as you yourself suggested, where prescription drugs are readily obtainable. She could have slipped previously crushed drugs into the milk herself, knowing her husband's daily ritual of drinking an entire pint at breakfast, waited for the drugs to take effect, killed him and only then drunk a quantity of the drug-laced milk herself, knowing traces of its presence would show up in any test. I imagine Dr Dally would have mentioned if he had been able to discern from the toxicology results whether there had been any major time difference in their separate consumption?'

Rafferty nodded and told him that, no, Dally hadn't mentioned anything of the sort.

'Anyway, as, if my scenario proves correct, there would probably have been no greater than half an hour's delay before Mrs Raine took her own draught, it seems unlikely,' Llewellyn added.

Rafferty again found himself agreeing. The logical mind was, he was sure, a thing of wonder. But it seemed, to him, to contain precious little humanity. No wonder – whatever trouble she had managed to get herself into – that Gloria Llewellyn was unwilling to have Dafyd find out about it.

However, for Llewellyn, the consideration

of his humanity or otherwise clearly held no deterrent to his relentless logical pursuit of the evidence. He was currently – with his wife Maureen's encouragement – studying for his upward progression on the police promotion ladder; Rafferty had little doubt that the Welshman would soon leave him trailing. It was unlikely that Maureen would be satisfied until Llewellyn reached the rank of chief constable...

'So,' Llewellyn continued, 'as that particular avenue of investigation is unrewarding, another might prove more fruitful – tracing the source of the Mogadon. Admittedly, if Mrs Raine obtained the drugs from some casual acquaintance who has since moved out of her life, we may never discover the identity of the supplier, but, on the other hand, if she obtained them on the internet...'

Llewellyn left the sentence unfinished, glanced at the still-technophobic Rafferty and asked, 'Would you like me to check out the computers and mobiles of the Raines and their family and friends for such possible purchases?'

'I was just about to suggest somebody did so,' Rafferty agreed. 'But it doesn't necessarily have to be you. I'd rather have you carry on with checking out the rest of the Renault Clio owners – it's important that we trace this scruffy type and find out just *why* he was watching the Raines' home. Even if he had nothing to do with the killing itself he might have valuable information about it.

'Jonathon Lilley has proved himself a bit of a techno-buff, so he can check out the computer angle – and not just the computers and other net-connected gadgets belonging to the Raines and their various acquaintances. We've already considered the possibility that – if she *is* guilty – Felicity Raine could have obtained the drug from someone else; the same thing applies when it comes to if she – or anyone else – used a computer in order to obtain them. And even though that check should be simple enough, perhaps you can give Lilley a hand when you've traced the man watching the Raines' home – is that likely to take much longer, by the way?'

'I shouldn't think so. The list of possibles has reduced considerably. There's only two left to check. I should have an answer later today.'

'OK. Well, finish that job first. It's too important to leave on one side. As I said, you can help Lilley with the computer checks when you've finished on the Clio angle. And that will, of course, mean Stephanie Raine, other family members or work colleagues with a possible grudge against Raymond Raine, and anyone else you can think of who might have some connection to the family. Tell Lilley to make a start on that line of enquiry before you set out again.'

Llewellyn nodded and headed off. He left Rafferty to his thoughts, thoughts which were an unsettling mix of wondering whether the still-silent Abra might decide not to return at all from her mission of mercy – if mission of mercy it was, rather than an excuse to disguise the fact that she had decided to leave him – and the worrying possibility that maybe Llewellyn was right and Felicity Raine *had* beguiled him.

Not only beguiled him, but by virtue of his reaction to her beguilement, somehow induced Abra to suspect it also. She had made several waspish comments since he had told her about the case. Certainly, before she had vanished off to Wales, she left him in no doubt that she felt he was too taken with the beautiful Felicity for her liking.

He sighed at this unhappy mix of thoughts and turned to ones less troubling. If Felicity Raine had obtained the Mogadon with the deliberate intention of murdering her husband it was unlikely she would have either obtained the drug from her GP or kept the pills once they had served their purpose. She could have thrown any tablets not used in any one of the rubbish bins *en route* from her home to the police station, having first made sure there was nothing on the bottle to identify her.

But whether she had or not, since in the interval said bins had been emptied by the private refuse firm contracted by the local council, they would now have no chance of finding them, though he would still check with her doctor. People who committed murder could make the most idiotic and basic blunders so it was always possible she *had* obtained them from her GP.

Armed with the toxicological evidence, Rafferty instructed the team to procure the general-practitioner details of every single one of the people even slightly connected to the case, as a priority. As he had remarked to Llewellyn, it should be a relatively simple matter to trace where the Mogadon had come from.

Meanwhile, anxious to get one of the pressing questions in the case answered, he picked up the phone and rang Dr Henderson, the Raines' GP, who had been out on his home visits when he had rung earlier. Fortunately, Dr Henderson had returned to the surgery.

Rafferty was thoughtful as he put the phone down. As he had expected, neither Felicity nor Raymond Raine had been prescribed the drug by their GP.

Dr Henderson had just confirmed what the painstaking search of the Raines' home had already indicated: namely that neither of the Raines had ever been prescribed any sleeping tablet and, as for other drugs, their medical records indicated it was long since

143

either one of them had been prescribed anything at all.

So where had the drug come from? And more to the point, *why* was it in their bodies?

Rafferty hoped Jonathon Lilley would soon find the answer to the first of those questions. And when he did, it just might help them find the answer to the second.

Eight

A day later Rafferty was no nearer to finding the answer to either question; worse, he was beginning to suspect that his careless remark to Llewellyn that tracing the supplier of the Mogadon should be a relatively simple matter was what had put the mockers on any hope of it actually *being* so.

Each of the general practitioners questioned with one or more patients on their lists who had any acquaintance with the Raines had emphatically denied prescribing Mogadon for them. Neither, as their earlier checks had revealed, was either Stephanie or Mike Raine on the drug.

Felicity hadn't been employed at all during her marriage to Raymond, so ex-colleagues were out. And, so far, so was family. They been unable to trace anyone with any family connection to her, though, as Felicity had told them she was the only child of two only-children who were both now dead, this particular search seemed fruitless and destined for failure. But fruitless or not, it was still on-going; all the lies and evasions of her in-laws

145

had succeeded in tarring Felicity with the same brush.

Rafferty read Stephanie Raine's statement through once again; interestingly, she made no mention that she was not a blood relative of Raymond, though admittedly, neither did she explicitly call Raymond her 'son'.

It was a small deception, but it struck Rafferty as being a deliberate one. What was she hoping to gain by this evasion? Was she perhaps hoping they wouldn't discover their true relationship and thus consider her – as Ray's loving mother – beyond suspicion?

Unlikely as it seemed that she could believe they wouldn't discover the truth, she was risking nothing. What could they actually accuse her of? Failure to contradict their wrong assumption?

Clearly, they weren't the only ones to have made the wrong assumption as the Raines' neighbour, Elaine Enderby, had believed Stephanie to be Ray's mother. He wondered why, and decided it might be a good idea to ask her. He checked her phone number and rang her.

Unfortunately Mrs Enderby was unable to recall how or why she had gained the impression that Stephanie was Ray's natural mother.

'I'm sorry, inspector. If it comes back to me I'll call you.' She paused. 'Actually, I've been meaning to ring you. There was something I should have mentioned before, but shock knocked it out of my head till now.'

'Oh yes? And what's that?'

'Well, actually, it was more a case of wanting to *show* you something. Perhaps you could come over?'

Intrigued, Rafferty put on his jacket and made for Elaine Enderby's house.

It was a pleasant day, with a fresh breeze cooling any hint of oppression. He was glad to get out of the station and revisit the idyllic spot even if, in his mind, it would be for ever tarnished by the murder of Raymond Raine.

Mrs Enderby greeted him warmly. She ushered him into her sun-bright kitchen and put the kettle on.

While she waited for it to boil, she said, 'I wondered after I put the phone down whether there is really any point in mentioning the diary now. Unless—' She gazed at him hopefully. 'Unless, that is, it might serve to help prove Raymond Raine *was* a violent man who abused his wife.'

'Diary?' Rafferty queried. 'What diary is this?'

'It's what I said I wanted to show you when you rang. I didn't mention before that every time I noticed fresh bruises or another black eye on Felicity's face, I made a note of it. I hoped such evidence might serve to gain her a better financial settlement should she ever find the courage to leave the brute.'

Of course, Mrs Enderby could have known nothing about the terms of the Raine family trust, Rafferty reminded himself.

She sighed and made the tea before sitting down at the table with Rafferty. 'It's too late for that now, of course, but maybe if she *did* kill him, it might get the charge reduced to manslaughter.'

She was right – such evidence of Raymond's abuse could well assist in reducing the charges against Felicity. He asked for the diary and Mrs Enderby was only too pleased to produce it, clearly hoping she might yet save Felicity from years in prison.

'At least Felicity seems to have good healing skin,' Mrs Enderby remarked as they sat companionably sipping their tea. 'The marks of Ray's abuse never seemed to last beyond a few days. Just as well, I suppose, seeing as he made such a habit of it,' she sadly commented. 'Wretched man always took off on some pretend business trip or other after assaulting Fliss.' She pulled a face. 'I don't suppose he could bear to look at her and see what he had done, though why that should be I can't imagine, as the man had the brazen gall of the devil himself.'

Rafferty sipped his tea. 'What do you mean?'

'I don't know whether he thought I was blind, stupid or just losing my faculties because of my advanced age.' She laughed at

148

this, being no more than fifty, and Rafferty laughed with her. 'Anyway, he obviously sensed my dislike and had the temerity to challenge me one day about why I was always so cool with him when we met. Well! The nerve of the man. You can imagine what I *wanted* to say. I had to bite my tongue to stop myself letting fly at him. But I thought he'd give Fliss another shiner if he thought she'd been telling me what he did to her, so all I said was, "You know why," and left it at that.

'Obviously I must have shot a dart in to his conscience, for he said nothing further about it.'

So Raine had not only been a bully, he had been brazen with it. An unpleasant combination. No wonder Elaine Enderby had wanted to let fly at him.

Rafferty finished his tea, thanked her for her hospitality and the diary and hurried back to the station. He was eager to compare the entries in Mrs Enderby's diary with those in Raymond Raine's business diary.

A few minutes of checking the two diaries side by side confirmed that Mrs Enderby had been right and that Felicity's bruises and black eyes invariably seemed to coincide with Raymond setting off on one of his business trips. Mrs Enderby's entries about Felicity's bruises covered a period of the past three and a half months. Why had he chosen such a time to deliver his blows? So she would have something to remember him by while he was away?

And what about Stephanie Raine? The discovery of her true relationship with Raymond was astonishing enough, but surely, if she had nurtured hopes of winning Raymond through murder, it would have made far more sense from her point of view if she had murdered *Felicity*. He had yet to question her about her continuing failure to mention her real relationship to Raymond or the fact that, with his death, her income from the trust would increase substantially.

He had just decided it was about time he addressed these and several other questions to Mrs Raine Senior when Llewellyn returned after his latest trip to check out Renault Clio owners. Rafferty dropped Stephanie Raine's statement as he took in Llewellyn's expression.

'You look like a man just back from a hot date. So what's the latest?'

'Something I think you'll find interesting – not least because it muddies the waters of Felicity Raine's possible guilt still further.'

Rafferty's eyes narrowed at Llewellyn's remark, but he sat back, careful to betray no other reaction. Once again, the brief spell of summer weather he had enjoyed earlier had vanished, replaced by another heavy, chilling downpour. Rafferty waited with as much patience as he could muster while Llewellyn divested himself of his sodden raincoat and umbrella and sat down.

Now, as Llewellyn reported, the Renault Clio owners had been narrowed down until only one name remained: that of a Mr Peter Dunbar.

But Mr Dunbar was no longer at the address the DVLC at Swansea had supplied. So Llewellyn had spoken to the neighbours at Peter Dunbar's old, Swansea-supplied address. 'I learned some interesting things,' he told Rafferty.

'Come on then, let's hear them.'

'After showing the photo of Felicity Raine and the one of Peter Dunbar that Swansea emailed over, I discovered that Felicity Raine and Dunbar had been married and that after Dunbar's business failed and he'd taken to drink, she left him. Couldn't stand his drunkenness, according to the neighbour. Dunbar promptly went to pieces. The marital home was sold prior to the divorce and Dunbar moved away – the next-door neighbour didn't know where. But—'

Llewellyn's pause heightened the suspense and was entirely unappreciated by Rafferty.

'Get on with it, man. I can't be doing with amateur dramatics when I've got the Super breathing down my neck for results.'

Llewellyn shrugged and continued. 'If Peter Dunbar – for whatever reason – had hoped to conceal his current location while he stalked either his ex-wife or Raymond Raine, he didn't make a very good job of it. I quickly traced him from the pile of credit-card statements that the new owners of his and Felicity's marital home had put aside. When I contacted the several credit-card companies that Dunbar used, they told me that most of Dunbar's recent spending was done here, in Elmhurst.'

'Considerate of him to provide his own paper trail for us, especially as – along with the Renault Clio evidence – it places him nicely in the town where his ex-wife lived with Raymond Raine.'

'Mm. Anyway, I had the foot soldiers show Dunbar's enhanced photo around the pubs here in Elmhurst – remember that Elaine Enderby said the man watching the Raines' home smelled strongly of drink?'

Rafferty nodded.

'Given that information, it seemed a fair possibility that Dunbar would be known in the local pubs. And he *was* known. We soon had a rough description of the area of the town where Dunbar was – from the credit-card trail – believed to live. A trawl around the streets quickly discovered Dunbar's blue Renault Clio with the partial registration number as described by Mrs Enderby.'

'You haven't questioned him yet?'

Llewellyn shook his head. 'I thought you

would want to be in at the kill, as it were.'

Damn right, thought Rafferty. 'You've done well, Daff. So, come on – tell me the rest.'

'As I said, Dunbar went to pieces when his wife left him. Apparently, according to the neighbour, he'd been going downhill for some time. His business had folded. He'd been drinking too much, staying out all night—'

'Yadda, yadda, yadda, as the Americans say. The usual stuff.' Rafferty, with his own unhappy memories of drinking too much because his late first wife *wouldn't* leave him, had little relish for a trip down Memory Lane. Now he asked, 'Anything else more potentially incriminating? Had he ever been heard to utter threats of violence against Raymond or Felicity?'

'Yes. Or rather, the neighbour said Dunbar didn't utter specific threats. They were more generalised ones, addressed to marriage wreckers and men who stole other men's wives.'

Although Llewellyn's reply provided an affirmative answer to Rafferty's question, it sounded unduly hesitant. Rafferty suspected Llewellyn thought he would pounce on it as evidence in Felicity Raine's favour.

Certainly, Llewellyn was quick to add, 'I have to stress that the neighbour I spoke to, a Mrs Lillian Anderson, an immediate next-door neighbour, who seems to have known both Mr Dunbar and his ex-wife quite well, said she thought Mr Dunbar's threats of violence were so much hot air. In her opinion they were said more to make a noise and make clear who was the innocent party in the break-up than because he really intended carrying out any threatened violence.'

'That doesn't gel with him lately taking to sitting outside the Raines' home,' Rafferty was equally quick to point out. 'Nor does it lessen the suspicious coincidence that Raymond Raine was murdered during Dunbar's stalking offensive. And if we take those two points with various other pieces of evidence, the case against Felicity Raine is no longer looking even remotely open and shut.' Which was a conclusion he had reached even before Llewellyn's latest discoveries.

Llewellyn couldn't argue with that. Well, perhaps he yet might, but at least he nodded at Rafferty's statement, his second admission that an element of doubt about Felicity Raine's presumed guilt had now crept in.

Several elements of doubt, in fact, that made Felicity Raine's conviction a thing of lessening certainty, including Dally's revelation that both the Raines had drunk the milk containing the sleeping tablets, and Jonas Singleton's revelation that Raine's cousin and business partner felt deeply wronged by Raymond hanging on to the extra 10 per cent share of the business which he felt rightly belonged to him. Now the discovery that Felicity's ex-husband, Peter Dunbar, also had reason to feel wronged – perhaps with greater cause – the sure thing that had so pleased Superintendent Bradley was unravelling before their eyes. And although part of him felt relieved that Felicity Raine wouldn't now be defenceless in the face of the charges against her, Rafferty was aware that Abra felt less than happy with his championing of Mrs Raine. Was that why she had gone off? he miserably wondered again, with Gloria Llewellyn's 'problem' no more than a useful excuse?

Rafferty didn't think he *had* championed Felicity particularly, but he was certainly keen for her to receive the full benefit of any element of doubt; perhaps it was that element which Abra – with that seemingly infallible women's intuition that most females seemed to rely on when it came to their menfolk – had picked up on. The fact that Felicity Raine was a very attractive woman only exacerbated the trait.

His ma was the same. She had always had an unerring eye for the tiniest misdemeanour, though why wanting to be certain that a suspect was guilty should be regarded in such a light eluded him.

Later, maybe; he would have time for these reflections but, as the Super had reminded him only that morning, the gore-hungry British public and the obliging tabloid press who provided them with most of the red meat they required were hotly demanding satisfaction and it was his job to provide them with it.

'Come on, then,' he said to Llewellyn. 'Let's go and see what Dunbar has to say for himself.'

Nine

Rafferty noted, as they drew up behind it and parked, that the car outside number 45 was undoubtedly the same one that Elaine Enderby had claimed was outside the Raines' house prior to Raymond Raine's murder. It was the same make and colour; even the partial registration number Mrs Enderby had supplied was the same. Not that he had for a moment doubted that Llewellyn's information would prove anything but accurate.

As they got out of the car and examined the other vehicle, Rafferty observed that the Renault's road tax was out of date and that the wear on all four tyres was below the minimum legal requirement.

'What do you bet he hasn't got any insurance or a current MoT either?' Rafferty remarked as they crossed the pavement and knocked on the door of number 45.

At first, there was no answer. After peering through the letterbox, Rafferty was about to knock for the third time when the door was abruptly wrenched open and a tired-looking,

157

unshaven man in his late thirties demanded, 'What do you want?'

The man, whom Rafferty presumed was Peter Dunbar, looked bleary-eyed. Given what Llewellyn had learned about his habits it seemed likely he was suffering from the effects of a raging hangover.

He certainly barked at them, before they could answer his question, in a voice furious enough to suggest he was currently suffering the usual morning-after punishment: 'I was asleep. You woke me up.'

Rafferty took in the crumpled shirt and trousers, neither of which looked particularly clean and which spoke eloquently of the too-familiar memory of nights spent comatose on the settee during his own miserably unhappy marriage, and said, 'I'm sorry, sir.' It was now well after eleven in the morning. 'Work nights, do you?' he enquired with every appearance of solicitude, which his own well-remembered and deadly stints of working through the long, dark hours while others slept ensured was sincere.

The man scowled and muttered, 'No.'

'You *are* Mr Peter Dunbar, sir?'

A wariness entered Dunbar's eyes. Rafferty guessed it had just dawned on him who they were and why they might have reason for calling on him.

'Yes. I'm Peter Dunbar. Who are you and what do you want?'

'Several things, actually.' Rafferty answered the second question first. 'But let's not chat here on the step. I imagine you know why we're here. Perhaps we could come in?' He took his warrant card out and held it under Mr Dunbar's nose before the man could voice any further objections.

Rafferty was interested to note the colour draining from Dunbar's blotchy red face. And although he was aware that the most innocent of witnesses exhibited signs of anxiety at having the police turn up on their doorstep, Peter Dunbar could not be included in such a category. At the very least, he was guilty of stalking the Raines around the time the wife-stealing Raymond was murdered. Certainly, if Dunbar *was* innocent, his reaction was way beyond the norm.

They followed Mr Dunbar as he turned abruptly on his heel and led the way down the dim, narrow hallway, which was lit only by the daylight filtering from the open door of a tiny kitchen at the rear.

Rafferty glanced around as they reached the back room. He couldn't help but note that Peter Dunbar's home looked – and smelled – as unkempt as the man himself. The furniture seemed to consist mostly of piles of cartons and tea-chests. It was as though, having made the effort to remove himself and his possessions from his previous, marital, home, Dunbar had not only run out of interest but also out of the energy required to unpack.

Almost hidden behind the piled-up boxes was an expensive-looking dark brown leather settee. It looked completely out of place in this tiny terrace, being more than a cut or two above it in terms of quality, and had obviously been purchased for a much larger room.

Rafferty found himself wondering if Peter Dunbar's recent financial downturn hadn't gone even deeper than Llewellyn had suspected. Had Raymond Raine – apart from stealing Dunbar's wife – also had something to do with that descent? Was that why Dunbar had been sitting outside the Raines' home at various odd hours?

If Dunbar's status *had* dropped as drastically as his current circumstances indicated, it would explain the incongruity of the large and expensive leather settee crouched in the back room of a small and scruffy terrace. And if Raine *was* the architect of Dunbar's emotional and financial freefall...?

As Peter Dunbar seemed to have lost his manners along with any previous good fortune, Rafferty didn't wait for the invitation to sit down that he guessed wouldn't be forthcoming, but pushed a couple of cartons out of the way, perched on the settee and gestured to Llewellyn to pull out his notebook and sit down.

As Rafferty watched, Peter Dunbar underwent several more colour changes. He suspected that for Dunbar the appearance of the notebook rendered their visit wholly official and completely unwelcome.

'I imagine you'll have read about the recent savage murder in Elmhurst?' Rafferty began conversationally.

Dunbar's head jerked up at the question. It was several seconds before he was able to put any kind of an answer together. 'What? No. I don't buy newspapers.' He pointed towards the nearest pile of cartons. 'And I haven't unpacked the TV yet.'

He thrust his hands deep in his pockets and leaned back against the nearest piled cartons as though keen to display an air of casual interest, and asked, 'What murder is this?' But the involuntary frown on his brow and the anxious flutter of the muscle in his cheek belied his relaxed stance. It indicated that he knew more about the murder than his quick denial proclaimed. But, of course, they already had reason to suspect this was so.

'You surprise me,' Rafferty commented, equally casually. 'I'd have thought you'd have heard about it – especially after we learned of your recent interest in the house belonging to the murdered man.'

Peter Dunbar's eyelashes began an involuntary blinking at this, but he said nothing in response, so Rafferty continued.

'Naturally, we assumed you must have known the victim or his wife. Or perhaps it was the house itself that interested you?' he suggested drily, though his glance around the room suggested he thought the latter unlikely.

Rafferty's last suggestion seemed to cause Mr Dunbar grim amusement. Not surprising, perhaps, given the size and opulence of Mr and Mrs Raine's home compared to Dunbar's current abode.

'You and your car were seen, Mr Dunbar, your registration number noted, covertly parked outside the home of Mr and Mrs Raymond Raine on a number of occasions shortly before Mr Raine was murdered,' Rafferty informed him before he could attempt any further denials. 'Perhaps – as we have since learned you used to be married to Felicity Raine, as she now is – you'd like to tell us what you were doing there?'

Dunbar slumped back, more heavily this time, against the piled-up cartons, his elbows digging deep into the top of a carton marked FRAGILE. He didn't seem to hear the ominous sound of what could only be breaking crockery.

'I suppose you'll find out,' he said finally in defeated tones. 'If you must know, I was hoping to catch Felicity alone. I wanted to try to persuade her to come back to me.'

Rafferty and Llewellyn exchanged glances at this.

'Persuade her to come back to you?' Rafferty repeated. 'Did you have any reason to believe that was likely?'

Dunbar nodded. 'She rang me. She wanted to apologise for leaving me so abruptly. She told me she felt guilty. But there was something in her voice that made me feel she wasn't happy. That gave me hope that she might consider coming back to me. We were happy once,' he told them with a wistful note in his voice that indicated he needed to convince himself as much as them that this had been so. 'I thought it was possible we might be again. I hoped—'

He broke off abruptly, almost choking on these last words. His breathing became so laboured that Rafferty stared at him in alarm. But Dunbar quickly got a hold on himself and waved away Rafferty's concern.

'I'm all right. I just get these attacks sometimes. The doctor told me they were caused by stress.'

Something else Dunbar might reasonably blame on Raine, was Rafferty's first thought. The damage Raymond Raine had caused Dunbar was piling up much like the unpacked removal cartons.

'I'm sure she would never have left me but for my unfortunate business reversals. After they occurred, I started to drink. Felicity didn't like it, of course. I suppose I wasn't very pleasant to live with. I'm not surprised she was caught by Raymond Raine's blandishments. He caught her, caught both of us, at a vulnerable time in our lives, in our marriage.' He tailed off after these revelations.

'I see. And did you manage to speak to Mrs Raine?'

'What?'

'You said that was the reason you'd been parked outside their house,' Rafferty reminded him.

'Oh. Right. Sorry. No, I didn't get to speak to her, although I saw her several times. But each time she vanished up the lane before I managed to pluck up the courage to call her name.' His shoulders hunched. 'I was scared she'd reject me, I suppose. Scared I'd imagined what I thought I heard in her voice when we spoke on the phone. After all, it was only a brief conversation.'

'What about *Mr* Raine?' Rafferty asked. 'Did you see him?'

Dunbar shook his head.

Rafferty wasn't sure he believed him, but, for the moment, he didn't question him further about it. He was more interested in discovering if Dunbar would admit to being parked in the lane on the morning of Raine's murder. Neither Elaine Enderby nor her husband had been able to confirm this important point; it being Jim Enderby's usual day off, the pair had enjoyed a lie-in.

'And was one of the several occasions when you saw Mrs Raine on the morning of her husband's death? Around seven, seven thirty last Monday it would have been.' Given Peter Dunbar's apparent emotional turmoil, he thought he might be in with a chance of a straight, possibly revelatory, answer. And so it proved.

'No,' Dunbar revealed. 'I didn't see her that morning. I – I must have nodded off. I remember waking with a start and a terrible crick in the neck after being slumped against the front passenger seat half the night.'

At least he'd admitted he'd been in the vicinity at the time Raine was murdered, thought Rafferty. His shot in the dark had paid off. Now he told Dunbar, 'You must realise, with Mr Raine murdered, that your behaviour looks suspicious? You had reason to hate him, to wish him some permanent harm. After all, you've admitted he stole your wife.'

Dunbar said nothing.

'When was it that your marriage broke up?' Llewellyn quietly interposed in to the silence.

'Nearly eighteen months ago.'

Rafferty raised his eyebrows. Raymond Raine hadn't wasted much time. He and Felicity had been married only fifteen months. The late Mr Raine's haste struck Rafferty as unseemly. It seemed likely it had struck Peter Dunbar that way also. And now someone had hastened Raine into the next world.

He found himself wondering again about the possible reasons for Felicity Raine's prompt confession to the crime. Had she had some reason *other* than her belief in her own guilt? Perhaps the desire to protect the hapless ex-husband from whom she had allowed herself to be 'stolen'?

'By the way,' Rafferty said, 'maybe I ought to mention that your road tax is overdue, twelve months overdue, in fact. Perhaps you haven't noticed as you've been busy with your house move – I know how these things can be overlooked.'

Dunbar looked startled that the conversation should move from the murderous to the mundane. There was more than a trace of relief there as well.

'Is it?' he asked. 'I – I hadn't realised. I hardly drive any more, you see, not since my accident. It was a bad one,' he revealed. 'And although it was several years ago now, I still haven't regained my confidence. Every time I climb behind the wheel, it brings it all back.'

Rafferty nodded. The accident and its on-going psychological problems could explain why Dunbar smelled the worse for drink when he drove himself to watch his ex-wife's home. Clearly, he needed to psych himself up in more ways than one...

He asked conversationally, 'How long have you lived here?'

'Six months? Seven?' He shrugged. 'I really can't recall exactly.'

Six or seven months and he still hadn't managed to unpack. Felicity leaving must really have hit him hard; hard enough to make him want to kill his rival? Rafferty wondered.

There again, he thought, seeing as Dunbar had failed to find the energy to unpack his belongings during a period of six months or more; failed, too, to update the address on his driving licence and credit cards; failed to change his tyres or renew his MoT, it seemed unlikely he would be able to summon the energy to commit murder.

Llewellyn had revealed that Dunbar's previous home, the one he had shared with Felicity, had been in one of the more upmarket areas of Habberstone, a busy market town four miles west of Elmhurst. Rafferty knew the area well. It seemed Dunbar had not just lost his wife. To judge by his current downsizing, he had lost everything.

'I think you must know the drill by now, Mr Dunbar,' Rafferty said as he stood up. 'Please produce your driving licence and other documents at the police station within the next few days.' Not one to kick a man when he was down, he added some advice: 'You might care to renew your tyres and MoT before you do so.'

Peter Dunbar nodded and asked, 'Is that it?'

He looked surprised when Rafferty confirmed it, a surprise not to be wondered at in the circumstances.

They let themselves out.

'It's fortunate for him that Mrs Raine confessed so promptly to her husband's murder.' Llewellyn repeated Rafferty's earlier thought as they climbed in their car. 'Even though she's since retracted, it's given him time to pull together a half-plausible tale to explain his presence near the murder scene. I, for one, certainly didn't believe his comment that he knew nothing about it till we told him today.'

Rafferty nodded as he started the car up, drew out and headed back to the station. 'And talking about that confession, having met her rather pathetic ex, doesn't it make you wonder if she had another reason – other than actual guilt, I mean – for making it in the first place? A guilty conscience can often inspire self-sacrifice of the most stupendous kind.'

As he concentrated on the road, Rafferty

sensed Llewellyn's serious dark gaze directed questioningly at him. Not for the first
time in their working relationship, he felt the
need to defend his latest theory.

'It's not impossible, Dafyd,' Rafferty remarked. 'After all, if she hadn't left him for
Raymond Raine, Raine would still be alive
and her ex-husband wouldn't be living out
of cartons and reduced to camping outside
her home. Maybe, if she feels partly responsible for the way things have gone for him,
guilt might encourage her to take the blame
for the killing herself rather than have her ex-
husband go down for the crime.'

Llewellyn still said nothing and Rafferty
pushed him for a response. 'You saw him.
He looks a broken man. I thought for a while
there that he lacked the energy to commit
murder, but maybe I'm wrong. I realised I
was assuming the inability to summon the
necessary energy to sort out mundane
household admin means that inability would
apply when it came to something more
emotionally charged. And jealous rage, even
in a broken man, can be the spur to do
something drastic when the blood's up. And
if he *did* kill Raine, she would realise what
her leaving had done to him. She must also
have realised that, in the state he's in, her ex
wouldn't be likely to survive long in prison.'

Llewellyn, the oracle of logic, spoke at
last. 'Surely,' he commented, the dismissal of

Rafferty's theory evident in his voice, 'that would be taking guilt over a broken marriage a little far?'

'Maybe,' Rafferty admitted. 'But it could also explain Felicity Raine's convenient amnesia about the event itself.'

'I rather thought Dr Dally had already done that. Didn't you say——?'

Rafferty broke in before Llewellyn could finish his sentence, unwilling to have his sergeant use his own words to contradict his theory.

'I want you to go back to the old address Dunbar shared with Felicity. Talk to the neighbours again. I'd like to find out a little bit more about his and Felicity's marriage.' Certainly, he thought, more than they'd known about it before Llewellyn had discovered its existence.

That had been careless, Rafferty acknowledged. Especially as they had already known how short was the duration of the Raines' marriage. Ray Raine had been thirty-two when he died and Felicity twenty-eight, although she looked much younger. In these days of marriages that barely lasted past the honeymoon, they were both of an age to have had previous marriages. Broken marriages too often caused another tragic breakage: that of life itself.

'While you're doing that, I'm going to arrange to question Felicity Raine again. In light of this latest discovery, I want to talk to her about Dunbar, ask her if she was aware he was watching her, her husband and their house. I'm curious to see what her reaction might be.'

Mrs Raine's legal representative, as Rafferty had anticipated, had quickly seized on her poor memory and general vagueness about her husband's death to persuade her to retract her confession. Part of Rafferty had felt a sense of relief at this. His uneasiness about this confession had grown with the passing of the days since Raymond Raine's murder. At least with the retraction, Felicity Raine would receive a full and thorough trial, should it even go that far, to establish what had really happened on that fateful morning.

She had already appeared before Elmhurst's magistrates and been remanded on a charge of murder to the largest women's prison in the district, it being better equipped than smaller local prisons to look after those, like Felicity Raine, who were considered at risk of self-harm and who were kept on suicide watch.

Rafferty was beginning to regret the murder charge. He had discussed it with the Crown Prosecution briefs earlier and they had agreed that it might now be wise to change the charge to one of manslaughter. What would they say in view of the latest evidence? he wondered, though he had a fair suspicion they would want to drop the case altogether.

Maybe, he thought, several days' experience of being a prisoner might have delivered the short, sharp shock that would trigger greater recall. Especially when she learned that they now knew about her ex-husband.

Felicity Raine, seated across the table from Rafferty and Llewellyn, looked slimmer and paler than ever. She seemed fragile, full of nerves, and jumped at the slightest sound.

Prison could do that to people, Rafferty knew. And the delicate Felicity Raine, who had the appearance of not being present at all half of the time, didn't appear particularly well equipped to cope with the worst of life's downsides. Altogether, her air of ethereal fragility had increased worryingly. She seemed to have no more substance than a will-o'-the-wisp that might vanish if he blinked. He was surprised she had agreed to see them without her legal representative being present.

He started gently. 'Why didn't you tell us you'd been married before?' he asked after they'd exchanged a few strained pleasantries.

She blinked and looked at him as if she didn't understand the question. But as she realised what he had asked, the ethereal look turned to one of watchful wariness, followed by a brief explanation. 'I'm sorry, but I don't understand what relevance my previous marriage has to my present situation.'

'Do you not?' Rafferty sat back, folded his arms and contemplated her for a few moments. 'It struck me that it might have a lot of relevance, especially as your ex-husband seems to have taken to watching you and the late Mr Raine.'

'Watching me? Peter?' She shook her head. 'You must be mistaken.'

'No mistake. He was seen, sitting in his car behind that little copse of trees opposite your house, on several occasions just before your husband's death.'

Strangely, Rafferty noted he had shied away from using the word 'murder'. It seemed altogether too brutal a word to use in Felicity Raine's fragile state. 'Surely you noticed him?'

'No.'

The brief reply, without any further curious questions, made Rafferty think he might be on to something with regard to her ex-husband's possible connection to the murder of her latest spouse. *Was* her previous ready confession an attempt to protect Dunbar? One prompted by feelings of guilt for having left him for Raine?

'Now, I have to say that I find it strange that you failed to spot him. Your neighbour and her husband noticed him on several occasions; Mrs Enderby even noted the part of his registration number that she could see and was still thinking about calling the police when she was distracted from this all too belated intention by the police activity outside your house.'

'Well *I* didn't see him inspector. I think I might notice if my ex-husband was stalking me. It seems unlikely.'

'Stalking? I don't think I said anything about *stalking*, Mrs Raine.'

She gave the faintest of shrugs. 'What you said, the way you said it – what other inference could there be?'

'Funny, because that's what *I* wondered. Perhaps it wasn't you he was watching – or *stalking*, to use your own word. Maybe it was your husband he was stalking?'

She tried to laugh off his remark as absurd, but her laugh sounded shaky. She glanced at him under her lashes, quickly, like a fawn fearing the hunter is getting too close, then looked quickly away again.

'Is it such a funny idea, though? After all, Mr Raine had stolen his wife.'

'Stolen?' She had the nervous habit of repeating his words back at him, he noticed. 'I wasn't *stolen* inspector. No one steals another human being unless they're kidnappers or terrorists and I can assure you that Raymond was neither. I went with him of my own free will. I divorced Peter of my own free will. No coercion was used.'

'All right then. Not *stolen* as such, but enticed away.'

This time her laughter was merrier and more convincing. It sounded like the treble of a small and delicate bell or the chuckle of a brook over smooth pebbles.

'You make Raymond sound like some fairy or goblin,' she told him, still smiling. 'He wasn't. I wasn't lured away by hypnotic spells or some pied piper's haunting tune, but by a man, a strong man I thought would take care of me better than—' She broke off.

'Better than your first husband had managed? Was that what you were going to say?'

'I suppose.' Again, she glanced quickly at him then away again. She admitted, 'I was weak. When my first husband's business went under, he found it difficult to cope. He felt a failure; he felt ashamed, I suppose, but mostly he felt angry. I didn't know what to do. I felt a failure too, you see. I couldn't help him. Not that he wanted my help. He seemed to feel that the fact that he might need it was even more degrading than his business failure.

'We drifted for weeks, months, making each other more and more unhappy. Then Raymond came along and made it clear he wanted me and wouldn't take no for an answer. It was as if a weight had been lifted from me. Suddenly, I didn't feel crushed by life, by demands and responsibilities I couldn't meet. I'm not a strong person, inspector.'

This time she met his gaze squarely, without looking away. 'I need someone beside me who is stronger than me. Not all women, even today, can be confident career types.'

Rafferty nodded. 'Tell me – I know you didn't have any form of employment during your marriage to Mr Raine, but, given your ex's business downturn, did you work at all during your first marriage?'

She nodded. 'I had a part-time job when I was with Peter. Nothing very grand. I tried to get more hours, go full-time, when Peter's business failed, but although I did increase my hours, my earnings were never going to make up for the loss of his. The fact that I had even sought more hours in order to bring in a greater income seemed to anger him more than please him. I felt I was in an impossible situation.'

Rafferty, like a dog after a particularly juicy bone buried he couldn't recall just where, returned to one of his earlier areas of exploration. 'You said before that you didn't notice your ex-husband sitting in his car watching the house you shared with Mr Raine?'

She shook her head.

'What about Mr Raine?'

'What?'

Rafferty was interested to note that the wary look was back in her eyes. 'I know you said that he hadn't noticed him either, but Mr Raine was a busy man, in and out of the house every day, following his business interests. I find it hard to believe that a man as sharp as Mr Raine wouldn't have noticed his love rival parked suspiciously behind the trees.'

'Well, if he did, he didn't mention it to me, which strikes me as unlikely.'

'Perhaps. Perhaps not. But I rather think he'd have noticed him, whether or not he chose to keep such information from you. Maybe he didn't want to upset you and thought he'd deal with your ex himself?'

Felicity Raine didn't attempt to agree or disagree. All she said was, 'As I told you, I don't know if Ray noticed him or not.' She gave a grim little smile. 'Do you know something, inspector? With you trying to blame my ex-husband for Ray's death, I'm beginning to wish my solicitor hadn't persuaded me to retract my confession.' She sighed. 'I must have killed Ray. No other explanation makes sense. Maybe I should retract my retraction. Accept my guilt for Ray's death and speed up the punishment of the court and my own period of atonement. At least, if I did that, I'd save Peter and others the trauma of being suspects in a murder investigation.'

'It's never a good idea to make such critically important decisions when you're upset,' Rafferty advised her. 'Speak to your solicitor again. Listen to his advice. Promise me you'll do that?'

She hesitated for some seconds. Then she nodded and said, 'Very well. But we both know what his advice will be, don't we? And I'm really not sure that it's advice I either want or should take any more.'

After an involuntary little shiver, she said, 'If you've nothing more you want to ask me, if I may, I'd like to go back to my cell now.'

'Certainly, but before you go, perhaps you'd satisfy my curiosity on something?'

For the briefest second she hesitated, before she gave a quick nod.

'You've retracted your confession, which is, of course, your right. But I wondered why you let yourself be persuaded to do so. You seemed sure enough of your guilt at first.' Though, even as he said it, Rafferty remembered it wasn't true; but Felicity failed to contradict him and he plunged on. 'What's happened to make you change your mind?'

She gave another little shrug. 'It's nothing that I can put a finger on, exactly. I can't really explain, beyond saying it's just that it's all so vague. When I told my solicitor that I'd suffered a period of unconsciousness before I came to and found myself and Ray – like

178

that, he managed to convince me that it brings in a large element of doubt that I *did* kill him.

'In fact the further away I get from that day, the more the whole thing seems like a dream. Or a nightmare. It's certainly seemed as if all this has been happening to someone else. Sometimes,' her voice cracked, 'sometimes, *I* don't feel real.'

Maybe it *was* truly just a nightmare for her and she hadn't killed her husband at all.

Since the lab had discovered that the two pints of milk that had been delivered on the morning of Raine's death had been tampered with and a quantity of crushed sleeping tablets inserted into both, the question of whether Peter Dunbar might have had a hand in this tampering was increasingly on Rafferty's mind. After delivery, the milk had probably sat on their doorstep for some minutes; long enough for anyone to tamper with it. And Dunbar had been there, on the spot, and with who knew what black thoughts curdling his soul.

Llewellyn, of course, had pointed out that Felicity might well have tampered with the milk herself in order to render her husband unconscious so she could kill him.

The post-mortem had revealed around a pint of milk in the dead man's stomach and Felicity Raine had openly revealed when questioned earlier that her husband invariably drank a pint of milk every morning. She told them he liked to line his stomach in preparation for the boozy lunches that were a regular feature of the fashion industry. She had also admitted that she didn't follow her husband's custom, having no boozy business lunches to attend. Her morning beverage was black coffee with either toast or cereal.

Certainly, as he had pointed out to Llewellyn, the blood test had revealed Mogadon in her system, sufficient to render her slight figure as unconscious as that of her husband. Though she might as easily have taken them *after* the deed, which, again, Llewellyn hadn't been slow to point out.

'Inspector?'

Rafferty roused himself from his internal debate. 'Sorry?'

'You said I could go if I satisfied your curiosity. Have I satisfied it?'

Not really, he felt like saying. But after staring at her for several seconds, his gaze locked with hers, he nodded and gave his unwilling consent for her departure.

Rafferty watched as, with a forlorn slump to her shoulders, Felicity Raine walked to the door and waited for the warden to unlock it and take her back to her cell.

He sat for several minutes after she had left, then, with a sigh of regret for he knew not what, he pushed back his chair and said, 'Come on,' to Llewellyn. 'Let's get back.

Maybe Jonathon Lilley's managed to unearth something from his email search.

'Even if he hasn't, at least now I can free you up to take some of the load off him. But before we see what Lilley's managed to unearth from the bowels of assorted computers, I think it's time we had another chat with Stephanie Raine. Like Michael, the victim's cousin, they both now stand in line for much improved inheritances. And, like him, she's another one who hasn't been totally honest with us.'

Ten

Michelle Ginôt answered the door as before.

And as Rafferty glanced at the subdued *au pair*, he caught the glint of gold at her throat. It was a piece of jewellery that looked familiar. But before he could recollect why this particular bauble should strike a chord, she had adjusted the delicate scarf at her neck, turned away and invited them into the drawing room, where she left them while she went to find Stephanie.

Did Michelle have a rich lover? Rafferty wondered as they waited for Stephanie to put in an appearance. She must have, he thought. Even though his glimpse of it had been brief, he thought the necklet had looked a costly piece; and, as they had discovered on checking Michelle's background, her family were not wealthy enough to buy her such a gift; and as an *au pair*, Michelle would scarcely have sufficient income to treat herself to jewellery.

Rafferty's gaze was drawn to the place where Ray and Felicity's wedding photograph had taken pride of place. The photo was no longer there, and now Rafferty found himself wondering what Felicity had looked like as Dunbar's bride. They hadn't found any photographs of her first wedding at their home; perhaps she'd tactfully discarded the photographic reminders so as not to offend Raymond if he should come across them?

Whatever the true depth of her grief for her murdered stepson, as soon as Stephanie appeared in the doorway, she wasted no time in polite conversation, but in a sharp voice immediately demanded what they wanted.

Rafferty took great delight in telling her. And after he had asked her why she had thus far signally failed to clarify her true relationship with Raymond or mention that his death would increase her income from the trust substantially, it quickly became clear that wounded innocence was her best ally.

'Really, inspector,' she protested, 'surely you understand that it never occurred to me to mention it? I was upset, naturally. You had just told me that Ray was dead – murdered by his own wi—'

Stephanie Raine's lips tightened on the bitten-off word 'wife', as if she couldn't bring herself to accord Felicity the status of Raymond's spouse. She sat down, without inviting them to do likewise, and stared up at them with a hint of defiance.

'I was in shock, naturally, as I'm sure my doctor would confirm. Besides, apart from anything else, I have always loved Raymond as if he was my own. He might have been almost a man grown when I first met him, but that's how I've always thought of him – as *my* boy. I suppose that's because, right from the first, we hit it off so well. It simply didn't occur to me to mention that he wasn't a blood relative.

'And even if it had occurred to me, for all I knew the police investigating his death would instantly seize on the wicked step-mother stereotype once they knew I would be financially better off after his death. Which is exactly what you're doing.'

Her carmine lips thinned. 'Of course, it was a possibility that played on my mind. Step-parents invariably seem to be cast in the worst possible light. How many times have we all watched as one or another step-parent of a murder victim appears at press conferences to appeal for the public's help, only to end up being charged with the murder? Besides, you must acknowledge that being told a member of one's own family has been murdered is not the sort of information one has broken to one every day. That is something you have to experience yourself to understand how deep the effect goes. It certainly doesn't increase one's clarity of thought.'

'Obviously not,' Rafferty agreed. 'Though I would have thought the fact that days have now passed since I broke the news of Mr Raine's death might have brought a little more clarity. And then, of course, you also failed to mention that your income from the trust your late husband and his brother set up increased substantially on Raymond's death.'

Stephanie bridled. 'I'm not sure I like your tone, inspector. Maybe we should be having this conversation in the presence of my solicitor?'

Before Rafferty could say anything, Llewellyn broke in. 'That's your choice, of course, Mrs Raine. But I think I can speak for Inspector Rafferty as well as myself when I say that we've found that most people with nothing to hide prefer to clear any confusion up as quickly as possible. Particularly in view of your stated fondness for the late Mr Raine.'

She looked a bit discomfited at Llewellyn's statement of the obvious and proceeded to backtrack.

'Well, of course I want to do that. But it seems to me you would be better advised in speaking to Felicity about *her* confusion. *I'm* not the one who confessed to murdering Ray in cold blood – *she* is. And Raymond is undoubtedly dead, yet here you are questioning *me* about our relationship and my possible motives for murdering him. Why are you trying to find a scapegoat when she's already admitted she did it?'

She turned back to Rafferty. 'Has she mesmerised you with her pretty face as she mesmerised Raymond and—' She bit off whatever else she had been going to add.

Rafferty suspected it would have been something along the lines of 'and the foolish, gullible first husband whom she was glad enough to leave as soon as the money ran out'.

Clearly, she had known about Felicity's first marriage, but, like her own true relationship with Raymond and her increased inheritance, had chosen not to mention it.

He thought he could guess why – so Felicity's embittered ex-husband wouldn't distract them from what she obviously considered Felicity's certain guilt.

'I don't think, in fairness, that it is quite that simple any more, Mrs Raine,' Rafferty quietly observed.

'Do you not?' Stephanie Raine's lips twisted in a contemptuous smile. 'It seems you really *are* as gullible as I suspected.'

As this was something that Llewellyn and Abra had also implied during the course of this investigation, albeit more subtly, Rafferty, unwilling to allow Stephanie to goad him into losing it, nevertheless found himself struggling to control his temper.

'Nor do I think this case is quite as clearcut as you seem to think it. It's usual, in a murder investigation, for the investigating officer to ask some basic questions – such as who benefits from the victim's death.'

Even as he voiced the words, he felt shame edge into his conscience that he should find a malicious satisfaction in making clear to Stephanie that she could certainly begin to number herself amongst the suspects. But he didn't allow his overactive Catholic conscience to prevent him from making the next observation.

'And as we know that Raymond's widow hasn't gained anything – has, in fact, lost out big-time – it behoves us to look at other possibilities. You, for instance—'

He got no further before Stephanie Raine's coolly contemptuous expression was replaced by the white heat of anger.

'You dare to try to lay Felicity's crime at *my* door?' She stood up. 'This conversation is going no further. If you wish to question me again, it will be in the presence of my solicitor. Now, I'm asking you to leave – unless you choose to arrest me?'

This last was said with a challenging air, almost as if she *wanted* him to arrest her. But Rafferty wasn't about to make that mistake. Stephanie Raine clearly wasn't short of money and would – if he was so foolish as to allow her to goad him into carting her off to the station – soon line up an expensive array of defence briefs.

From her expression and the contained fury in her eyes, Rafferty guessed she was holding herself back only with difficulty. He suspected she longed to give in to the impulse to give him a resounding slap across the face or mark him with her long, carmine talons.

Part of him wished she would give into the impulse – then he *would* have an excuse to arrest her and give her a taste of a night in the cells, like Felicity, whom she had been keen enough to have incarcerated. Instead, she resorted to the woman's eternal weapon, that of ridiculing the foolish male.

'She *has* got you mesmerised, hasn't she?' she taunted. 'Clever Felicity. It might be amusing if it wasn't so tragic. Admit it, inspector: you'd do anything to get pretty little, fragile little Felicity out from under, no matter who you have to pin Raymond's murder on to do it.'

Rafferty, who knew he would be wise to say nothing further, failed the wisdom test and replied indignantly, 'That's not true. It's—'

'No? I suggest you examine your conscience, inspector. You *are* a Catholic, I presume, with a name like Rafferty?'

Unwillingly, Rafferty nodded.

'Then try looking below the surface, below Felicity's pretty face, and you'll see something not nearly so pretty. You'll see poor Raymond's murderer.'

For Rafferty, it had been an uncomfortable interview. He and Llewellyn returned to the station and Rafferty sat at his desk staring into space.

Stephanie Raine had suggested he look beneath the surface and now he did just that. But it wasn't below the surface of Felicity's pretty face that he tried to peer, but that of Abra.

Once again he asked himself why she still hadn't been in contact with him. It was a question that had plagued him for several days now.

He looked across at Llewellyn as he industriously ploughed through the latest reports, and he opened his mouth. But then he closed it again without saying anything.

What was the point in worrying Dafyd when he couldn't tell him anything? Abra had said that, whatever family problem it was that had taken her away, Llewellyn didn't know anything about it.

Rafferty frowned pensively down at the expenses claim he was meant to be filling in. Blasted things always left him out of pocket, as his receipts had a habit of disappearing – when, that was, he remembered to get them at all.

He sighed heavily. So heavily that Llewellyn raised his studious head from the paperwork and asked, 'What's the matter? Don't tell me you've lost yet another twenty-pound receipt, but held on to the one for fifty pence?'

'How well you know me.'

Llewellyn was right, of course. It *was* always the receipts for larger amounts that vanished. But this time, it wasn't the loss of another £20 expenses receipt that was troubling him, but the growing suspicion that he had lost far more. He was becoming convinced that he had carelessly lost his greatest treasure, Abra and her love. This line of thought immediately connected to another and he found himself asking, 'How's your mum, Dafyd? It's ages since I've seen her. I really liked her when we met.'

Llewellyn looked surprised by this abrupt change of subject, but he answered readily enough. 'She's in reasonable health, I suppose, considering her time of life. Keeping busy, you know.'

But Rafferty *didn't* know, that was the problem. The trouble was, how could he extract from Llewellyn information that he presumably didn't even possess?

He gave it his best shot; who knew what a fishing expedition might turn up?

'A good-looking woman, your mum. I've always said so. Do you ever wonder whether she'll marry again?'

Llewellyn stared at him. 'Marry again? No. She loved my father too much to ever consider such a thing.' Llewellyn frowned and looked questioningly at Rafferty. 'Why do you ask? Has my mother said anything to yours? I know our mothers have become quite close.'

'No. Of course not,' Rafferty told him quickly – a shade *too* quickly, to judge from Llewellyn's concerned expression. 'I was just wondering, that's all,' he finished lamely.

Nothing more was said after that. But ten minutes later, it was Llewellyn who was sighing and being distracted from his work and Rafferty realised that all he had achieved with his failed fishing expedition was to place a – probably unnecessary – anxiety in his sergeant's head to go with the one in his own.

That evening, as he sat in the flat that was still empty of Abra, Rafferty stared morosely into the glass of Jameson's whiskey; its warm alcohol reflected his anxious gaze back up at him. But tonight he was able to find no solace in drink.

Even the flat, which Abra had transformed from its previous spartan bachelor look, failed to improve his mood. She had taken the place in hand since their meeting; the first thing to go had been his gaudy picture of Southend by night. Now, instead of his tired and mismatched furniture and curtains, they had expensive cream leather settees which Rafferty lived in fear of spilling something on. The carpets from which his ma had tried and failed to remove the stains had been taken up and disposed of; instead, the solid-wood floor underneath had been sanded and a warm varnish applied, much to his ma's disgust.

'It looks as if you can't afford a decent carpet,' she had complained when she had first seen the transformation. In her youth – and Rafferty's – the lack of a carpet, or sizeable rug at least, in the living room had indeed signalled a shaming poverty.

But whatever his ma might say, the flat had never looked so good: the tired, multi-coloured curtains had gone, to be replaced by wooden blinds varnished the same shade as the floor, and several large lamps provided a far more subtle illumination for the glowing colours of the pictures Abra had bought than the harsh centre light would have done. She had even organised the removal of the old gas fire and the reinstatement of the chimney so they could have the occasional open fire.

Yes, the flat looked beautiful; even Nigel, his upwardly mobile estate-agent cousin, would be unable to find much to sneer at now. But without Abra in it, it felt empty, soulless and unhappy; much like me, thought Rafferty.

And as he recalled Stephanie Raine's

taunts, he felt even more unhappy and slammed his glass down on the coffee table.

OK, he told himself, you have doubts that Felicity Raine did for her old man. Justifiable doubts, no matter what Llewellyn or the vengeful Stephaine Raine might have to say to the contrary. You're the man in charge, so you have to check them out, even if that means upsetting Abra, the applecart and whatever – *who*ever – else would be more than happy to see Felicity Raine conveniently tried and convicted.

It may well be that your brain – and other parts – are beguiled by her beauty. But even if they are and she's as guilty as hell, one of the first rules of a murder investigation is to find out about the victim. No matter what Stephanie Raine might have implied, it was still good police procedure to check out the victim and see if there might be anyone else – other than his wife – who might have had it in for Raymond Raine. And they *had* found others, several others, in fact, all with more than enough reason to wish him dead.

Apart from Michael and Stephanie Raine, who both stood to gain financially from Raymond's death, Llewellyn had also found another strong possibility in the cuckolded Peter Dunbar. And, for all they knew, there might be others whom Raymond Raine had treated badly. After all, not only had the Raines' neighbour and Sandrine Agnew,

Felicity's friend, told them they suspected he beat Felicity, but Raymond had also hung on to what his cousin, Mike Raine, undoubtedly regarded as his rightful equal share in the family business.

Ray Raine's behaviour to these two most important people in his life – his wife and his business-partner cousin – gave rise to the possibility that there were others to whom he had acted with a less than generous heart.

Maybe he ought to set his Welsh bloodhound to sniffing out the existence of more cuckolded husbands, resentful business colleagues or frustrated, lust-filled women of mature years who might have yearned after Raymond, as he suspected Stephanie had done? If he did so, he might just uncover something that would either get Felicity Raine out from under altogether, or prove her guilt once and for all.

With that thought to sustain him, Rafferty headed for his empty bed. He had just climbed between the cold sheets when, from the living room of his flat, he heard his mobile ring out. His heart started hammering with expectation as he asked himself who would be likely to ring him at this hour, who but the station – or Abra?

The thought caused him to leap out of bed and race for the phone.

Eleven

As Rafferty snatched up the mobile and said, 'Hello,' he felt flooded with a feeling of euphoria that Abra had at last remembered his existence. Just don't sound pathetic, he reminded himself as he spoke her name.

'Abra, sweetheart,' he said. 'What's happening?' In spite of his resolution of only seconds ago, he found himself demanding, plaintively, 'Why haven't you rung me? I thought—' He stopped abruptly.

'Thought what?' Abra immediately asked.

'Nothing. It's not important. You've rung now and that's all that matters.' He would rather Abra remained unaware of what he *had* thought ... He was only too conscious how much she hated it when his insecurities surfaced.

'I'm sorry I haven't managed to ring you before now, but you wouldn't believe the time I've had with Gloria. And I forgot to bring my mobile charger in the rush to get up here and Gloria's been in such a state that I didn't like to leave her to go into town to buy a replacement. Gloria doesn't have a phone in the house and she wouldn't let me ask the next-door neighbour if I could use hers. Anyway, it's taken me all this time, but I finally managed to persuade her that I really had to contact you and that in order to do so I needed to go shopping.'

It was on the tip of Rafferty's tongue to ask if she had never heard of public phone boxes, but he didn't want to start an argument, not now when she had finally rung him. Of course, Abra was younger than him, still in her twenties. He supposed it would never even occur to the mobile-besotted younger generation that such things as public phones were there to be *used* rather than just furnishing the street. The thought made him feel very old.

'You've certainly been a woman of mystery lately,' he remarked, striving for a lighter tone. 'I was beginning to think I'd have to get the Welsh boyos in blue to track you down. So how's Gloria?'

'Much the same. She's the reason I'm ringing, actually. Sorry it's so late. I hope I didn't wake you?'

'No. I'd only just turned in. Another long day at the coalface.' He again opted for the light tone, but this time it was the wrong choice as Abra immediately seized on his words.

'You're still on the Felicity Raine case, I gather? I've been reading about it in the papers.' She didn't wait for him to answer, but just added, 'Then the late night figures.'

Rafferty recalled Abra's thoughtful expression as he had kissed her goodbye on the morning of the day she had left for Wales. Her feelings of antipathy towards Felicity Raine had grown overnight; he knew she thought his concern for the woman was bordering on the obsessive and he had been unable to convince her otherwise.

'Funny that this Felicity Raine should turn out to be far from the innocent damsel in distress you imagined when you were gearing yourself up to be the valiant knight errant who freed her from captivity,' she commented. 'Tell me if I've got it wrong, Joe, only didn't she divorce her first husband and marry the second before the ink was dry on the divorce papers?'

Reluctantly, Rafferty confirmed it. 'I wouldn't believe everything you read in the papers, Abs. You know they always like to put the worst possible spin on things.'

'Mm.' She didn't sound convinced, he noticed. 'And now she's charged with murdering the second husband.'

As Abra had, with some relish, pointed out, Felicity Raine was hardly the stuff that would-be knights errant would be likely to champion. Rafferty thought that was all the more reason for *him* to do so. But he had no desire to talk further about Felicity Raine, certainly not with Abra, and he hurried on before she could say anything else on the subject.

'So, how are you? Have you managed to sort out your Aunt Gloria's little problem? When are you coming home?'

Abra laughed. But her laugh sounded strained to Rafferty's ears.

'So many questions. The answers are: OK, no and I don't know, in that order.'

Her third answer caused Rafferty's previously hammering heart to receive what felt like a mortal blow. 'You don't know? But—'

'Let me explain, Joe. I promised Gloria I'd say nothing to you or Dafyd – or anyone else for that matter – but just before she went to bed tonight, she had a change of heart, about telling you, at least. The truth is Gloria's got a shoplifting charge hanging over her.'

'What?' Rafferty was too stunned by this revelation to say anything further for several seconds. Whatever else he might have been expecting – from Gloria signing up with a mature version of the Folies Bergères to Abra telling him it was over between them –he had never considered the possibility of the morally upright Dafyd Llewellyn's mother getting in trouble with the law.

Dafyd's widowed mother had married a Methodist minister and although she had been a dancer and a bit of a girl in her youth and was still an outgoing, people person, he had never thought her likely to cause her family any concerns of a criminal nature. That had always been *his* family's role...

'So, what's she done, then?' he asked. 'Helped herself to some expensive jewellery?'

'Hardly. She is a Methodist widow, remember? Though I can see it's a good job you're not going to be responsible for the case as it's clear you'd have her convicted before she could say, "It's a fit-up, Your Honour,"' Abra reproved him. 'Whatever happened to innocent until proven guilty? Or does that only apply to good-looking young women like Felicity Raine?'

Before Rafferty could protest his own innocence, Abra went on. 'Anyway,' she said, 'at least she's yet to be charged, though I think it's only a matter of time before that happens.'

Rafferty was too shocked to say anything else for the moment, which was perhaps just as well. It gave him the chance to gather his wits before he tactlessly blurted out something else that he shouldn't. 'So how is she?' he finally asked. 'Is she OK?'

'What do you think?' she asked. 'When she's about to be charged with shoplifting and has my upright cousin Davy for a son? Of course she isn't OK.' He heard her take a deep breath. 'I'm sorry, Joe. I didn't mean to snap at you. It's just that I've been trying to cope with this on my own and it's been a bit of a strain. When I finally managed to replace my charger and Gloria put aside her scruples for long enough to borrow my recharged phone, I thought she was finally going to ring Dafyd, but not a bit of it. Instead, she rang your ma and had a long heart-to-heart with her about her arrest, though at that stage, she still refused to let *me* confide in anybody. But I finally managed to get her to agree that I could tell you. I think she's more upset and worried about Dafyd finding out about this than she is about the charge itself.'

'Understandably.' Worry about Dafyd finding out about criminal behaviour was something Rafferty could empathise with. 'Poor Gloria. You've rung him now, though, surely? It wouldn't be right to keep it from him. How did he take it?'

'He hasn't taken it one way or the other,' Abra revealed. 'He still doesn't know. And never will, if Gloria has her way.'

'But surely she realises he'll find out sooner or later?'

'I suppose she must, deep inside. How can she not? But at the moment, she's intent on burying her head in the sand. She refuses to let me ring him.'

Abra's voice lowered conspiratorially. 'She's in a bit of a state, to be honest, Joe.

She's been going through The Change and having a bad time of it. I wonder if that's what caused her to take the stuff from the supermarket. She's told me she's been sleeping poorly for weeks. She's been having these night sweats that wake her half a dozen times a night. And although she insists she's innocent of this shoplifting charge, she's admitted that she's been getting a bit forgetful and muddle-headed through tiredness. And then there's the video footage.'

'*Video* footage?' Rafferty repeated.

'Yes. She's bang to rights, Joe. I'm at my wits' end to know what I can do. Unless a miracle happens, I don't think there's any doubt but that she'll be charged. And although Aunt Gloria insists she's technically innocent, that she didn't *intend* to steal, the police here seem to have no doubts. And Gloria keeping banging on that she's innocent isn't helping, to be honest. But in a way she's right. She *is* innocent. I'm convinced she's telling the truth when she says she didn't deliberately set out to take things without paying for them. She's just so tired with not sleeping. I don't think you could call it proper stealing. I don't know what to do, Joe. But I really can't come home yet. You do see that, don't you?'

Abra's voice wobbled and Rafferty, conscious of how badly he had let her down once already this year, and unwilling to do so again, put aside his personal anxieties and hurried to reassure her.

'Of course I do, sweetheart. It sounds as if Gloria needs someone there for her right now. Your mother...?'

'She's away on holiday with Dad. Just about everyone in the family's away. It *is* August, after all. Besides, she doesn't want them to know about it either.'

'Yet you said she's spoken to Ma about it?'

Abra confirmed it.

'I wonder,' he said. 'What would she say if I got Ma to agree to travel up there – to add a bit more womanly support and all that? Might be just the ticket, and no one can say that Ma hasn't had occasion to learn something about the law and all its processes.'

At least as talented as his ma at ferreting out information, since they had been together Abra hadn't taken long to extract from Rafferty most of the juicy details of these learning processes.

'It would certainly take some of the worry off me,' Abra agreed. 'Would she come, though?'

'Oh, I think you can leave that to me,' Rafferty promised airily. 'I can be quite the persuader when I set my mind to it – I'm not Ma's blue-eyed boy for nothing.'

'It's true that Aunt Gloria might listen to and be comforted more by an older woman,' Abra murmured. 'Whatever I say just seems to get her goat. As I said, there's video footage, so there doesn't seem much question but that once she *is* charged she'll be found guilty. God knows what she'll do if she really thinks Dafyd is likely to find out about it. Just make sure *you* don't let anything slip.'

'Mum's the word,' Rafferty agreed while he marvelled at the strange turns of the wheel of fate.

Dafyd Llewellyn had been strictly raised, on his minister father's insistence, with a staunchly moral outlook on life in which wrongdoing was never anything but wrong, and always deserved punishment.

Rafferty, with his own family's predilection for breaking laws they regarded as unimportant, had had several anxious episodes himself in keeping news of their actions from Llewellyn. It was ironic that he should now be charged – unfortunate word in the circumstances – with keeping news of *Llewellyn's* family's wrongdoing from him.

He sighed. He hated to be put in this position. He just hoped Dafyd never found out about it – or that his DI had known about it and said nothing to him.

Abra said she was tired; she had had another trying day and wanted her bed.

'OK, love. But promise me you'll ring me around ten tomorrow morning at work?'

Abra promised.

'I'll drop in on Ma first thing in the morning on the way to the station and exert my fabled charm to persuade her to travel up to Wales. Though I don't anticipate any problems. I know how much she likes Gloria. I'm sure she'll be only too pleased to provide whatever she can in the way of support.' Rafferty paused, then said, 'Blow me a kiss, Abra. You don't know how much I'm missing you, sweetheart.'

Abra blew several kisses and, in spite of her professed tiredness, they made a lingering farewell.

With the depressing thought that it could be several days yet before Abra was able to return home, Rafferty poured another large one and recrossed the hall to his bedroom, only to be hit again by how much he was missing her. The flat felt like a shell of a home without her presence, the bedroom just a place to sleep. Maybe, he thought, when she returned, they'd have another go at making babies together...

Though, after their last experience in that direction, which had caused his entry into Abra's bad books, he didn't dwell on how Abra might take the suggestion.

Rafferty rang his mother first thing the next morning to say he was coming over before work for a chat about Gloria's little problem.

'I'll look forward to it,' she said. 'I'll have the kettle on ready, son. And I've got a nice bit of back bacon and some free-range eggs. They should set you up nicely,' she said before he said he had to go and broke the connection.

Set me up for what? Rafferty wondered after he put the phone down. But he forgot the question as he showered and prepared for the day and the murder investigation that was still awaiting resolution.

Ma said little until Rafferty had got himself outside the enormous breakfast she had cooked for him and which consisted not only of well-buttered toast on the side and the already promised back bacon and eggs, but mushrooms, black pudding, tomatoes, baked beans and sausages.

Once he'd eaten his fill, she sat back, poured a third large mug of strong, well-sugared tea and observed, 'I thought you and Dafyd were friends.'

Rafferty did a double-take. 'Why do you say that, Ma? We are. You know we are.' More or less, anyway. Most of the time, he silently amended, until Dafyd starts coming over all superior.

'Only it's wondering I've been why it is you aren't rushing up to Wales yourself to sort Gloria's little problem out.'

'Me? But I'm in the middle of a murder investigation.'

His ma pulled a face. 'As if they aren't ten

a penny – greedy people killing one another for money, as likely as not. Friends and family are more important. There'll always be another murderer awaiting your attention. And since Dafyd Llewellyn married your cousin, his mother Gloria is friend and family both.'

'Well yes, exactly. I know that. It's why I suggested to Abra that *you* would be a big help up there.'

'Me? Sure and what use would I be? I could comfort Gloria, obviously. But poor Gloria needs something a bit more substantial than *comforting* right now. She needs someone to sort this out for her and make sure she's *not* charged. It's not as if I'd have any *official* standing. Unlike you. No, it would make far more sense for you to go up there and use some influence.'

Bemused, stuffed from the filling breakfast that had left his thought processes sluggish, Rafferty wondered what influence his ma thought he could possibly bring to bear amongst the Welsh force dealing with Gloria's case. It wasn't as if he knew anyone up there. 'But—' he began.

'The Lord knows that it doesn't seem to have sunk in with poor Gloria that once charged and up in court the local press will probably report the case, unless something big happens that throws small events like Gloria's off the news pages.'

'I know,' Rafferty agreed. 'And there's not much chance of that unless someone sets off stink bombs in that expensive new hot-air factory they've got for that Welsh Assembly or whatever they call themselves. I'd do it myself,' he joked half-heartedly, while taking the opportunity to remind her that he was a trifle busy at the moment, 'only, as I said, I'm a bit tied up right now with this murder case.'

Ma waved aside his murder case and his stink bombs and carried on as if he hadn't said anything.

'That's why it's essential to make sure there *is* no court case. And you're the only one who can do that. If you set off as soon as you've finished your breakfast, you could have it all sorted out by teatime.'

Rafferty wished he shared his ma's conviction about his skills of persuasion. He'd thought he'd have little problem in persuading *her* to go to Wales, but he hadn't managed that too well...

'Anyway,' he said, as he slurped the last of his tea, ready to head for the station and its different demands, 'I've got to get to work. As I told you,' he reminded her for the third time, 'I've got this murder case and the Super, as ever, is snapping at my heels for a result. Let's just hope that if Gloria *is* featured in the local rag up there, some kind soul doesn't take the trouble to send the cutting to Dafyd.'

'Don't say such things, Joseph. You're tempting the fates. I'm trying not to think about that possibility. Gloria's in enough of a state as it is.

'No.' Ma stood up, swept his empty plate and mug from under his nose and said, 'As I told you, there's nothing for it but for you to go up there and sort it out. I'd come up with you, but the bedroom arrangements in Gloria's house being what they are, there wouldn't be room for me as well.'

Rafferty frowned. What was his ma on about now? he wondered. He knew very well that Gloria's home had three bedrooms and could accommodate his ma, himself and Abra, so why—?

His mother broke into his musing. Her next words revealed she had grudgingly permitted him a few hours' grace to get on with solving the murder.

'All right, son. I can see this morning's no good for you. That being the case, I'll tell Gloria you'll drive up there tonight, after work. They'll be expecting you.'

'But—'

But his ma had sailed off to the kitchen with his breakfast dishes, leaving his protest trailing in her wake.

Rafferty tried to telephone Abra or Gloria before his mother contacted them, to tell them it was impossible for him to travel to the other side of the country just now. But he could raise neither of them. He could only hope his ma was having similar luck...

But half an hour after he reached his office, he realised when he lifted the ringing phone and found Abra at the other end that his ma must have called on all the Catholic saints to aid her. For Abra was bubbling over with relief and Rafferty knew his ma had well and truly dropped him in it. He had been set up – done up like a kipper.

'Your ma said you're coming up,' Abra explained, delight and relief filling her every word. 'Oh, Joe, it's such a weight off my mind, I can't tell you.'

Put on the spot, Rafferty couldn't find it in him to disappoint her, especially when her attempted laugh turned into a relieved sob.

'It will make all the difference your coming up here and having a professional word with the officer in charge of Gloria's case. He's called Detective Inspector Jones. I haven't managed to see him yet, but I remember Dafyd saying some time ago that there was a DI Jones at the local station here that he was great friends with. It must be the guy in charge of the case. Only, of course, Gloria refuses to say she's Dafyd's mum in case he insists on calling Dafyd. But if you were to speak to this DI Jones, face to face...'

Abra's voice faltered again at that point.

After all the strain she had suffered during the previous few days, Rafferty suspected tears wouldn't be far behind. And he knew that, whatever else he did, he couldn't fail her a second time, not after he'd failed her so miserably over their lost baby earlier in the year.

'Sweetheart. Don't cry,' he begged. 'As Ma told you, I'm coming up.'

God help me, he thought, because I don't know how I'm going to manage it – or square it with Llewellyn without revealing the real reason for this sudden trip.

'Only it won't be till tonight as I'll have to organise a few things on the murder front. And it'll have to be a flying visit,' he warned her.

'That's OK. Hopefully, a flying visit will be all that's needed.' Her voice lowered, lovingly. 'Thanks for this, Joe. I know it's difficult for you. You're a darling, you know that?'

Rafferty agreed that he was a darling.

'Gloria will be so relieved and delighted when I tell her.'

After chatting a while more Abra said she supposed she had better let him get on with the murder case he was about to temporarily abandon.

'OK, love. Anyway, I expect to get there sometime in the wee small hours.'

'I'll leave the key under the flower tub to the left of the front door,' Abra told him before they made a second lingering good-bye.

Rafferty was left with the conundrum of wondering what Llewellyn was going to say when he explained that although they were in the middle of a murder inquiry, he had to make a little overnight visit on a private, family matter. Somehow, Rafferty doubted that his sergeant was likely to echo Abra's cries of delight...

Twelve

'The late Mr Raine seems to have gone in for some unorthodox practices,' Llewellyn reported later that morning while a bemused Rafferty was still trying to figure out not only how he'd been bamboozled into making a flying trip to Wales, but also how he was going to explain his absence to Llewellyn. He just hoped Superintendent Bradley didn't get to hear of it...

Llewellyn had been out, on Rafferty's instructions, to look more deeply into Raymond Raine's character and doings. Rafferty roused himself from thinking about Abra, Gloria, his ma's organising capabilities and the best route from one side of the country to the other when there was no direct motorway route, to pay attention. 'Go on,' he encouraged.

'And the unorthodox behaviour he went in for wasn't solely confined to the world of business.'

'So, what are we talking about here? More cuckolds like Peter Dunbar?'

Llewellyn nodded. 'I'm certain of several.

It seems the late Mr Raine felt it his duty to cut a Casanova swathe through his firm's female workforce. At the last count, as I understand it, he'd paid for three abortions and two discreet transfers of cash.'

Rafferty whistled.

'Though, in fairness to him, these events seem to have transpired before he married Felicity.'

'That's all right, then. So how did you manage to unearth these titbits? You haven't taken to getting all dragged up and listening to gossip in Raines's ladies' loo, by any chance?'

Llewellyn raised an eyebrow. 'Is that your usual procedure, sir?' he quietly enquired. 'I suppose, unlike your Catholic upbringing, my Methodist childhood didn't equip me for high-camp apparel, though even I have to agree the male priests in the Catholic Church do wear some fabulous frocks. Quite where the embrace of poverty enters the plot, however, has always eluded me.'

'Me and all,' Rafferty muttered.

'That aside, I simply used good detective work to acquire my answers.'

'OK, Dafyd. You've done well. He certainly sounds to have been a bit of a lad, our late Raymondo.'

'A bit of a *beast* would be more accurate in my book.' A glimmer of – something – shimmered in Llewellyn's eye. 'He really did seem the kind of man to use other people as commodities.'

'Makes you understand why Felicity topped him. If top him she did.'

'No,' Llewellyn immediately contradicted. 'I wouldn't go that far. If she objected to his behaviour, she had the option of divorcing him as she had her first husband. Although divorce is not something—' Llewellyn stopped himself mid-sentence and finished simply, 'There's never an excuse for murder.'

'Never' was too strong a word in Rafferty's lexicon. He could think of one or two people who – from his point of view, at least – would be greatly improved if they were held coffin-fast for all eternity. The Super for inst—

He cut the thought short. He had no time for indulging in private fantasies right now. 'Anyway, as I said, you've done well, Dafyd. You'll have done even better if you've managed to put names to the numbers of not-to-be mothers and the other ladies he paid off.'

'I got those, certainly. I have never subscribed to the view that doing half a job is sufficient.'

There was something about Llewellyn's body language as he handed over his list of names and addresses that convinced Rafferty that what he next confided wouldn't be to his liking.

He was right, as he learned after Llewellyn responded to his invitation to, 'Go on, then.

I can see you've got some other juicy morsel you're just dying to tell me all about. So let's have it.' He guessed it would be something about Felicity Raine. I'm such a good guesser, I should go on one of those game shows on the telly and win a fortune, Rafferty thought less than a minute later, after Llewellyn quietly acknowledged there *was* something else and proceeded to share it.

'It seems to be common knowledge – at least amongst the more senior members of staff at Raines – that Mr Raine hadn't acted entirely honourably when he persuaded Felicity to leave her first husband for him.'

'Is there ever anything honourable about running away with another man's wife?' Rafferty enquired.

'No. Obviously not. But it wasn't that aspect to which I was referring.'

'Well, go on, then. Spit it out. What did he do? Organise some white slavers to kidnap her from her husband's bed? If that's what's doing the gossip rounds amongst the Raines' old family retainers, it's not how Felicity tells it. She admits she was at fault.'

Rafferty's Welsh retainer began to get uppity. 'Do you wish to hear what I've learned, or not? Sir?'

'Oh, don't go all stiff-necked on me, Dafyd. If the wind remains in this direction, you'll stay like it. Just tell me.'

'Very well. But you'll have to understand

215

that nothing was said outright. It was all hints and subtlety.'

'I'm sure you can translate for those of us who don't do subtle.'

Llewellyn's lips thinned at this, but apart from sighing faintly, he gave no other indication that his DI was getting seriously up his nose.

'As I said, it seems that Mrs Raine married her late husband without being made privy to the fact that Mr Raine didn't actually *own* shares in the family firm. As we know, Jonas Singleton told us that Raymond Raine would only inherit his – admittedly major share – if – when – he produced issue. So if one of the male principals named under the trust terms, the two cousins Raymond and Mike Raine, failed to have children, the family firm would revert to the cousin who *did* perform his familial duty. And as the late Mr Raine is—'

'Late – it means Felicity will get nothing. We know that.'

'Quite so. But – and this is the part I felt was the most important – Mrs Raine *didn't* know that. Mr Raine had never confided in her the facts of the trust, partly, I believe, because he didn't want to lose face by having her know he wasn't the boss of all he surveyed even if that seemed, on the surface, to be the case.'

Rafferty, suspecting there was more to

come, said, 'Come on, Dafyd. Why don't you just spit the rest out?'

'Very well. Mrs Raine had no reason to suppose she wouldn't come into a substantial fortune on her husband's death. We already know she didn't apply to the Probate Office for copies of the wills of the brothers who founded the business. And as she's succeeded in muddying the waters, to the extent that she's far from being the only suspect in spite of her confession—'

'*Retracted* confession,' Rafferty automatically corrected. 'And I hardly think it's fair to blame her for the fact we've discovered several other possible suspects.' It was odd, he thought, that the usually far from impetuous Llewellyn should in this case seem more eager than he usually was himself to pin the murder on a particular suspect. It was almost as if they had exchanged roles and personalities.

Llewellyn ignored his interruption. 'She may well believe that if – when – we drop the charges against her, she will soon be a very rich and very merry widow. I think someone ought to inform her of the true facts and what her actual position will be.'

'Do you now? And who's going to do that?' Rafferty wondered aloud. 'Can't say I fancy it, myself. I know – why don't *you* do it? After all, you'll enjoy breaking the bad news so much more than I ever could. Must be that dour, killjoy Methodism of yours. *You* tell her.'

Feeling that his present predicament and the need to travel all the way across the country to Wales to try to sort out Gloria's problem was somehow Llewellyn's fault, he wanted to punish him. It was unfair of him, he knew – unwise, too, in view of the fact that he had yet to break the news of this little trip, but that didn't stop him. Unsure whether he was disgusted with himself, with Llewellyn or with his ma for being such a devious woman, Rafferty turned away and walked straight out of the office.

'So, how did she take it?' Rafferty demanded upon Llewellyn's return from breaking the news of her poverty to Felicity Raine.

'Surprisingly well,' Llewellyn admitted.

Rafferty grinned. 'Bet that knocked the wind out of your sails.'

Llewellyn didn't rise to the bait.

'So, come on. What exactly did she say?'

'Not much really. She seemed remarkably philosophical about losing her home and any hopes of a wealthy inheritance. She even said she probably deserved it as a punishment for deserting Dunbar when he really needed her.'

'By the way,' Rafferty told Llewellyn. 'Something else turned up while you were out. Two somethings in fact. We had a call from the Australian police. They were able to exonerate Ray and Mike's cousin, Andrew Armstrong. Apparently, he hasn't left Oz for over a year.'

'And what was the other thing?'

'We've finally traced Felicity's father. Turns out he's not dead after all.'

Rafferty's digging into Felicity Raine's family background had sprung from his determination never again to get his wires crossed with regard to relationships, as he had with that of Stephanie Raine and her stepson. Along the way, this determination had been tempered by his desire to find someone – anyone – with whom Felicity could claim kinship. In her situation, she must feel desperately alone and in need of someone to care about her. So he was delighted when his digging had finally turned up trumps shortly before Llewellyn had returned. They now had an address to go with the name – Frederick Franklin – of Felicity's father.

When he'd realised Franklin was still alive, Rafferty had been astonished the man hadn't contacted them on learning of his daughter's plight. He was pleased for Felicity's sake to learn she wasn't, after all, entirely alone in the world. Though when he arrived at the prison to let Felicity know the good news, he felt somewhat deflated when she looked more upset than delighted at the

219

discovery.

'Why on earth did you bother looking for my father?' Felicity asked, in the first show of vivacity he had seen her display. 'If it was for my sake, I'm afraid you've been wasting your time. If I were you, I wouldn't waste any more of it by going to see him, which I imagine is what you're thinking of doing?'

Rafferty admitted it was.

'There's really no point, inspector,' Felicity assured him. 'We haven't set eyes on each other for several years. I really thought he must be dead by now as he wasn't a young man when I was born and his dietary habits were always far from healthy. But even though he's still alive, I can't imagine what you think he could tell you that would help me.'

Neither could Rafferty – now. But after going to all the trouble of looking for Mr Franklin, he might as well see the man. Though he couldn't help but think how dreadfully sad it was that Felicity, with no one else in the world to call her own, should show no interest at all in seeing her father. In fact, when he pressed her to do so, she dug her heels in.

'No. There would be no point. We've never really got on,' she told him. 'We put up with one another while my mother was alive, but after she died I didn't visit any more. Believe me when I say we both prefer it that way.

Please don't think me terribly churlish after all the trouble you must have taken to find him, but I assure you he won't thank you if you turn up there with my tale of woe. He won't be interested. He certainly won't come prison-visiting, if that's what you're hoping for.'

That was exactly what Rafferty had been hoping for, but he decided not to admit as much to Felicity.

'That's for you and your father to decide,' he told her. 'But at least he's entitled to know what's been happening, whether he decides he wants to see you or not.'

'Do I really get no say in it?' she asked in a plaintive voice from which tears weren't far away. 'Please, inspector, I'm over eighteen. Am I not at least allowed a say in who is informed of my situation? I've lost so much already – whether or not through my own fault – please let me retain a semblance of dignity by keeping my father in ignorance of my present situation for as long as possible. I'm begging you.'

Rafferty would have been happy to oblige her on the point, but for the fact that he wanted to speak to Mr Franklin anyway and question him about Felicity's marriage to Peter Dunbar. Even if, as Felicity claimed, she and her father had never been close, surely the man would be able to tell them something they would be unable to get from another source?

He already felt like an insensitive brute in the face of her distress. To stop her becoming even more upset, he simply told her a little white lie and said he would think about her request.

'Thank you, inspector. You're very kind. I appreciate it.' She reached out a slender hand and rested it on his arm for a moment before she quickly withdrew it – perhaps worried that even this light touch might break some arcane prison rule she was unaware of and she would be penalised.

'Why did you tell her that?' Llewellyn asked once Rafferty had finished recounting what had happened while he was out of the station.

'God knows,' Rafferty replied. 'I felt such a heel for not being able to agree to her request. I suppose I thought, What she doesn't know won't hurt her. And if her old man acts as couldn't-care-less as she claims, I can't see there's any harm done, as it's not as if he's likely to contact her to let her know we've spoken to him.'

Frederick Franklin lived in a run-down block of council flats in Burleigh, in the north of the county.

Felicity must indeed have been a late baby, as she had told them, Rafferty realised once Frederick Franklin answered their knock and they'd introduced themselves and given a brief explanation as to why they had come. Franklin looked to be approaching his seventies.

Mr Franklin frowned as if he was still trying to get his head around what Rafferty had told him. 'You said this was about my daughter and her husband?'

Rafferty nodded.

'I don't know what you think I can tell you,' Mr Franklin said. 'I haven't seen my daughter for several years, not since my wife died. What did you say she'd done? Murdered her husband? Why ever should she do that? God knows I never had much of an opinion of Peter Dunbar, but he was harmless enough.'

Rafferty was astonished to discover that Felicity's father seemed unaware that she and Dunbar had divorced, but then he reasoned that the divorce and her remarriage had happened after her mother's death and she had said she had had no contact with him since. He thought it past time someone broke the news to him. He was just sorry it had to be him.

'Your daughter is no longer married to Peter Dunbar. They divorced early last year. She's been married to a Mr Raymond Raine for around fifteen months. That is to say—'

Rafferty, aware from Mr Franklin's bewildered expression that he was making a ham-fisted job of his explanation, paused briefly to regather his forces before he went doggedly on.

'She *was* married to him, that is to say. Unfortunately, her husband died last week – he was murdered, in fact, a crime to which your daughter confessed, although she has since retracted her confession. At the moment, she's on remand, charged with the murder of her husband. Her *second* husband that is, Raymond Raine.'

Unsurprisingly, Mr Franklin still looked bewildered. When he regained the power of speech, he asked, 'Why on earth would she kill Pe – whichever of her husbands it was?' He shook his head. 'Modern marriages,' he muttered. 'I suppose you'd better come in,' he ungraciously invited.

They followed him into an untidy living room. Mr Franklin sat himself back down in an armchair in front of the TV, where obviously he had been immersed in the day's horse racing.

He picked up his copy of *Sporting Life*, glanced longingly at it, then with a look of regret put it down again. 'Young people nowadays seem to jump in and out of their marriages as easily as my generation get in and out of a bath.' With a grimace, he touched his stiff leg, which Rafferty had already noticed, and added, 'Easier.'

'Your daughter didn't tell you she had

divorced her first husband and remarried?'

'Clearly not. We were never close. Like chalk and cheese, if you want the truth. If her mother had still been alive, doubtless she would have told *her*.'

Rafferty stared curiously at the grizzled features of Mr Franklin; he could see no sign that Felicity Raine had inherited her delicate beauty from her father. Although he was short, like his daughter, being no more than five foot five or six, all resemblance ended there. Where Felicity was slender, her father was stout; and whereas Felicity seemed other-worldly Frederick Franklin was so much of *this* world that one glance around the living room of his first-floor flat revealed a fondness for most of the human vices. The television was currently showing horse racing at Newmarket; clearly, Frederick Franklin had placed several bets as, beside the cigarette-end-filled ashtray and the half-empty bottle of gin, the day's *Sporting Life* was open and several runners were marked in each race. There was no sign of any other newspaper.

Felicity's father, like her ex-husband, appeared to be a man who was one of life's weaker vessels; certainly, the flat and its cheap contents didn't indicate that his gambling habit was anything other than the unlucky sort. Evidently, he was no more skilled at fatherhood either, for he asked no more questions about his daughter and her plight and made no enquiries as to her welfare or otherwise.

No wonder Felicity hadn't troubled to keep in touch, Rafferty thought. Clearly, there was nothing for her here.

Frederick Franklin must have realised he would be unable to return to his racing until he'd posed a few questions for them to answer, as he said, 'Well, go on, then. Tell me exactly what happened.'

Quickly, Rafferty explained the events of that fatal Monday morning.

'She knifed him, you say?'

Rafferty was pleased to note this had startled him out of his complacency.

'It's the first I've heard of it.'

Astonished, half pitying, Rafferty said, 'Surely someone – neighbours, friends – would have told you what was happening in your daughter's life?'

'The neighbours never met Felicity. And although they learned from my late wife that we had a daughter, they had no reason to suppose this Felicity Raine, you tell me she's now called, was her. For that matter, neither had I. Mind, I always told the wife Felicity was too pretty for her own good and that spoiling her as she did would make matters worse. Bound to come to a bad end, as I told her.'

'You don't seem to have any doubts that

she did it.'

'Should I have?' Frederick Franklin stared at him. 'I thought you said she'd confessed and you'd charged her? Why would you do that if you didn't think she did it?'

Good question, thought Rafferty. 'Things are not always as straightforward as they might at first appear,' he explained. 'In fact a number of other possible suspects have since come to our notice. And as I believe I said, your daughter's retracted her confession.'

Rafferty, distracted by the still-playing television, sat down in front of it, picked up the zapper from the arm of Mr Franklin's chair and turned the sound down.

He noticed Mr Franklin's frown at this action and ignored it. But before Rafferty could explain further, he saw that he had lost Franklin's attention. His gaze had strayed to the silent television screen and the steaming horses pictured thereon.

However, once he'd ascertained the names of the winners – none of which was apparently his, to judge from the way he pulled some betting slips from his shirt pocket and ripped the top one in half then half again – he turned his attention back to Rafferty.

'So – did she do it or didn't she? It's over a week ago now, you said. Surely you've managed to find out which applies?'

Rafferty sighed. He hoped Llewellyn was taking note of this latest example of the perversity of human nature and would alter his outlook accordingly.

He explained the sequence of events that had contrived to delay the start of the case. 'So when your daughter promptly collapsed after making this confession, she was hospitalised and comatose for three days. We were unable to interview her, so we've had less time than you think.'

'So why are you wasting time with me? I'm sure my daughter's already told you we haven't had any contact for several years. I can tell you nothing. So what, exactly, is it that you want from me?'

'For myself, nothing,' Rafferty told him bluntly. 'But I thought, as her father, you might offer Felicity some comfort. I can organise a visit to the prison where she's being held on remand—'

Mr Franklin interrupted him. 'Has she asked to see me?'

Rafferty was forced to confess that she hadn't.

'I didn't think so. She made clear to her mother and me that she intended to make her own way in the world. I thought she was ashamed of us. Certainly, I've barely set eyes on her since the day she married Peter Dunbar.' He shook his head. 'The Lord knows where my wife and I got Felicity from. I'm a plain man, as you can see, and my wife, if anything, was plainer. Felicity was always a changeling from the day she was born, though she was a determined one, always straining to be off somewhere we knew not where, off on her own, without having her old parents dragging after her. Eventually, she got her way and we let her go.'

'She must have been quite young when she and Mr Dunbar married,' Llewellyn remarked.

'Aye, she was that. Barely twenty. But she had always been a magnet for the boys from the time she was thirteen or fourteen. She thought, I suppose, that she'd had enough boyfriends to recognise the one she wanted when he appeared. Her mother tried to tell her no good would come of it, that her character hadn't finished forming yet, all the usual stuff you churn out to youngsters determined on going their own way. For all her efforts, Felicity went ahead and married him anyway. And now you tell me she divorced that one and married another fellow who's now dead?' He shook his head. 'It's a rum do and no mistake.'

Strangely, Frederick Franklin didn't seem particularly surprised by these events.

'She was always a secretive little thing,' he now revealed. 'Even as a small girl. But reserved with it. That's why I was astonished when she said she wanted to train for work in the theatre. I thought she meant she wanted to be an actress, but no, she wanted to train as one of the backstage staff, powdering people's shiny noses or some such. It didn't seem much of a job to me, but she said it would give her the chance to travel and to work in the West End, and it would provide her with far more regular work than being an actress. I suppose me and the wife were relieved at that, as actresses have such rackety lives.

'But then, I suppose she started to find that line of work not as exciting as she'd hoped because she threw it all up a few months before she gained her certificate and decided she wanted to marry Peter Dunbar. Older than her, he was, too. Me and the wife didn't approve, but, as I told you, that didn't stop her.'

He glanced again at the still silently flickering TV screen and sighed heavily over all the exciting horse races their intrusion was making him miss.

Quickly, before his attention strayed again, Rafferty said, 'I realise now that, as you were unaware your daughter had divorced Peter Dunbar and taken Raymond Raine as her second husband, you can't tell me anything about *that* marriage. But in a murder investigation, every piece of information, no matter how seemingly irrelevant to the case, can be helpful. So if you can tell us anything – anything at all – about her marriage to

Peter Dunbar?'

'I'm not sure that I can, to be frank.' He snorted. 'Saw little enough of them once they married. But what little I *did* see made me think they were an ill-matched pair. Never understood what she saw in him. I said to the wife that she must have married the fellow for his money, though the wife wouldn't have it. She told me Felicity had confided the business had been in trouble for longer than she'd let on, yet Felicity had stood by him even when the money started dribbling away. But I still think she married him for his money. She must have done, to my way of thinking,' he insisted. 'I was damned if I could see why else she would have wanted to marry him. Man had no drive, no backbone either. No backbone at all. Hardly surprising both Dunbar and his business collapsed. Nothing holding them up, d'you see?'

The words 'pot', 'kettle' and 'black' entered Rafferty's head. Although he had no idea what line of work Mr Franklin had been in before his retirement, to judge by his less than luxurious home it didn't seem likely that he had been noticeably successful at it, whereas Peter Dunbar *had* achieved something substantial, even if he had lost it all, whether through misfortune or mismanagement.

Rafferty saw little point in remaining any

longer. After asking for and obtaining Mr Franklin's telephone number and telling him he would keep him apprised of developments regarding his daughter, he and Llewellyn left. He heard the volume turned up on the TV before they reached the front door.

'Well, that was a waste of time,' Rafferty complained to Llewellyn as they left the cramped flat and walked down the stairs to the car. 'No wonder Felicity chooses to pretend she has no family. If I had a father who made clear he preferred his horse racing to his daughter, I reckon I'd have done the same.'

'I wouldn't say it was entirely a waste of time,' Llewellyn contradicted him.

Rafferty, suspecting that Llewellyn was just continuing his earlier contrariness, refused to give him the satisfaction of seeking further enlightenment about what – if anything – Llewellyn thought he had learned. Trying to play the Great Detective again to my Dr Watson, he suspected, and decided not to take up his allotted role.

Besides, later, when he had had time to think about things, he felt he was finally beginning to get an inkling of who had killed Raymond Raine and why, which surely entitled *him* to the superior role?

But until this inkling grew to something approaching proof, he decided to keep his thoughts to himself. As he glanced at his watch and saw that it was already getting on for midday, he suggested they grab some sandwiches.

'We can eat them in the car.' Rafferty hesitated, then burst out, 'By the way, I've been meaning to tell you. I have to go away on a family matter. Only overnight tonight and a chunk of tomorrow.'

'Going away? But what about the case? We haven't yet reinterviewed Mike Raine. Surely you can stay around for long enough for us to question him as to why he lied to us? After all, he is the one who stands to inherit the bulk of the Raine family business. I would have thought that would be more pressing than some family problem. To my mind, the only family business more pressing when we're in the middle of a murder investigation would be a life-and-death matter.' Quietly, Llewellyn asked, 'Is one of your family seriously ill?'

Rafferty, annoyed at being cross-questioned, said shortly, 'No. It's another matter entirely. Anyway,' he said, 'I'd have thought you'd be glad to be in charge of the case. You've seemed keen enough to be the main man before.'

'Maybe. But there's no satisfaction in being in charge for so short a time. All it means is that one would have to carry on running the investigation in the way the temporarily absent officer has organised it.'

Llewellyn's voice and expression made it clear that, given the choice, following Rafferty's way of organising things was the last thing he would do.

'Well, I can't do anything about it *now*,' Rafferty insisted. He felt riled that Llewellyn should choose to have a go at him when it was *his* mother who was the cause of his being called away; although, of course, his own had, as usual, managed to put her two-penn'orth in. 'I told you. I'll only be away overnight and a chunk of tomorrow. We'll fit Mike Raine in tomorrow afternoon. I should be back around mid-afternoon, if not sooner. Ring Raine later and make an appointment for around four o'clock.'

Thankfully, before Llewellyn could voice any further protests, Rafferty's mobile went off. He snatched it from his pocket, half expecting it to be Abra again. But it was Jonathon Lilley. He listened for a little, then excitedly asked, 'You have? Good man. Where are you? OK, we'll see you at the station in an hour or so.'

'That was Jonathon Lilley,' he told Llewellyn. 'And although his poking about in the innards of computers has yet to bring any results on the Mogadon front, he's found out something else that's sure to please you.'

From Llewellyn's downturned mouth, Rafferty got the distinct impression that nothing he said at the moment was likely to please his sergeant. For a second he felt tempted to tell Llewellyn why he was *really* going to Wales. But then he thought of what Abra would say if she found out he'd spilled the beans and decided against it.

'Come on,' he said as he reached the car and climbed in. 'I told him we'd meet him back at the station. The sandwiches will have to wait.'

Thirteen

Llewellyn got into the passenger seat and asked, 'So what has Lilley found out?'

'I gather it's something that could possibly implicate Felicity Raine. Though, before you get *too* excited, it's only fair to tell you it could just as easily implicate Mike or Stephanie, especially, in her case, if she's been playing a more subtle game all along than we might have given her credit for.'

Rafferty put his foot down and drove to Elmhurst in record time, much to the disapproval of Llewellyn, who prided himself on being a cautious driver.

Lilley was waiting for them in reception and all three walked up to Rafferty's office.

'So let's have the rest, Jon,' Rafferty invited when they had all sat down.

Strangely, given her stated aversion to her daughter-in-law, Stephanie Raine had not only forgotten to mention that Raymond had been her stepson rather than her natural child, she had also managed to forget her conversation during a rather drunken dinner party she had held several weeks before

Raymond's murder, at which she had carelessly revealed the password to her computer's email account.

This information, Lilley told them, was supplied by a Mr Gerald Huntley, a friend of Stephanie who had been present at the dinner party. He had told Lilley that the subject of computer passwords had come up during the meal and Stephanie had boasted that she had no trouble remembering her password because she used the same one for every one of her internet accounts. She had even apparently blurted her password out for all her guests to hear.

'Mr Huntley said he warned Mrs Raine Senior that using the same password for everything was very unwise, as was revealing it to others. He commented that it was fortunate she was amongst friends and family rather than in a restaurant with maybe a few of the listening ears belonging to the criminal fraternity. He said that he told her that if someone got into her system and knew or was able to discover what should be secure information, they would be able to clear out her bank and savings accounts as well as access other sites, the contents of which she would presumably prefer to remain confidential. She didn't take his warning seriously, apparently, and just laughed it off.

'Mr Huntley said he's been worried about

it ever since, especially in view of Felicity Raine's presence that evening and the subsequent publicity regarding her confession and its later retraction. He learned about the drug that was in Raymond's system from Stephanie and that we have yet to trace its source. He wondered if Felicity might have used her mother-in-law's computer to buy it.'

Lilley's normally serious grey eyes were shining with excitement at the thought that his discoveries might prove vital. 'He was sufficiently worried that such might be the case that he decided the information might prove significant to the investigation.'

'Good for Gerald Huntley,' said Rafferty. He supposed Stephanie Raine had wasted no time in poisoning Huntley's mind against Felicity. Still, if the information was true and not something Huntley and Stephanie had dreamed up between them, it might help move the investigation forward.

While Mr Huntley's computer, as the fair-haired Lilley now confirmed, had proved innocent of orders for the drug found in Raymond's and Felicity's bodies, the question that remained – now that they knew that Stephanie was not Raymond's natural mother – was whether Stephanie's so far unchecked computer might contain the drug order they had so far sought in vain.

Gerald Huntley had given Lilley the names

of the other party attendees: both Felicity and Mike Raine had been present that night. Either of them could have made a mental note of the password for future reference.

'Certainly, Felicity Raine must have had easy access to her mother-in-law's computer,' Llewellyn observed.

'So must her mother-in-law,' was Rafferty's tart comment. 'Seeing as it was her machine. And it seems likely that Mike Raine could have accessed it as well without much difficulty. Let's have the guest list,' Rafferty said to Lilley: 'we might as well find out if Uncle Tom Cobbleigh and all had access.'

Lilley handed the list over.

Rafferty quickly scrutinised it. Beside the names of the guests as yet unknown to them, Lilley had noted what relationship they had to the Raines. As well as Stephanie herself, Raymond and Felicity, the dinner guests had included this Gerald Huntley, whom Lilley had delicately described as Stephanie's sometime gentleman friend, Mike Raine and Sandrine Agnew; the latter had presumably been invited to make up the numbers and make sure the male/female ratio round the table was the same.

Rafferty found himself wondering if the dinner party had been staged solely for Stephanie to have an independent witness to the fact that Felicity would be able to access her internet account with no difficulty. But for her to do this, she would have to know that Raymond was to be murdered, as well as know he was to be rendered unconscious before he was killed.

Strangely, in her eagerness to incriminate Felicity, Stephanie Raine seemed blind to the fact that she herself had even more opportunity than Felicity to use her own computer to order the drug.

Though, why would she? Rafferty asked himself. No one they had questioned had said other than that she doted on Raymond. And no one, other than Elaine Enderby, the Raines' close neighbour, had commented that Stephanie's behaviour towards Raymond had been 'inappropriate'. But then, in passing their home as she must often do, she would have the opportunity others lacked to hear unguarded conversations during the bright summer evenings.

Unless Raymond had spurned some far from maternal advances from Stephanie, he really couldn't see that Stephanie would have a good enough motive for wishing him dead. There again, while Elaine Enderby hadn't said Raymond had dismissed her affection, she had said that he seemed amused by it.

But if rejected lust hadn't been a factor, he thought it unlikely that, for Stephanie, the cash on its own would be a sufficient spur for murder. She clearly didn't lack for money and, equally clearly, her love for Raymond seemed sincere, even if it was inappropriate.

But then Felicity, like Stephanie, also claimed to love the dead man. The killing of a spouse was a far more regular occurrence that the killing of one's grown-up stepchild, but even so...

Of course, as he remarked to Llewellyn after he had thanked and dismissed DC Jonathon Lilley, the sooner they accessed Stephanie Raine's computer, the sooner they might be able to discover if in fact the drug *had* been ordered from it. To this end, he suggested they get themselves over to Stephanie Raine's home immediately.

Somehow, in spite of their previous, less than friendly encounter, Rafferty had a feeling, whether or not his suspicions about the dinner-party conversation were proved correct, that Stephanie Raine would welcome this visit.

'Tell me, Mrs Raine,' Rafferty asked Stephanie. 'Do you own a computer?'

Unsurprisingly, she nodded, clearly happy to confirm it.

'We'd like to check it, if we may. We have yet to find the source of the Mogadon in your stepson's body and as my officer has now checked every other computer owned by any known friend of your stepson and his wife, I wondered whether anyone might have had access to your machine and used it to order the drug from the internet.'

'Felicity, you mean?' she murmured with an air of innocence while she directed a wide-eyed stare at him.

Rafferty, unwilling to gratify the woman's spite, said nothing. He didn't need to, for Stephanie Raine was racing ahead all on her own.

With an eagerness in her voice that she clearly found difficult to suppress, she told them, 'Felicity certainly had access to my computer. She and Raymond were often here for lunch and so on, so she would have had plenty of opportunity to order anything she liked on my machine.'

'Where do you keep it?' he asked.

'It's upstairs.' Stephanie hurried towards the door and said, 'Come along. I'll show you.'

After gaining Stephanie Raine's permission, Llewellyn turned the computer on.

Rafferty noted that the password was not conveniently stored on the hard drive, but had to be typed in each time the internet was accessed via the internet service provider – which, in Stephanie's case, was AOL. Given Stephanie's declared carelessness, this struck him as an odd thing for her to do.

'Could you let me have your password, please, Mrs Raine?' Llewellyn asked, careful to follow Rafferty's instruction that he not give Stephanie Raine the satisfaction of discovering from them what she might – or might not – have forgotten during what sounded to have been an evening of drunken pleasure.

'Of course. It's "rayray". All lower-case. Perfectly easy for Felicity to guess, particularly as it was my pet name for him.'

Fortunately, Stephanie didn't seem to have an addiction to sending emails or signing herself up for regular bulletins from various sites, so Llewellyn's check through her emails didn't take long.

'Here it is,' he said, after another ten minutes. He printed out the confirmation of the order for the Mogadon.

It was, Rafferty noted, ordered in Felicity's name and with her credit-card details. Would this turn out to be another nail in her coffin? Rafferty wondered. Another prison door slamming on her future?

But, as Stephanie had been happy enough to point out when she had been doing her best to convince them that Felicity would have ready access to her computer, the same surely applied to Stephanie when it came to having ready access to Felicity's handbag and credit card. It was unlikely that Felicity would feel the need to take her bag with her when they went into the dining room to eat.

'So when was this order sent?' he asked Llewellyn as he peered over his shoulder.

'The order was sent at one p.m. on Saturday the twenty-third of July,' Llewellyn told them.

That was just over two weeks before Raymond's murder and three weeks after the dinner party, Rafferty worked out. He again peered over Llewellyn's shoulder. 'And what about the delivery address? Was it the same?'

Llewellyn shook his head. 'No. The drugs were delivered to Mr Nicholas Miller at his home here in Elmhurst. Felicity's handyman/gardener,' Llewellyn reminded him.

'How could I forget?' How could he forget, either, that Miller was also *Stephanie's* handyman/gardener? And possibly, given Elaine Enderby's comments about the 'extras' Miller provided his lady customers, he fulfilled a role that was something more than either.

'Can you remember who visited the house that day?' he asked Stephanie. 'And who could have had access to your computer at the time the order was made?'

As if aware that she had already betrayed an unattractive eagerness to tie Felicity's name to any wrongdoing, she hesitated, then said, 'I'll have to check my diary. It's in my bag downstairs. I'll just go and get it.'

She was back in less than a minute. 'Yes, here it is. I threw a barbecue that day. Everyone was here. I remember the weather was gorgeous.'

'When you say "everyone", would that include all the guests at your dinner party?'

'Of course.' After a slight pause, she couldn't resist adding, 'Including Felicity.'

Rafferty, unwilling to gratify her desire that he share her eagerness to condemn, said quietly, 'Perhaps you could let me have a list of their names?'

'Certainly. The guest list is downstairs.'

They trailed after her down the stairs to the living room where she opened a small desk, rummaged through a wallet file with pockets labelled INSURANCE, INVESTMENTS, UTILITY BILLS and so on, then rummaged through further, as-yet-unfiled piles of chaotic paperwork that were promptly consigned to the floor filing cabinet, before she finally managed to produce the list.

There were thirty names on it, Rafferty noted. All would have to be questioned.

'And did Felicity – or anyone else – spend any time alone upstairs?'

Before Stephanie had a chance to reply and further damn her daughter-in-law, Michelle burst into the room. She shot Stephanie a look of dislike and before Stephanie had the chance to say anything, told them that Felicity had certainly *not* gone upstairs that day; she had used the downstairs bathroom and that once only.

'You're sure about that, Mademoiselle Ginôt?' Rafferty asked. 'You must have been busy with so many guests.'

'*Non*. Madame, she hire the caterers. I do nothing but relax.'

'Even so, I presume everyone would be mingling. You could not have watched Felicity Raine all afternoon,' Llewellyn objected.

'What is this *mingling*?'

'It means *mêler*, Michelle,' Stephanie told her, adding triumphantly, 'and you're right, sergeant, Michelle could not possibly have watched Felicity all the time.'

Michelle opened her mouth, but Stephanie forestalled her.

'You spent most of the barbecue flirting outrageously with my guests,' she told Michelle. 'I remember because I had to speak to you about it. You were an embarrassment.'

Michelle pouted, but said nothing further.

'Let's get over to Nick Miller's home,' Rafferty said after they had left Stephanie Raine and Michelle Ginôt to indulge their simmering hostility. 'I'm keen to find out about this delivery he took in and whether he noticed Peter Dunbar watching the Raines's home. One of them must have done, and with Felicity denying that either she or Raymond noticed him, we might have better luck with her handyman.'

'Surely he'll be at work,' Llewellyn protested.

246

'Well, I know that,' Rafferty retorted. 'But I need to find out where he's working, don't I? With a bit of luck his wife will be at home. It's worth a try, anyway.' He paused, then said, 'Remind me. Where is it he lives again?'

Llewellyn told him.

'OK. But put your foot down, Dafyd. And that's an order. I'm starved. We'll get some lunch as soon as we've spoken to Mr Miller.'

Nick Miller's home and garden were far from being good adverts for his business, Rafferty noted as he walked up the weed-littered path and knocked on the wooden front door with its worn varnish. His own father had been the same, he remembered; if it hadn't been for his ma, who could turn her hand to most things, the Rafferty family home would have looked sorely run-down.

Mrs Miller looked as neglected as her home and garden. She was very thin, with straggly bleached blond hair as much in need of a colour job as the front door. Her clothes looked threadbare and seemingly as worn down by life as the rest of her.

She gazed at them from lacklustre eyes. 'Yes?'

'We wanted to speak to Mr Miller.' After introducing Llewellyn and himself and showing her his warrant card, Rafferty said, 'It's in connection with the murder of Mr Raymond Raine.'

247

She immediately bridled and demanded, 'What's that got to do with my Nick?'

'Nothing, as far as I'm aware. But we need to speak to him urgently about another aspect of the investigation.'

'He's out. Working.'

'So where am I likely to find him?' Rafferty asked.

She frowned. 'Let me see. It's Tuesday today, isn't it?'

Rafferty nodded.

'You'd better come in. I'll have to check his diary.'

They followed her down a dim hallway to a back living room that was as uncared-for as the rest of the house.

She walked across to a cupboard in the corner, opened a drawer and pulled out a diary. Flipping through the pages, she crossed back to Rafferty. 'Right. Well on Tuesday mornings he does a Mrs Tindall at Rose Cottage, in Springmeadow Lane. He usually finishes there around one o'clock.'

It was after 12.30, Rafferty noted from the clock on the mantelpiece. Just in case he missed him at Rose Cottage, he asked, 'And what about Tuesday afternoons? Who does he work for then?'

'His regular Tuesday-afternoon customer died last week. I can never remember the new one's name. Hang on,' she said as she flipped through the diary. 'Here we are,' she said. 'It's a Mrs Johnson that he goes to on Tuesday afternoons now.' She handed the diary to Rafferty, who took the opportunity to flick through the entries for the rest of the week.

All of Nick Miller's clients were female, he noticed, and he recalled that Elaine Enderby had mentioned this little titbit. Interesting. He found himself wondering what the recently deceased customer had died of and before he closed the diary and returned it, he 'accidentally' let it slip open to a date a couple of weeks earlier to check the name of the previous Tuesday-afternoon client.

To his surprise, he saw that it was Sandrine Agnew. But Ms Agnew hadn't died a week ago. He had spoken to her himself on Thursday evening. As far as Rafferty was aware, she was still very much alive. He hoped so, anyway, as he wished to question her and the other guests to get their take on Stephanie Raine's dinner party.

So why, he wondered, had Nick Miller told his wife that Sandrine Agnew was dead? And why had Ms Agnew accepted her premature demise and the loss of her gardener? Reliable gardeners and handymen weren't so thick on the ground that you allowed one to remove you from his client list without protest. Unless she had found someone she preferred and had been willing to lose his services? Or perhaps, given her presumed lesbian sensibilities, it was simply that she had found the mucho macho Miller too much to stomach on a regular basis?

'Tell me, Mrs Miller, do you and your husband act as a kind of *post restante* for his customers?'

'Post what?'

'It's just that we noticed that one of his customers ordered some goods and gave this as the delivery address,' he explained.

'Oh that. Many of Nick's customers are away from home a lot and miss important parcels. He just lets them use this address for convenience as I'm mostly at home to sign for anything that needs a signature. My Nick's a very obliging man.'

From her expression, Rafferty guessed that Mrs Miller's husband was altogether far too obliging to his lady customers for his wife's liking.

'And have you signed for anything in the last few weeks?'

She shook her head. 'But often I wouldn't need to. And the postman, and the delivery couriers of the firms that Nick's customers order goods from regularly, know to leave things in the greenhouse round the back if there's no one in. We never bolt the side gate. Anyone can go round and collect their parcels.'

Which meant that whoever had ordered the Mogadon would know they would have no problem picking it up without being seen, as long as they chose their moment carefully.

Another glance at the clock told him he'd better get moving if he didn't want to chase over to the other side of town where Miller's new afternoon client lived.

As they parked up, they saw Nick Miller's muddy blue van at the kerb and Miller himself balanced on a ladder on the pavement, stripped to the waist and wielding a set of expensive electrical hedgecutters.

Miller was what Rafferty suspected his ma would call a 'fine figure of a man', with his flat stomach and the tanned and muscular physique that rippled in a way guaranteed to please the ladies as he wielded the cutters.

Careful not to surprise him while he was up a ladder using a potentially lethal tool, Rafferty stationed himself to the side of the ladder, cleared his throat and waited for Miller to notice him.

'We meet again.' Miller turned the hedge-cutters off and climbed down the ladder. 'What do you want? I've already told you all I know.'

'Have you, though?'

Miller scowled, and looked from Rafferty to Llewellyn and back again. 'What's that supposed to mean?'

'Merely that I remember your saying when we last met that you were unable to recall anything of significance. Perhaps now your memory's had time to recover, you've recalled something useful. Maybe the fact that we've some new evidence might help jog your memory.'

'New evidence?'

Was it his imagination or did Miller look suddenly anxious? 'Yes,' Rafferty said. 'We've now learned there was a man in a car watching Mr and Mrs Raine's home. I wondered whether you had noticed him?'

A look of relief crossed Nick Miller's face. He nodded. 'Felicity – Mrs Raine – told me this man had been watching the house. She confided that the man was her ex-husband and that he had threatened violence against her and Mr Raine.'

Like her stepmother-in-law and her cousin by marriage, Felicity Raine too had now been caught out in a lie. Rafferty wondered what she had hoped to achieve by lying about the man. He felt disappointed in her, a disappointment he took out on Nick Miller.

'And you didn't see fit to tell us about this man threatening violence?' he demanded. 'Not even after Mr Raine was murdered?'

Nick Miller, young, handsome and with as many female clients as he could accommodate, looked them over with a lazy confidence and told them, 'It was none of my business. If Felicity suspected her ex had attacked Mr Raine she could have gone to the police herself. Obviously, she didn't suspect him, even though she seemed scared of him. She asked me to have a word with him and warn him off. That was a couple of days before Raymond died. She told me she didn't want to ask Mr Raine to speak to him as she was worried it would turn nasty.'

He paused before adding, 'She wasn't wrong.' Miller smirked and looked even more pleased with himself, if that was possible. 'Her ex called me a few choice names when I walked over and spoke to him. I thought he was going to throw a punch at me at one point, but when I told him he was welcome to try, he took one look at my muscles and backed down. He seemed to think she and I were on more intimate terms than that of mere boss and employee. I wouldn't have kicked her out of bed, but Mrs Raine was always very businesslike and never so much as glanced beyond my face – not like *some* of the bored housewives I look after.' He smirked again. 'Anyway, I told her ex he had it all wrong and that the only service I provided for Mrs Raine was keeping her grass trimmed and her weeds under control.'

He frowned. 'It's funny, now I think of it, but he didn't seem to know her new name. "Mrs Raine?" he said, as if it was news to him. "So it was that bastard who stole her away from me.'"

Rafferty was surprised to discover that Dunbar hadn't known the identity of the man who had seduced his wife until shortly before Raine's murder. How could he not have known? He had been watching the house for some days – surely he had seen Raymond Raine and recognised him?

They left Nick Miller to his hedge-cutting and made for the prison again, to learn what Felicity Raine had to say for herself. Rafferty's stomach grumbled, but he told it that lunch would have to wait.

Felicity Raine was paler and slimmer than ever. She appeared shamefaced as she admitted, 'I know it was cowardly of me to leave my first husband in the way I did, but I just couldn't stand another row. That's why I took my chance and left Peter when he was out of the house and just left a letter on the kitchen table. He knew Raymond socially, of course, it was through Peter that I met Ray, but he didn't know I was having an affair with him. The next time he heard from me was when my solicitor wrote to him saying I wanted a divorce. Ray's name didn't come into it.'

Rafferty was beginning to feel sorry for Peter Dunbar. 'I see. But that doesn't explain why it should have come as such a shock to learn your new married name when

Mr Miller warned him off. Surely your ex-husband must have seen Mr Raine driving in and out of the entrance?'

'Well no, actually. I doubt it. Raymond always used the back entrance. It was handier for his office. So unless my ex realised we had two entrance drives, one each, front and rear, it's unlikely he ever saw Raymond. The rear entrance goes directly to the garage which is concealed behind a high hedge at the back of the house and can't be seen from the road.'

It was nice to get one thing at least cleared up. 'Tell me,' Rafferty now said. 'You told me that you and Mr Raine had been arguing a lot before his death?'

She nodded.

'Did you argue on the morning of his death?'

'Yes.' She dropped her gaze. 'God forgive me. I'd gone out to answer the door. Raymond followed me to the door to continue the argument. The delivery driver who had rung the bell was so embarrassed at the way Raymond was behaving that he forgot to get my signature for the parcel.'

Rafferty was beginning to get a clearer picture of that fateful morning. The Raines' front drive was fairly short, the front door easily visible from the road and from behind the copse of trees where Peter Dunbar was watching. Now he asked: 'And was this parcel delivered before or after the milkman arrived?'

Felicity frowned in thought, but then, as if just understanding the reason for his question, she exclaimed, 'No! You don't still think that Peter had anything to do with Raymond's death? The idea's absurd.'

Was it, though? Rafferty wondered. The man had been cuckolded and humiliated. When he had finally discovered the identity of the man who had stolen his wife, and the fact that he must have been the last to know it, it wouldn't have been surprising if he had wanted revenge on both of them. Killing Raymond and setting Felicity up to take the rap would have seemed the perfect vengeance. And even though it seemed they had now traced the source of the drug used on Raymond Raine, it would be interesting to learn if Peter Dunbar had ever been prescribed Mogadon...

'Please, if you'll just answer the question. Was the parcel delivered before or after the milkman's arrival?'

Felicity Raine's brow wrinkled. When her gaze met his, she looked suddenly anxious and not nearly as certain as she had been. She wrung her hands, as though unable, like Lady Macbeth, to clean the blood of her guilt from them. Her voice, when she finally answered, sounded stricken as she admitted, 'Before. The parcel was delivered a good

half-hour before the milkman usually arrived. But—'

Rafferty held up his hand. 'Please, Mrs
Raine. At this stage, all I'm interested in is
the facts. What conclusion they lead me to is
something I'll discover in due course.'

Still, he thought, it was interesting that it
was only a couple of days before Raymond's
murder when Peter Dunbar discovered the
identity of the man who had enticed Felicity
away from him. Maybe, finally seeing Raine
again in the flesh had proved too much for
him. He had had two days to brood and
scheme since Nick Miller had revealed the
truth. Had the temptation to pay back the
man who had cuckolded him proved too
great?

'I promise you I'm not the sort of man to
run ahead of the facts and start coming to
conclusions about who might be the guilty
party.'

Beside him, Llewellyn made a strangled
sound, as if he was choking on the biscuits
Rafferty had begged from the prison governor to fill the hunger gap caused by their
missed lunch.

But as Llewellyn had eaten none of them,
Rafferty knew this wasn't the reason for the
choking fit. He thumped him, harder than
necessary, between the shoulderblades to
clear the non-existent blockage and said, un-
kindly, 'If you can't manage to eat biscuits

257

without choking on them, Dafyd, you should leave them for those who can,' before he stood up, thanked Felicity Raine for her time and information and knocked on the door to be let out.

Fourteen

When Rafferty finally arrived home after another demanding day, he put a frozen lasagne in the microwave. While it cooked, he jumped in the shower and threw some things in a bag for his trip to Wales. He was out of the door in less than half an hour.

The cross-country trip from Essex to Gwynedd in Wales, Llewellyn's old stamping ground and where his mother still lived, was as difficult as he had expected it would be. There was no direct route from Britain's east to west coasts and he had to pull over constantly and consult the map; it was the only time he'd thought a satellite navigation system, with its accompanying bossy female voice, might prove itself useful rather than Big Brother intrusive.

He finally reached Gloria's home around one in the morning. As he parked, he glanced up at the bedroom windows; they were in darkness, as was the rest of the house apart from the hallway where, through the square glass panel in the front door, he could see that a light had been left on in expectation of his arrival.

Even though Abra had said she would leave the key under the large flower tub to the left of the front door, he had thought – hoped – that she, at least, would have stayed up to greet him.

He sighed and lifted the flower tub. Sure enough the key was there. He let himself in and after he had paid an urgent visit to the bathroom and had a wash and brush-up, he found the kitchen, made himself tea and ate the beef sandwich that Gloria or Abra had prepared for him.

With his hunger sated, Rafferty revived a little. He thought of Abra lying upstairs in her lonely bed and immediately brightened. He climbed the stairs with a light but eager tread. Confronted by four closed doors, one of which he already knew to be the one to the bathroom, he wondered which one was Abra's.

After opening one door and looking in on a Gloria who was muttering restlessly in her sleep, he tried again and got lucky.

After using the landing light to get his bearings as to the room's layout, he shut the door, shed his clothes and climbed in beside the warm and sleeping Abra, nuzzling her neck and murmuring her name.

She woke up the instant he put his cold hands around her bare flesh.

'Ow!' she complained. 'It's you. Get off,

you sadist.'

'That's a fine greeting for a man who's just arrived on his white charger to rescue the damsel in distress,' he commented.

Abra snorted. 'White charger?'

'OK. It's a white Cavalier with the odd rust spot. Have you any idea how difficult it is to get a white charger nowadays? Anyway, never mind that. Give us a cuddle.'

Abra obliged. Soon Rafferty, too, was as warm as toast as Abra's naked body put some much-needed heat into his. He was just beginning to feel he was finally getting the welcome he deserved, when Abra suddenly broke off her embrace, sat up and said, 'I almost forgot. It's no good, Joe, you've got to go.'

Bewildered, Rafferty said, 'Go? Go where? I've only just got here, for Pete's sake. I'm not going anywhere—'

'I don't mean you've to go home, pea-brain. Only across the landing to the other spare room.'

'And why would I do that?' Dumbfounded, Rafferty also sat up. Then he laughed. 'You're joking, right? You had me going there, for a minute,' he admitted as he snuggled back down in the bed and pulled Abra with him.

Abra struggled back up and yanked his head off the pillows. 'I mean it, Joe. I'm not joking. I'm sorry, but I know my Aunt

Gloria. For herself, she wouldn't care in the slightest that we're not married but are sharing a bed in her home. But because of my late uncle—'

'The Methodist minister?'

'The very same. My uncle took a dim view of unmarried couples sharing a bedroom, so Gloria thinks it would be an insult to his memory if she allowed it in his house.'

'But,' he began. 'But we *live* together for heaven's sake—'

'I know. It's rough on you. Rough on both of us. But I think we ought to respect her wishes. It's only for the one night, after all.'

The one night he'd expected to have Abra back in his bed ... But after his long day's work, followed by the tiring drive, Rafferty had no energy to argue. Besides, deflated by Abra's unexpected ejection of him from her bedroom, even the energy he had summoned for love-making dissipated. Though at least now he understood his ma's reference to the bedroom accommodation in Gloria's house not being sufficient to house her as well. She might have explained it to him, he thought resentfully. But of course, as she would have known, if she had explained then he might not have so readily submitted to her machinations to get him to Wales.

Suddenly, he felt deadly tired. Without more objections, he gathered his shoes and clothes together in a heap and crept across the landing to his lonely single bed.

Rafferty woke reluctantly from a deep sleep around seven the following morning. He showered, shaved and dressed, then went downstairs to the welcome aroma of grilling bacon.

The two women were both up before him. Abra put a pot of tea on the kitchen table as he entered the room, then glanced at him with a teasing smile and asked, 'Sleep well?'

'Like a top,' he retorted. 'I didn't have your freezing feet to contend with, remember.'

Abra pulled a face as he bent forward to kiss her. He gave Gloria a quick peck, too.

She was showing the strain of the previous few days, he noticed. It was less than a year since he'd last seen her, but she seemed to have aged five years in that time.

'How are you, Glo?' Rafferty asked. 'I was so sorry when Abra told me what had happened.'

Gloria shrugged and gave him a brief, faltering smile. It was a mere shadow of the vivacious grin he remembered from Christmas. 'I suppose I'll live. I feel so stupid, Joe. It was such an idiotic thing to happen.'

'You're in good company, Gloria. You'd be surprised how many people have found themselves in a similar position after a fit of absent-mindedness. These huge supermarkets aren't always user-friendly.'

She tried another smile to show her thanks at his attempt at comfort. Again it quickly faded. 'But sit down and have your breakfast.' He heard the forced brightness as she placed a plate piled high in front of him.

'I thought you'd like a fry-up after that long drive.'

'Mm. Looks good.' He picked up his knife and fork and attacked the breakfast with gusto.

Ten minutes later, replete, he sat back and picked up his second mug of tea. 'What did you say was the name of the officer in charge of Gloria's case?' he asked Abra.

'Jones. Detective Inspector Jones. As I told you on the phone, by a stroke of luck it came back to me that Dafyd mentioned him ages ago. They used to be great friends, as I recall.'

It was nice to get some good news at last, Rafferty reflected. 'Sounds hopeful,' he said. 'With this Inspector Jones being a friend of Dafyd, we stand a good chance of persuading the local cops not to press charges. Have you managed to see this DI Jones yet?' he asked Abra.

She shook her head. 'He wasn't in the station either time I went to speak to him. Hopefully, you'll have better luck, especially now Gloria's agreed you can reveal she's Dafyd's mum. Though you'll have to make this DI Jones promise not to contact Dafyd.'

Rafferty nodded and glanced at his watch. 'No time like the present. But perhaps I ought to ring first and check he's in.' He pulled out his mobile.

Abra found her handbag and produced a slip of paper. 'That's the phone number.'

Rafferty's brief telephone call established that Inspector Jones was in the station, had no morning appointments and was able to see him. After another trip to the bathroom to clean his teeth, he shrugged into his jacket.

'I'd better be off,' he said. 'The sooner I see this DI Jones, the sooner we'll get you out from under,' he told Gloria.

The light of hope entered her eyes at this.

'Thanks, Joe. It's good of you to drive all this way and try to sort this out for me.'

'No problem.'

He was about to add that Dafyd would have done the same for him when he realised that Dafyd trying to use his professional influence to get charges dropped against a Rafferty family member was about as un-likely as him turning into a serious boozer. It was the reason *he* was here, after all, and why Gloria had agreed to Abra telling him what had happened. It was clear that even Gloria considered it unlikely that her son wouldn't turn all sanctimonious on her if she were to tell him the truth.

Confident that Llewellyn's old friend would be able to smoothe things over, Rafferty got the directions from Gloria and made for the police station.

As he drove through the narrow streets, Rafferty caught the occasional glimpse of the remains of a ruined castle on a ridge about a mile outside the town. Not much more than the keep remained. He had read something of the great medieval castles of Wales, built either by the native Welsh princes to defend themselves against the hated English, or by their main persecutor, Edward I. He had even found the time to check if any were near Gloria's home. Maybe if he sorted Gloria's little problem out quickly, he might be able to spare half an hour to look it over.

His gaze rested briefly on one of the tourist information signs and he learned that this particular castle had been built in the thirteenth century by Llywelyn ab Iorweth, as the Welsh called him. The name translated in to English as Llewellyn the Great, he read.

Wouldn't you know it, he thought with a wry grin, that the name Llewellyn would have the epithet 'Great' attached to it. It would be all he needed for Llewellyn to start claiming he was descended from royalty...

DI Jones turned out to be a sallow, thin-faced man in his mid-thirties with eyes that were set too close together. But Rafferty didn't let his first impression put him off. Looks were often deceptive, he reminded himself – hadn't he and Dafyd got off on the wrong foot when they first began working together? And DI Jones had agreed to speak to him privately.

As he followed Jones down the corridor to his office, Rafferty rehearsed again the words he thought most likely to persuade the Welsh DI to agree not to charge Gloria.

'But—' Rafferty, reduced to incoherent spluttering only five minutes later, stared uncomprehendingly at DI Jones after his carefully worded request had been denied. 'What do you mean, you can't help? I thought Dafyd Llewellyn was a friend of yours?'

Jones gave what Rafferty could only describe as a smirk.

'Oh, no, Inspector Rafferty. You've been badly advised. Dafyd Llewellyn and I were never friends. You must have me confused with ex-DI Dai Jones. Thick as thieves the two of them were. He retired two months back. *He* might have been prepared to abuse his position to help family and friends escape punishment for their wrongdoings, but I'm not.

'No.' DI Jones rocked back on his heels and directed a look of self-righteous piety at Rafferty. 'The law must take its course and

I'm here to make sure that it does. Now.' He strode to the door, pulled it open with a sharp jerk and gave Rafferty a smile that he didn't like the look of. 'Doubtless I'll see Mrs Llewellyn in court.'

'Doubtless,' Rafferty muttered as he strode past Jones, wishing as he did so that the word didn't sound such an unwelcome echo to that which had featured in Sam Dally's invitation to the latest post-mortem.

Deflated, Rafferty wondered how he was he going to tell Gloria and Abra that he'd cocked up big-time. Too late, now, he realised what he should have done was make some discreet enquiries before he arranged the appointment with Jones. If he had, he would have learned the facts that DI Jones had just told him with such relish. Common sense should have told him that the police-station personnel would not necessarily have remained the same since Dafyd's transfer to the Essex force. In the police service, as in life, nothing remained static.

Maybe he ought to find out where the retired DI Dai Jones lived and see if he could still exert some influence on Gloria's behalf? After all, according to the other DI Jones, Dai had only retired two months ago and, in spite of his previous reflection that nothing remained static, Dai Jones might well have some good mate in a position of greater authority than Poison Ivy Jones and who might be willing to pull a few strings.

However, when he re-entered the police station, after first making sure the current DI Jones wasn't around, he discovered that finding Dai Jones wasn't going to be that simple.

'Dai Jones is retired from the police service,' the young constable behind the desk informed him.

Rafferty nodded. 'I know that. But I want his advice on a case,' he told him.

'And what case would that be, sir?'

'I'm not at liberty to discuss it,' Rafferty said. 'It's hush-hush.'

'*Hush-hush*, is it?' The young officer seemed to find this amusing and he told Rafferty, 'I think you'll find that Dai Jones's whereabouts are also *hush-hush*. The inspector told me I'm to give you no information on that particular topic. He said he thought you'd come creeping back looking for Dai Jones's address. He told me he thinks you're some sort of *subversive* and not a policeman at all.'

As Rafferty had managed to leave his warrant card back in his flat in Elmhurst, he was unable to contradict the young officer, whose Welsh lilt flowed most lyrically. Rafferty suspected he was putting it on for all he was worth, to remind Rafferty that he was an outsider – and an unwelcome, subversive, *English* outsider at that.

Too late, he recalled Llewellyn explaining

something of the reasons for the Welsh antagonism towards the English, which nowadays still occasionally inclined them to burn down English holiday cottages. King Edward I was one reason, of course, as he had ruthlessly crushed Welsh independence and littered the landscape with his mighty castles. The local-government reforms in the seventies hadn't gone down a bundle either. And although Llewellyn's county, Gwynedd, taking as it did the name of the ancient capital of north-west Wales, was a more imaginative name choice than some, the resentment over the reforms made by their English rulers in faraway London still simmered beneath the surface.

Clearly, he was not going to find out where Dai Jones lived from the local police. Though it was ironic really, he reflected, as, apart from being born in London, he wasn't English at all. His bloodlines were Irish on both sides. Perhaps he should have explained that, he thought, and encouraged a little Celtic fellow-feeling?

But he suspected it was too late now; and it was unlikely that treating them to a third dose of his London accent would encourage them to belatedly embrace him as a fellow-Celt. More likely to act as a red rag to the Red Dragon, as it had already done twice over.

He abandoned the idea and left the police

station to find a phone box. But when he looked at the endless listings for 'Jones' in the directory he almost gave up.

He glanced at his watch. Time was getting on. He had told Llewellyn he would be back in Elmhurst by late afternoon; but if he didn't manage to trace this Dai Jones pretty quickly there was little chance of that.

Maybe he should accept the situation. He *did* have a murder to solve, he reminded himself, and Gloria's problem, although upsetting for her, was trivial in comparison. For all he knew, *his* Jones wasn't even listed and Dai not even his correct first name but his second.

Yet he had given Gloria and Abra his word that he'd do his best. After telling himself not to be a faint heart, he quickly glanced round to see if anyone was watching him – he wouldn't like to risk someone reporting him and giving DI Jones the satisfaction of charging him with malicious damage. But the High Street was deserted. Surreptitiously he tore the pages listing the Jones entries from the directory and stuffed them in his pocket. He'd find the nearest pub and use his mobile; at least he could have a pint or two while he worked his way through the listings.

Two hours and two pints later, Rafferty still hadn't traced the elusive Dai Jones. If he could have used official channels it wouldn't have been a problem, but he'd already made himself high-profile enough in Dafyd's home town; if Dafyd ever found out he'd been here he'd certainly wonder what had brought him. He would start asking questions of the neighbours and the local cop shop and then Gloria's little secret wouldn't be a secret any more.

He checked his watch again. It was long past time he started thinking about driving back to Elmhurst. He didn't want Llewellyn to be able to complain that he had broken his promise on his return time, though it now looked as though he wasn't to be spared that particular irritation.

To ward off the worst of Llewellyn's ire, he phoned him and asked him to put the appointment with Mike Raine back a couple of hours. Before Llewellyn could voice any complaint, Rafferty remembered the ruse Abra had used to get out of having to make further explanations before she took off for parts west. Quickly, he told Llewellyn the reception was poor and cut him off. He left the pub and drove back to Gloria's house to confess his failure.

It was an hour later, after another meal and an emotional parting from Abra, when Rafferty set off on the long drive home. He felt relieved and guilty in about equal measure that Gloria had been so understanding of his failure to help her.

He had hoped the task of speaking to Dai Jones and enlisting his help would be a quick and successful one; he'd never thought he wouldn't manage to speak to the man at all.

Apart from seeing Abra again, the entire trip had been a waste of time. And although he would continue to try to trace Dai Jones and get him onside once he arrived home, he felt it unlikely he would trace the man before Gloria was charged, especially as he had to concentrate on the murder. And after driving for hours he was not going to be in the freshest state for conducting the interview with Mike Raine...

Think positive, he advised himself. But no sooner had his mind formed the words than it provided a vivid reminder of the trouble he had got into the last time he had thought positive. With him, it seemed, positive thinking had a strange knack of leading to negative experiences. Maybe it would be better if he didn't think at all and just concentrated on his driving and the magnificent mountain and lakeland scenery that surrounded him and for which this part of Wales was justly famous.

Between the rugged mountains, the dramatic passes which had been natural allies to the Welsh princes all those centuries ago as they conducted their guerrilla warfare against the English, and the serene lakes, it was the sort of spectacular scenery designed to make a mere mortal feel very humble and insignificant, as Rafferty discovered to his chagrin. The Welsh police, unfortunately, had had the same effect.

Fifteen

Tired and still smarting from his humiliating failure in Wales, Rafferty got back to his Elmhurst flat at around quarter to six that evening. He rang Llewellyn and told him he'd meet him at the Raines' family offices. He remembered to pick up his warrant card before he left. Just in case their questioning should encourage the second confession in the investigation...

He had cut it fine, but at least neither Mike Raine nor Llewellyn would be able to complain that he was late for the rearranged interview.

The business premises of the Raines family fashion firm, with its décor of black, grey and silver and accents of white and scarlet, looked as sleek and upmarket as on their last visit. So did Jane the receptionist, who clearly hadn't forgotten them, as a chill descended as soon as they entered the building and approached her desk.

Rafferty flipped open his warrant card and, for the second time, revealed the information that had found no favour first time round. 'We have an appointment with Mr Raine.'

As before, they were told to take a seat.

After learning how the cousins must have been encouraged by the terms of the trust to view one another as rivals, he thought it would be understandable if there had been no love lost between the pair. And Mike Raine had clearly lied to them about not knowing the identity of Raymond's solicitor. It had been a stupid lie, and Mike Raine hadn't struck him as lacking intelligence. What had prompted it? he wondered. Maybe he'd learn the answer shortly.

Rafferty kept a curious eye on the receptionist's body language as she picked up the phone. The flirtatious manner with which she reported their arrival indicated she was speaking to Mike Raine rather than his secretary. Along with her earlier hostility, it strengthened the suspicion raised during their previous visit that she might have designs on the cousin whose future looked so much rosier now than it had but a short time before. Was Jane ambitious to produce the Raine family heir now that Raymond's wife could no longer do so? he wondered.

Jonas Singleton had made clear that, as trustee, he felt no inclination to shield the younger Raine cousin or any other family member should any of them turn out to have had a hand in Raymond's death. In fact, he had gone out of his way to fully explain Mike's position both before and after Raymond's death.

Understandable if Mike had felt bitter about the unfairness of his situation as the junior partner. Had he decided he would prefer to be top dog, and set about murdering Raymond in order to achieve it?

But if he had, why on earth hadn't he made a proper job of the planning? The way he had just blurted out the thoughtless lie about not knowing who Raymond's solicitor was was surely more indicative of panicked innocence? Besides, he'd put up with his cousin lording it over him for more than two years. So what had changed?

Mike was twenty-seven and was not only unmarried but without a partner of any sort. In fact, their questioning of Jonas Singleton had revealed that Mike Raine lived alone. Yet, in spite of this and the fact that he had no girlfriend there had been no hint that he had homosexual leanings, which was something Rafferty had wondered about, given that the rag trade was largely run by homosexuals.

Jonas Singleton, he recalled, had let slip that Mike would make sure Felicity was looked after financially. And as he thought of Felicity's haunting beauty, he wondered if *she* was the catalyst for change. Did Mike have leanings in that direction?

Certainly, to Rafferty, Mike's evident concern for Felicity's financial well-being indicated a degree of tenderness. And now, if he suspected that Felicity *had* killed Raymond, Mike, at last about to take what he must regard as his proper place in the firm, had even more reason to feel tender towards the woman who might well have made that rise possible.

Could Felicity and Mike together have conspired to bring about Raymond's death and Mike's inheritance? Having failed to provide Raymond with the heir to the Raine kingdom Felicity might have thought that throwing in her lot with his successor might be a good idea. If Mike had a yen for Felicity and if his feelings were reciprocated, they could provide him with an additional motive to the basic, business one, to remove Raymond. And with Raymond gone, who knew to what – or whom – else Mike might aspire?

If only Felicity, as though determined to sacrifice herself to some savage god, hadn't made that hasty confession. Because although, as he had prophesied right at the beginning of the case, she had soon been persuaded to retract, that confession had coloured and influenced his conduct of the case right from the start when she had stumbled into the police station reception in her bloodied dress, soaked to the skin and, in a voice that made clear she could hardly herself believe that she had done the deed, told them she had just killed her husband.

From recollecting the recently discovered Raine family history, Rafferty was dragged back to the present by the still-cool voice of the receptionist.

'Mr Raine is free now,' she told them. 'You may go up and he will meet you at the lift on the sixth floor as before.'

The receptionist had failed to mention that Mike had removed himself from his smaller office to his late cousin's much larger corner suite.

The phrase 'dead men's shoes' ran through Rafferty's mind as they followed Mike into the plush office with its own private bathroom and settled in the informal seating area rather than around the desk. Was this an attempt to disarm them? Rafferty wondered as he again mused on what explanation Mike Raine would come up with for lying to them. For all his boyish looks and seeming openness, the lie had exposed Raine as a man ready to deceive. It made Rafferty wonder just what treachery might be concealed beneath that youthful exterior.

Mike Raine interrupted his thoughts. 'Your sergeant didn't say exactly why you needed to speak to me again, inspector.'

'Did he not? I'm sorry. It was a simple matter really. I would like you to explain something to me.'

Mike Raine shrugged. 'If I can.'

Rafferty thought it was likely to be more a case of whether he *would* and whether his explanation would be the truth. 'It's a perfectly simple matter,' he said, 'though one that has intrigued both Sergeant Llewellyn here and myself since we discovered it. We would like to know why you lied to us.'

Mike blinked. '*Lied* to you? I don't understand. Lied about what, exactly?'

'You told my sergeant when he telephoned you that you didn't know the name of your cousin's solicitor.'

Mike Raine stared at him. 'Is that all?' – as though he had feared Rafferty was going to refer to something else entirely. Then he recollected himself and asked, 'Did I?'

'Yes, you did. I'd like an explanation.'

Mike stared at him. Then he began a rapid blinking while his eyes darted all around the room. For a moment, Rafferty thought the man was going to make a bolt for the door. But then he got a grip and visibly calmed himself.

'I can't imagine why I would do such a thing.'

Rafferty could – if Mike *had* murdered his cousin, he might have welcomed the delay such a lie would cause while he thought his actions through further. Yet Rafferty had to admit that the delay – given his ready admission to having no alibi, which, fortunately for him, had been readily contradicted by his secretary – had gained him little. The receptionist-cum-fill-in-secretary was clearly a far from disinterested party. Rafferty had the feeling she would have sworn the moon was made of green cheese if it would get Mike Raine out from under.

'I'm sorry,' Mike said. 'I really don't know why I said such a thing. I don't even remember doing so, but I accept that I must have.'

'Yes, Mr Raine. You did. We have, of course, since learned that you and your late cousin shared the same solicitor.'

Mike Raine shrugged. 'Well, yes. Of course we do. I can't have been thinking straight, inspector, or even listening straight for that matter, after the shocking news your sergeant gave me. Besides' – he smiled his disarming boyish smile – 'what difference can all this make now? You have Felicity's confession that *she* killed Raymond. Poor Felicity.' He looked at them with an expression of bewilderment. 'Who'd have thought little Fliss would do such a thing? It's hard to make sense of it. I don't know what to think any more. I simply don't know what to make of it.'

'Snap,' Rafferty felt like saying. Only pride and professional prudence required that he keep his tongue discreet. It wouldn't do for any of the suspects to know how far at sea he felt, nor that, rather than swimming for the shore, he felt increasingly as if some powerful undertow was at work which was sending him further towards deep water with each movement he made.

Fortunately, Mike seemed oblivious to Rafferty's inner turmoil.

'And although I feel dreadfully sorry for her if she was so unhappy that she resorted to murder, I don't understand why you're continuing the investigation. Unless – unless—?' Mike paused, then the rest came out in a rush. 'Unless you think she had an accomplice?'

As Rafferty didn't choose to satisfy his curiosity on the matter, Mike's gaze swivelled searchingly between him and Llewellyn. And although the office was cool, sweat broke out on his forehead. Then his gaze slid away from them and fixed on a point beyond them. For a few brief seconds, Mike looked as if he might burst into tears. Was he imagining losing what had taken him so long to acquire?

If he was, he chose to follow Rafferty's example. With a smile, he said, 'I admit the thought of being Felicity's partner in anything is a very attractive one, but I'm afraid I must disappoint. Unfortunately, the divine Felicity never put such a proposition before me.'

The recovery had been swift. Rafferty

wondered if he had imagined that moment's blind panic that had frozen Mike Raine's mobile face. Had he really just clutched at the opportunity to delay their investigation, as Rafferty believed? And was he now using his shock at the news of Raymond's murder as an excuse for his earlier information failure?

If he felt he had need of such a delay it could indicate that Mike had had some involvement in his cousin's murder. And if he one day had a child, he stood to benefit from Raymond's death more than anyone. Certainly more than Felicity – who had lost everything, even her home and her freedom. Yet why had she made that confession?

Rafferty was beginning to feel that both he and the case were going round in circles of the ever-decreasing sort. If he wasn't careful, he'd disappear up his own fundament.

Although Mike had freely confessed to having no alibi, he seemed untroubled by this, or that the one belatedly supplied for him wasn't entirely unprejudiced and still left him placed in an invidious position. Rafferty decided that troubling Mike Raine might be a good idea. It might help him get to the truth.

'By the way...' He wondered what Mike's reaction would be when he told him that Felicity had retracted her confession. He thought it might startle Mike into some unwise revelation and he studied his face closely as he said, 'Were you aware that Mrs Felicity Raine has retracted her confession?'

Clearly, he hadn't known. For a fleeting moment, before the shutters came down, Rafferty had caught the sudden fear in Mike Raine's eyes. Though whether the fear was brought about by guilt, or by anxiety that his convenient alibi would make him of more interest to the police than he might have hoped to be before the retraction, wasn't clear.

'So you see, the investigation is now wide open. We shall, of course, need to look deeper in to all the alibis given to us and consider all the possible motives, of which yours, you must admit, looks pretty strong – financial gain and increased power are two of the prime motivations for murder. And you possess both of them.'

Maybe, if, as Rafferty suspected, Mike had also lusted after Raymond's wife, they would have the grand slam of motives in the one suspect. Though, against that, was the knowledge that Felicity had failed to confide in Mike about either her confession *or* its retraction. He couldn't help but wonder why this was.

'There's one other matter that I wanted to speak to you about.' Rafferty turned the screw. 'Since we last spoke to you we've learned that you felt your cousin had unfairly deprived you of your full share in the business. That would be enough to make any man angry and want to do something about it. Was that the effect it had on you, Mr Raine?'

For a moment, Mike said nothing. Then he conceded that his ill-luck *had* angered him.

'Of course it did. Naturally, I wanted what should have been mine – what *would* have been mine but for my late father's last illness and the sudden and unexpected death of my uncle. Wouldn't any man? That's why I came in early on the morning he died. I thought if I forced Raymond to at least acknowledge my industry and that I was an asset to the firm he might relent and agree to let me have back what in the normal course of events would have been mine by right – the ten per cent of the business which would have brought me up to a full fifty per cent share.'

Rafferty found Mike's explanation less than convincing. From what he had so far learned of Raymond Raine, giving others what they considered their due didn't immediately strike him as being in character. He was, if what Elaine Enderby and Sandrine Agnew said were true, not simply a jealous wife beater but a secretive man who kept things close to his chest and who didn't voluntarily give up the things he considered his possessions. The late Raymond Raine struck Rafferty as likely to possess a ruthless streak that he doubted the younger Mike could have matched, especially when it came to an ego contest about who made the greater contribution to the family firm.

In fact, he felt Mike's determination to take the confrontational approach would, with Raymond, have been the worst possible way to go about getting his 'rights'. And Mike must surely have realised that? He had presumably known the older man all his life and must have had regular exposure to his cousin's determined personality. So what, he wondered, had been different about that particular morning that he believed he would be in with a chance of persuading his cousin to do the 'right' thing?

He asked Mike the question, but Mike simply smiled that winning smile of his again, the peevish look that had made a fleeting appearance now gone, and replied that he had no particular reason – apart from natural justice and the proper rewarding of those who increased the firm's profits – for thinking that Raymond would see things his way.

'Anyway,' Mike continued, 'you seemed interested to know if I was the one who murdered him. In my defence, as you must also know, I'd worked with Raymond for several years and managed to resist any temptation you seem to think I might have had to kill him. Why would I have chosen to kill him now? Nothing had changed.'

'I don't know, Mr Raine,' Rafferty told him. 'But if you did, I'll not rest till I find out the whys and wherefores.' He stood up. 'We'll see ourselves out.'

As Rafferty returned to the car park with Llewellyn, he asked, 'Still no theories you'd like to share with me?'

Llewellyn, never one to rush in with an unconsidered comment, pondered for several seconds before he remarked, 'Only the one. *Cherchez la femme.*'

'Not still harping on that theory? It seems to me there are far too many *femmes* in this case already, without looking for any more.'

As they drove back to the station in their separate cars, Rafferty mentally reviewed the means, motives and opportunities of each of the suspects in the investigation. And as he did so, for the first time he began to see a pattern emerging.

But then he was brought up short at the realisation that the pattern he thought he saw lacked one vital factor. Without that one element, the pattern collapsed.

Sixteen

The following morning, when Rafferty, with Llewellyn hard on his heels, entered the police-station reception, it was to learn from Bill Beard on the desk that he had visitors.

Beard pointed to the two women sitting at the far end of the reception waiting area.

Rafferty recognised Stephanie's French *au pair*, Michelle Ginôt, and Felicity's plump champion, Sandrine Agnew. They hadn't noticed him enter and with their heads close together, whispering, they had a distinctly conspiratorial air.

As he studied them, he recalled Llewellyn's *'Cherchez la femme'* comment and wondered whether his sergeant might not have the right idea, but the wrong target.

He walked over to the two women. 'Mademoiselle Ginôt. Ms Agnew. I believe you wish to see me?'

They both nodded.

'What can I do for you?' he asked.

'I am troubled, inspector,' Michelle told him. 'I liked the *pauvre petite* Felicity. I would not wish for her to remain in the prison when the ozzers they are plotting against her.'

'Plotting? Who precisely is plotting? And what are they plotting?' he asked. From the look of these two as he had entered reception, they might well have been doing some plotting of their own.

Rafferty noticed that Michelle had used the past tense when she spoke of Felicity Raine; he wondered if she was being prophetic or if her less than perfect English was to blame. Either way, she made it sound as if Felicity had not simply lost her freedom, but her life. Which, he supposed, she effectively had.

'Perhaps we should go up to my office?' he suggested. He nodded at Llewellyn to accompany him; the women's air of being about to confide something explosive made him want a witness.

Michelle nodded and she and Sandrine Agnew followed Rafferty and Llewellyn up the stairs.

Sandrine Agnew spoke up once they were seated. She was again dressed in a very mannish way, he noted: tailored trousers, practical lace-up shoes and yet another tweedy jacket.

She explained that as she was a good friend of Felicity's, Michelle had asked her to accompany her to the police station to help her explain something she had overheard.

Rafferty, looking at the almost masculine Sandrine Agnew, couldn't help but wonder what the pretty, feminine and totally French Michelle thought of the young woman at her side. But Michelle's manner betrayed her feelings for the plain, large-boned and plump Sandrine and her masculine attire. Beneath the surface gratitude that Sandrine had agreed to accompany her to the police station, Rafferty detected a measure of – what? Pity? Contempt?

After shushing Michelle, who had once again started on about *'la pauvre Felicity'*, Sandrine Agnew said, 'Let me explain why we've come to see you, inspector. Michelle told me that she's worried Felicity is being set up. Frankly, so am I.'

'Go on,' Rafferty invited.

'Michelle came to see me this morning – she knows that Felicity and I are friends – and confided that she had overheard Stephanie on the phone late last night. She didn't know to whom Stephanie was talking, but from what she says, I suspect it must have been Mike Raine. Anyway, Michelle told me she hadn't been able to sleep. I think she finds Stephanie's house a little frightening at night,' she added as an aside. 'It's large, fairly isolated and very quiet. Far from what she's used to as she comes from a big Parisian family. I gather she's taken to raiding Stephanie's drinks cabinet as a cure for her insomnia.

'Anyway, I digress. She was just rounding the bottom of the stairs when she heard Stephanie's voice.'

Rafferty nodded. 'And what did she hear, exactly?'

'Michelle thought herself quite alone as she crept down the stairs in search of her nightcap. But then she heard Stephanie's laugh. And when she rounded the bottom of the stairs she saw the light in the drawing room. She heard Stephanie quite clearly, she assures me.'

Rafferty sighed quietly to himself as he waited impatiently for this rigmarole to reach some conclusion. He just hoped this revelation of a late-night conversation hadn't been made up by Michelle as a way of getting back at Stephanie for telling her she had been an embarrassment at the barbecue, though, hopefully, the phone records would be able to prove that the conversation had at least taken place. Though how they'd prove that the conversation Michelle was going to quote had done so, particularly if Stephanie and Mike contradicted her, he did not know.

Perhaps Sandrine Agnew heard the sigh, for her plain face reddened and she drew her short, square-built body together, sat further forward on her well-fleshed buttocks and said, 'I gather Stephanie sounded pleased with herself. As if she'd pulled off some tremendous coup, and with Felicity as the obligatory sacrificial lamb.'

Sandrine's cheeks reddened some more, but this time Rafferty felt the cause was anger that anyone – especially Felicity's step-mother-in-law – should fail to be consumed by grief at Felicity's plight.

Rafferty already suspected that the plain and mannish-looking Sandrine Agnew held something of a torch for Felicity Raine. A love certain to be unrequited, he thought with a fleeting pity. Though clearly Sandrine Agnew wasn't one to lightly give up on a cause, even when it appeared hopeless.

'Anyway, Stephanie sounded very hyper. Michelle told me she heard her say quite clearly, "Let Felicity take the blame." Then she laughed and said, "It's not as if, being childless, she's now got anything to lose, unlike us. With Raymond dead, I feel I must grab whatever else I can. Besides, it's plain the police would be glad to have the case cleared up quickly."'

Rafferty winced. He was sufficiently put out to see that Sandrine Agnew saw no reason to argue with Stephanie Raine's assumption that he felt the necessity to defend himself.

'Catching the killer is always going to be near the top of the wish list of every police-man investigating a violent, non-accidental death,' he agreed in a firm voice. 'But most of us place the capture and conviction of the *right* person in the top spot. We don't get any satisfaction from jailing the innocent.' He paused. 'Was that all Stephanie Raine said?' It didn't seem to amount to much, he thought.

But Sandrine Agnew shook her head.

'No.'

She pulled a sheet of paper from the pocket of her tweed jacket and held it up close to read. 'Hang on.' Her face cleared. 'Here we are – I made notes so I didn't miss anything. Stephanie went on to say, "And they *do* have her confession. And while she may have retracted it, I'm sure, between us, we can concoct something to encourage them to push on with the murder charge. And then you and I will both be home and dry."'

Sandrine Agnew sat back and fixed Rafferty with small, near-sighted brown eyes. 'It's clear to me that Stephanie at least has been plotting to make sure Felicity takes the blame for Raymond's death. Although,' she was honest enough to admit, 'from her responses to Mike's replies it seems he's not anything like as keen to plot against Felicity as Stephanie is. Anyway, what are you going to do about it, inspector?'

Rafferty studied her anxious but determined expression and wondered how Sandrine had managed to convince herself that

Michelle, with her poor grasp of English, should have understood what Stephanie Raine had said at all, never mind be word-perfect when she recounted its contents to her.

Anxious not to antagonise her and reinforce her belief that the police, once they had charged someone, wouldn't be over-interested in their guilt or otherwise as long as they got a conviction, he explained patiently, 'First, I want to be sure that Mademoiselle Ginôt is certain about what she heard. Her English—'

'Her understanding is better than her spoken English,' Sandrine was quick to reassure him.

That hadn't been Rafferty's experience. But he felt he must attempt to offer some reassurance.

'I'll make some enquiries,' he promised. 'I'll speak to Michael and Stephanie Raine, though I hope you and Michelle appreciate that it's unlikely Mrs Raine will think kindly of Mademoiselle Ginôt when she learns that she not only eavesdropped on her conversation, but then divulged its contents to you, my sergeant and me.'

Michelle immediately demanded of Sandrine that she explain what Rafferty had said, thereby negating Sandrine's claim for the French girl's ability to understand more English than she could speak.

Once she grasped what he had said, Michelle said, '*Pouf* – and for a second, Rafferty thought she had taken to sexist name-calling out of frustration – but then she added, 'What do I care for Stephanie and the work that I do *pour elle?* Such jobs are twenty to a euro. The agency they will find me anozzer.'

'The agency may not find you something else immediately, Mademoiselle Ginôt, especially if Stephanie contacts them and gives you a poor reference.

'Obviously, as Mademoiselle Ginôt's a witness in this case, I do not want her leaving the country should Mrs Raine ask her to pack her bags,' Rafferty advised Sandrine Agnew.

'Don't worry, inspector. It's not a problem. Michelle can always come and stay with me.'

Michelle didn't look too thrilled at the prospect, thought Rafferty. 'Just as long as we're kept informed of her whereabouts.'

To his surprise, Sandrine Agnew seemed satisfied with his response, for she got up, gathered her bag and Michelle together and said thank you to Rafferty and Llewellyn, and 'We'll wait to hear from you,' and left without further ado.

'What do you make of that, sir – Joseph?' Llewellyn asked.

Rafferty shrugged. 'God knows. Though it struck me as unlikely that little Mademoiselle from Armantières, with her less-than-wonderful grasp of the lingo, took in all that late-night conversation and was able to report it to Sandrine Agnew verbatim.'

Llewellyn nodded. 'Exactly what I thought myself. Didn't you say that the first time you spoke to Mademoiselle Ginôt she got her yesterdays confused with her other days?'

'Mm. It seems to me that either young Michelle's English is about to put mine to shame or she's been prompted, encouraged and had words put in her mouth by Ms Agnew – presumably she's hoping this evidence will help get Felicity released and that Felicity will be suitably grateful.'

Llewellyn nodded sagely. 'Love, they say, does the strangest things to a person's ability to reason.'

Ain't that the truth, thought Rafferty, whose reasoning ability since Abra had taken off for points west had dipped way below that expected of a detective inspector, as the Super hadn't been slow to tell him.

He had seen more than enough of Stephanie Raine and her determined spite to last him a lifetime, but he supposed he had no choice but to face the music again. He sighed, sure Mrs Raine Senior could be relied upon not only to take umbrage that he had come to question her on the word of her own *au pair*, but, of course, to also deny any conspiracy against Felicity.

'I suppose we'd better get over there and hear what Madam Stephanie's got to say for herself. We'll speak to Mike Raine afterwards.' No doubt, he thought, with a similar result.

Stephanie Raine turned out to have plenty to say for herself, none of it helpful, unfortunately.

'Of course I deny saying such things. And I shall continue to deny it, as it's not true. What that girl thought she was doing, sneaking about the house in the middle of the night, spying on me—'

'I believe she suffers from insomnia,' Rafferty put in on behalf of the absent Michelle, who, he learned, had yet to return. He didn't envy her reception when she did so.

'Well she can suffer from insomnia elsewhere from now on. I'll not tolerate someone spying on me in my own home and then lying about what I said, as I shall tell her the minute she returns.'

Just then, the front door banged. Stephanie immediately strode to the drawing-room door. 'So it's you. Come in here this instant.'

A sulky-looking Michelle trailed into the room after Stephanie.

After haranguing the unfortunate Michelle for five minutes, Stephanie told her she could take her things and leave. 'And you needn't expect a reference from me. I'll explain exactly why to that agency when I speak to them.' Stephanie stared hard at Michelle, who had made no move. 'Well? What are you waiting for? I told you to pack. I meant now, not tomorrow or next week. I want you out of my home immediately since you've proved you can't be trusted.'

After directing a vituperative volley of what sounded like French swear words at Stephanie, Michelle turned on her heel and flung out of the room.

After that, they made their excuses and left, though as they were about to turn out of the drive, Rafferty said, 'Hang on. I've just remembered a couple of things I think Stephanie and Michelle might be able to provide answers to. In private,' he added as Llewellyn made to follow him. 'I think I'm more likely to get truthful answers if there aren't any witnesses. Wait for me here. I doubt it will take long.'

After questioning Stephanie again about the barbecue she had held in July, he went looking for Michelle. He found her in her flat over the garage. It took only a few minutes to get the truth out of her, less to retrieve the expensive trinket she admitted stealing.

Satisfied that his theory was now advancing better than he had dared hope, Rafferty resolved, as he still felt he had some ground to make up on the case-resolution front, to keep his thoughts to himself for a while longer. And even if several more supportive elements had been added to the pattern he had discerned, he was painfully aware that it still lacked that one essential, additional ingredient to round it all off perfectly. So when Llewellyn questioned him on his return to the car, he revealed nothing of his conversation with either Stephanie or Michelle.

Instead, when Llewellyn showed signs of tight-lipped annoyance at Rafferty's uncharacteristic discretion, he changed the subject and said, 'I wonder if there's much point in speaking to Mike Raine. Stephanie will have got on the blower to him as soon as the front door shut behind us and he'll have his story ready.'

'Perhaps,' was Llewellyn's stiff comment. 'Perhaps not. But as Ms Agnew said she thought he wasn't as ready to fall in with Stephanie Raine's plans as she might like, it's possible he'll share what he knows.'

'Unlike some people' was the implication Rafferty had no difficulty in discerning behind Llewellyn's frosty demeanour.

'In any case, it will surely be instructive to hear what he has to say for himself,' Llewellyn added, in the manner of one teaching Granny to suck eggs.

But Llewellyn was wrong. Their conversation with Mike Raine wasn't instructive at all. Although Mike, unlike Stephanie, was perfectly polite, he simply backed up what she had said.

'I have to say that your willingness to investigate the misheard evidence of the linguistically challenged Michelle indicates a certain desperation, inspector,' was Mike's comment. 'I hope it doesn't mean that my cousin's killer will remain unconvicted for the foreseeable future.'

So did Rafferty.

Rafferty's mobile rang ten minutes after their return to the station. He was thankful that Llewellyn, still in something of a huff, had taken himself off when he saw that the caller was Abra. Now what? he wondered as he snatched the mobile up.

'Abra. How are things? What's the news on the Gloria front? I suppose she's been charged now?'

'No. That's what's so weird. I don't know what that horrible DI Jones is waiting for, but he told me in very lofty tones that there had been a delay in charging her. This delay's obviously not down to him, as from what you said it sounded as if he couldn't wait to make sure Dafyd's mum had a criminal conviction.'

'How is she?' he asked.

He heard Abra sigh. 'Not any better for

this delay,' she said. 'I think she just wants it all to be over. And now, to go with the lack of sleep, she's hardly eating. Ironic that it should have been two tins of peaches the supermarket security staff found in her shopping bag.'

'That's all she took? Two tins of peaches are what's caused all this upset and misery?'

'That's all. And she doesn't even *like* bloody peaches, which shows how forgetful she's become. God, Joe, I feel so angry about it all. Anyone with an ounce of common sense and a smidgin of humanity would have seen that, rather than being a habitual thief, she's unwell. I feel like punching that sanctimonious DI Jones in the nose.'

'The law can be an ass, Abra. God knows I see enough examples of mulish stupidity every working day to make me despair. But why not encourage her to do something to help herself while she's waiting for this business to be over? Getting her GP to put her on HRT might be a good place to start. Otherwise she might have this – or something very like it – to be gone through again.'

'God forbid. Though she was on HRT before. She only came off it because of all these journalistic scaremongers spreading the gospel that HRT increases the risk of breast cancer and other health problems. Better, to my mind, to deal with the health problems you *have* got than start worrying about the ones you don't have and likely never will. If it wasn't for them, she'd still be the Gloria of old and not a soon-to-be convicted criminal.'

While Rafferty felt sorry for Gloria, whom he liked, he also wanted Abra home. He missed her terribly.

'Persuade her back on the HRT, Abs. You'll never get home otherwise.'

Rafferty became conscious of an awkward silence on the other end.

'Abra? Did you hear me?'

'Yes. I just wish I could obey, oh my lord and master. Only Gloria's taking a bit of persuading. I'm sure I'll talk her round to returning to the medication before long. Only even if – when – I manage to persuade her of its benefits, it'll take a few weeks to kick in.'

Rafferty was dismayed. 'A few *weeks*? But—'

'Keep your hair on, Joe. It may not be as bad as that. Hopefully I'll be able to get home next week, as Mum and Dad should be back from their holiday in the Algarve. Joe? Are you OK with that?'

I'm going to have to be, he thought. But he was just being selfish. Abra was right: Gloria's need of her was, at the moment, greater than his own.

'I'm fine, Abs. Just promise me you won't stay there a day longer than you can help?'

'Scout's honour.'

'And can you let me have the phone number of Gloria's neighbour so I can at least get in touch?'

'I've bought a new charger for my mobile,' Abra assured him. 'I did tell you.'

'I know. Even so, I'll feel happier if I have a back-up number. You know what you're like for forgetting to charge your phone up.'

'Rather better than you are, if the truth be told.'

As this was undeniable, he said nothing further on the subject.

Nor did Abra. She simply provided the neighbour's number as he had requested and told him to cheer up.

'After all,' she added, with a hint of her normal mischief, 'as we both know that it's pretty unlikely that Dafyd *won't* find out about Gloria's pending conviction one way or another, you can always look forward to being the first to rub his nose in the fact that his mum's a super-criminal. Just imagine how much fun you're going to have with that little titbit.'

'I wouldn't dream of it,' Rafferty protested.

But perhaps his protest was a bit too quick, a bit too vehement, for Abra teased, 'Oh yeah? Come on, Joe. After all the times Davy's high moral principles have put you on the spot with regard to *your* mum. Not to mention most of the rest of your family.'

Rafferty decided a change of subject was way overdue.

'Just you look after yourself,' he ordered. 'And tell Gloria I'm still working on getting in contact with Dai Jones. Love you,' he added.

'Ditto.'

But, he admitted to himself as he came off the phone, Abra was right about one thing. He *would* find it a temptation to just blurt out the truth to Llewellyn. Especially when he was being crabby, like now. And even though he felt genuinely sorry for Gloria, he suspected it *was* inevitable that Llewellyn would learn about her conviction from someone, and that probably sooner rather than later.

And as it was likely to be the only chance he would ever have to come over all superior with his high-moral-ground sergeant he wasn't sure he would be able to resist the temptation – especially the next time Llewellyn dissected one of his theories with that infuriating logic of his.

It wasn't as if his record for resisting temptation was exactly up there with Jesus H. Hadn't he sworn only two cases ago that he would abandon wild theorising? He hadn't taken long to fall from grace and fail to resist that particular vice, after all...

But now, he thought, he'd better have another go at getting hold of the ex-DI Dai

Jones. He'd come up with what he thought a very cunning plan to persuade one of his Welsh opposite numbers to give him the information: ringing the Welsh police station and pretending to be a Welshman, one of 'us', as opposed to one of 'them', the hated English.

He found the slip of paper that Abra had given him on which she had scribbled the police station's telephone number. And after five minutes spent practising his accent, his 'boyos' and his 'isn't it?'s, he picked up the phone and tapped out the number.

He didn't recognise the voice at the other end. It certainly wasn't the cocky young copper who was so determinedly Welsh that he probably had a coal mine buried deep in his valley. It wasn't DI Jones either – not that he'd struck Rafferty as the sort to lower himself to answer the phone in reception.

No, this one sounded early-middle-aged and spoke politely to Rafferty – though that, of course, might just be the influence of the accent.

But, Welsh accent or no, he still didn't get anywhere. What was it about this Dai Jones that had everybody so keen to keep any information about him under wraps? he wondered.

He spun his chair round to face the desk and replace the receiver – and met Llewellyn's startled gaze.

Had he heard any of his conversation? Rafferty wondered uneasily. He certainly couldn't have heard the first bit when he'd mentioned Dai Jones's name as he'd been facing front at the time and knew Llewellyn was out of the room, so he decided to bluff it out.

'I was just having a competition with a friend to see who could do the worst Welsh accent,' he explained weakly.

'Oh yes?' Llewellyn raised an eyebrow. 'I think you won.'

He hadn't, though, Rafferty knew. He was still no further forward on the Dai Jones front. But at least Gloria still hadn't been charged. Rafferty couldn't understand why there was such a delay in what was a routine shoplifting charge. But he was too glad of it to ponder further on the whys and wherefores. It gave him a bit more time to try to help her out of the hole she was in.

Seventeen

While he might not be making any advance in helping Gloria, Rafferty at least felt he was making progress in the Raine murder investigation. If only it didn't still contain that one fatal flaw, his latest theory would be nigh-on perfect.

He had just relented and decided to share his thoughts about this theory with Llewellyn when the office phone rang. He sat up straight, suddenly alert, when he recognised the voice of the governor of the prison where Felicity Raine was being held on remand.

He listened for a few seconds, asked some questions and then replaced the receiver. 'That was Mrs Collins, the prison governor,' he told Llewellyn. 'Apparently Mrs Raine has collapsed. She's been rushed to hospital. The Accident & Emergency here in Elmhurst. We'd better get over there.'

As he walked towards A&E reception, from the corner of his eye, Rafferty caught a glimpse of a familiar face in the crowded waiting room. He stopped. Then he saw that the familiar face of Sandrine Agnew was accompanied by Michelle Ginôt. What were they doing here? he wondered.

But then, as he got closer and saw they were wearing matching expressions of anxiety, it struck him that they must know about Felicity Raine's admission.

'What are you doing here?' Rafferty immediately demanded as he reached their seats. 'I take it you've heard the news?'

'About Felicity? Yes,' Sandrine Agnew confirmed.

'Who told you?'

Sandrine Agnew hesitated, then blurted out, 'I'm a volunteer at the hospital and have a friend who works in A&E. She recognised Felicity, was aware of her present circumstances and that she's a friend of mine.' Sandrine raised her plump chins in defiance of Rafferty's clear disapproval. 'I hope I haven't got her in any trouble, but I thought Felicity might be glad of my support since she's unwell.'

Rafferty glanced around him. Suddenly he noticed they had a fascinated audience among the other waiting patients and he lowered his voice. 'I'm sure. But I hope you understand that she's still a prisoner?'

Sandrine Agnew nodded. 'But not for much longer now, I think, inspector.'

Rafferty raised his eyebrows at this. 'Why do you say that?'

'You have only to look at the other suspects this investigation has thrown up – each of whom has motives for wishing Raymond dead and far more to gain than has Felicity from his death. Michelle and I have already told you about her overhearing Stephanie and Michael colluding to make sure Felicity is convicted and—'

'A collusion they both deny,' Rafferty interrupted to tell her.

Sandrine shrugged this aside as if it was no more than she had expected. 'To quote one of the parties in a previous court case – "They would say that, wouldn't they?" They have everything to gain and nothing to lose by making such a denial.'

She paused, then asked, 'Inspector? May I see Felicity? I need to know for myself that she's all right. None of the other hospital staff will tell me anything and my friend's gone off shift now.

'I'm not a relative, of course,' she remarked with a trace of bitterness. 'As if any of Felicity's relatives ever cared enough about her to even turn up here, as I—' she hesitated, glanced at Michelle with a frown, as though unwilling to acknowledge her presence and shared concern for Felicity, and murmured, 'and Michelle, have done.

'Inspector?' Sandrine prompted when Rafferty failed to respond. 'You haven't said whether or not I can see Felicity,' she reminded him.

Rafferty considered. Then he thought, Why not? It might turn out to be helpful. At least as far as he and the solution to this case were concerned.

'OK,' he said. 'But first I must find out how she is myself. Then, as long as she is well enough and the A&E consultant, the prison guard and Mrs Raine herself agree to your visit, you can have a few minutes with her.'

'Thank you, inspector.' Sandrine smiled. It made her plump face almost pretty.

After Rafferty had had a word with the consultant and he and Llewellyn were allowed to pass through to the curtained area to speak to Felicity Raine, he became aware of a feeling of *déjà vu* as he saw her lying on the trolley. Her clothing was bloody, as it had been the first time he had seen her, though this time the bloodstains were lower down the material and not nearly as plentiful as when she had walked into the police station and announced she had murdered her husband. Surely, he thought, as he stared at the bloody material of her dress, she wasn't about to report that she had murdered someone else? But all of a sudden, he knew what had happened. And as he realised that his theory no longer had a fatal flaw, he quietly asked Felicity, 'Did you lose your baby?'

She looked warily up at him as if she suspected his motives for asking the question, but then she relaxed back against her pillows and shook her head. 'No. They were able to save him. It's going to be all right.'

'Him?' he queried. 'So you are far enough along in your pregnancy to have the scan tell you the sex?'

Felicity didn't respond. Instead, she laid her hand lightly on her stomach and smiled.

She might, in reality, be a murderess, as Rafferty now knew without a shadow of a doubt, but he very much feared she was a murderess who would not only get away with her crime but also secure her son's inheritance from the trustees.

He believed Llewellyn was right when he said that she had sufficiently muddied the waters and spread enough doubt about her guilt, while increasing the suspicion of other suspects, to encourage the Crown Prosecution Service to look again at the case against her and decide to drop all charges.

Felicity Raine had played her part – that of bewildered, horrified, guilty innocence – to perfection. As her own father had said, Felicity had had men falling adoringly at her feet because of her beauty since her early teens. She well knew how to use her looks and air of fragility to hook them in, use and manipulate them and then, when it suited her, discard them as she had Peter Dunbar when he lost his money and his business. She had done the same with the father who knew her too well and Raymond Raine also, whom she had manipulated out of this world so she could inherit his money in right of her child, without having either his husbandly demands or husbandly neglect to trouble her.

How skilfully she had managed to spread the net of suspicion outwards from herself, to her mother-in-law, Raymond's cousin Mike, Sandrine Agnew and her deluded ex-husband. Even Nick Miller, the handsome gardener, had felt the fearful breath of suspicion.

Her second husband she had falsely had labelled a wife beater, making the lie the more convincing by denying it and applying appropriate theatrical make-up to provide the black eyes and the bruises.

No wonder, Rafferty thought, that she had begged him not to go to see her father; for it had been the information that she had trained as a make-up artist and worked in the theatre that had acted as an irritant in Rafferty's brain, causing the first stirrings to make him wonder whether, as the unlikely Gloria Llewellyn had been caught out in a crime, maybe the equally unlikely seeming Felicity might also turn out to be guilty as charged.

Rafferty gazed steadily at the still-smiling

Felicity. 'It seems congratulations are in order,' he said. 'And not only for your pregnancy, I think. You've been very clever.' But not, he hoped, clever enough to get away with murder.

'Clever?' she echoed as she gazed up at him from eyes that were limpid grey pools of innocence. 'What do you mean, inspector?'

'Allow me to explain. You managed to almost make me believe in your innocence, in spite of all the evidence. I even defended you. And although my suspicions against you have been growing for some days, the discovery that you're pregnant really clinches it. But then, of course, all the wicked things you have done would have purpose – unless you enjoy evil for its own sake – only if you had reason to believe you would inherit Raymond's share of the trust. And as the only way you could do that was by having Raymond's baby—'

He broke off as he heard a gasp behind him. He turned and saw an ashen-faced Sandrine Agnew standing behind him. He hadn't heard her approach the semi-curtained trolley. She must have tired of waiting for Rafferty to return and tell her she could spend some minutes with Felicity and – given her status as a volunteer at the hospital – no one had tried to prevent her approaching the cubicle.

Now she hissed at Felicity, 'Pregnant? How

can you be pregnant? You told me you hadn't slept with Raymond for months. You hated him, you said. You told me you were longing to leave him and come to live with me.'

A look of alarm crossed Felicity's face. 'Be quiet, Sandrine,' she ordered.

'What is the matter?'

Unnoticed during the hubbub of Sandrine Agnew's distressed questioning of Felicity, a curious Michelle had joined Rafferty, Llewellyn and Sandrine around Felicity's trolley.

'How are you, Felicity?' she asked before she took in the red stains on her dress and, with typical French grasp of such matters, she exclaimed, 'You were *enceinte*?'

'She is still *enceinte*, from what I've just heard,' Sandrine told her in a voice faint with hurt and betrayal.

Felicity was quick to soothe her friend's distress. She glanced down; again her hand went to her stomach. 'Yes. I'm pregnant. But I wasn't sleeping with Raymond – not willingly, anyway. You know how violent he could be. He raped me, forced himself on me.' She gave a convincing sob and let a steady stream of tears flow down her pale and tragic face.

The tears convinced Sandrine, who seemed only too keen to be convinced. The previous look of suspicion vanished immediately. 'Oh my dear,' she murmured as she

314

put a tender hand over Felicity's. 'Don't upset yourself. We can bring up the baby together.' Sandrine's plain face suffused with the rosy glow of pleasure. 'We'll be a proper little family.'

Rafferty knew he was losing any control he might have had over this bedside scene. At Felicity's ready lies, Sandrine's anxieties were willingly thrust aside. He knew he had to do something, say something, if he was to have any chance of preventing Felicity, through her child, from getting her hands on Raymond's majority ownership of the Raine family fortune.

Over my dead body, Rafferty swore. He was determined to trap her into telling the truth for once. That way, the Crown Prosecution Service would have no cause to either drop the charges against her altogether, or lower them from murder to manslaughter, as he suspected they yet might. He couldn't be sure what they had would be enough to secure a conviction or even ensure that she stood trial. He knew that he must try to get her to convict herself from her own mouth. If he failed, even if she did still face a courtroom in a manslaughter charge, he couldn't be sure that Felicity's acting skills and air of vulnerability wouldn't sway a jury. He knew there was a more than average chance that Felicity Raine would succeed in getting the entire case against her overturned, if indeed it even went that far.

Rafferty shook his head. No. He was not going to allow that to happen. Felicity Raine was as ruthless a killer as Rafferty had ever met; she deserved the rope around her pretty neck, but as that was no longer possible, for the crimes – both criminal and moral – that she had committed, she should serve sufficient time behind bars to ensure the bloom went from her skin and the natural gold of her hair faded till it needed artificial assistance. That way, she would be less likely to so easily find more victims in the future...

And after unashamedly browbeating Michelle Ginôt into telling him the truth, Rafferty believed he knew just how he could achieve his aim. And now, even as Felicity raised her tear-stained beauty beseechingly towards Sandrine and told her, 'It's you that I love and want to be with. It's only thinking of our plans that keeps me sane while I'm waiting for the police to discover my innocence,' Rafferty put his hand in his jacket pocket and pulled out the gold and diamond necklet that he had retrieved from Michelle and that she had confessed she had unhooked from Felicity's neck and stolen the first time Felicity had shared her bed in the little flat over the garage.

He held it up so they could all see it richly glittering under the harsh hospital lighting. Its very glitter seemed to speak of betrayal and sin.

'Do you recognise this?' he asked Felicity as he continued to hold the necklet up high.

For an infinitesimal moment, Felicity's gaze narrowed, then, as though calculating what, from her point of view, would be the best answer, she admitted it.

'Yes. Of course. It was Raymond's wedding gift to me. I lost it some weeks ago, before Raymond's...'

For the first time, it hit Rafferty how Felicity's sentences, when she mentioned her late husband's name, would always drop off in that delicate manner, as if to imply the word 'murder' could no more sully her lips than the act of murder could sully her hands.

It was just another of her little tricks, of course, like using her theatrical make-up training to create her own bruises and black eyes. Like gulling Elaine Enderby and the infatuated Sandrine Agnew into helping to create the tapestry of deceit that branded Raymond a wife beater.

When he had questioned Elaine Enderby he had discovered, as he had prodded her memory and her diary, that coincidentally Raymond had always left home on some business trip around the times of these injuries. Likewise, Felicity's bruises had always vanished shortly before his expected return.

It was only a small matter, but it had niggled him sufficiently to consider what it might imply. As did the pretty Michelle's apparent lack of male suitors. Man-like and British, it had never occurred to him that the French girl might be other than heterosexual. And when Stephanie Raine had said that Michelle's flirtatious behaviour at the barbecue had been embarrassing, he had assumed it had been the *men* with whom Michelle had flirted. How Stephanie had laughed at his naïve assumption. His ears were still blushing from the humiliation.

Rafferty swung the delicate little necklace in the air and said, 'It certainly disappeared, but you didn't lose it, Mrs Raine; it was stolen from you. Stolen as a keepsake by Michelle Ginôt the first time you and she became lovers.'

For a brief second, Rafferty had managed to surprise Felicity sufficiently to get through her defences to her black, murderous heart. And Sandrine Agnew had seen it. He watched as Sandrine, puzzled at first, then anxious, looked from Felicity to him and back again.

'Felicity,' she said uncertainly, 'is it true what the inspector said? That you and Michelle were sleeping together?'

'Don't be silly, Sandrine,' Felicity responded as, from beneath her thick lashes, she darted an anxious glance towards Michelle. 'Of course it isn't true. The inspector's playing games because he knows his case against me is falling apart. You must know it's you that I love and want to be with. I wish you'd make some effort to find Raymond's real killer,' she said to Rafferty, 'because I can't stand much more of this. And now, in my condition, all this stress is unlikely to be good for my baby.'

As he saw Sandrine's anxiety fade for the second time, Rafferty knew he was losing the advantage he had gained by producing the necklet. At Felicity's ready reassurance, Sandrine had been only too willing to suspend disbelief. Frantically he sought the words that would enable him to regain the upper hand. But before he could think of anything to say that might sufficiently disconcert Felicity into blurting out even part of the truth, Michelle Ginôt added the spark that was guaranteed to rekindle the hot embers of Sandrine Agnew's jealousy.

Michelle pouted and rounded on Felicity with full Gallic outrage. '*Non*,' she said, in her voice all the contempt of generations of French for perfidious Albion. 'You did not it lose, Felicity. Do not keep lying to your naïve friend. *Sandrine est vraiment crédule, n'est-ce-pas? Et toi, tu es très cruelle.*'

Strangely, Michelle's mongrel mix of French and English sounded more sincere and truthful than all Felicity's language-fluent lies.

'I steal it,' Michelle insisted. 'I undid it

from your neck last time you were in my bed, just as *l'inspecteur* said. I wanted a keepsake I could wear close to my heart. But now—'

Michelle spat at Felicity with all the earthiness of her peasant forebears. Her aim was remarkably accurate. The stream of spittle hit Felicity full in the face.

'Now, I want nothing of such keepsakes. I am glad *l'inspecteur* he take it from me. When I remember you laughing and telling me how *odieux* you found the love of the fat and gauche Sandrine, I think – I think, what it is that you must say about *me*?'

Sandrine's previous rosy glow at the thought of playing happy families with Felicity and her baby faded. Now she went deathly pale. Abruptly, she pulled her hand away from Felicity's as though scalded. 'No,' she said in a voice suddenly breathy with shock and pain.

For the briefest moment, Felicity's ready tongue failed to come up with a response to Michelle's claim. But she quickly recovered her wit.

'Surely you can't believe what Michelle claims?' Felicity whispered, in a breathy little voice of her own, as though equally stricken. But this time her fluent lies were not so readily believed.

Sandrine glanced from face to face before she asked, 'Have you doubly betrayed me,

Felicity? Did Raymond really rape you, as you claim? Or were you sleeping with him as well as with Michelle while you held me at arm's length? What of the promises you made to me when you asked how you might best get rid of your husband?'

'Be *quiet*, Sandrine,' Felicity ordered again, fear clearly evident in her voice. 'Do you want to ruin everything?'

Sandrine Agnew gave a bitter laugh. 'Ruin everything?' she repeated. 'For me, everything is already ruined. And I'll *not* be quiet,' she told Felicity.

Sandrine deliberately turned her back on Felicity and her pleas and faced Rafferty. 'I wish to make a statement,' she said. 'I colluded fully with Mrs Felicity Raine in planning the murder of her husband.' Her face almost crumpled but visibly she got hold of herself.

'I wanted Felicity to leave him, you see. I didn't want his money, but apparently *she* did, which explains why she put me off time after time, saying he would never let her leave him and that we would have to kill him if she was ever to be free of him and his abuse.

'Yet, it is clear to me now that, all the time she fobbed me off with more lies and promises, she was trying to become pregnant by him so she could inherit his fortune through his child.'

'Shut up, you stupid, fat bitch!' Felicity shrilled, as her demure and delicate air collapsed in the face of Sandrine's simple honesty.

Sandrine Agnew, Felicity's previously adoring puppy, turned red, then white. Before either Rafferty or Llewellyn could stop her, she had flown at Felicity and hit her with such force that Rafferty suspected this time she would have a black eye for real.

They managed to drag Sandrine away.

'You – bitch,' she echoed Felicity's name-calling in a barely heard whisper of horror. 'You lied to me. Yes. Lied like you lied to all the rest.'

Sandrine pulled her arms away from Rafferty's and Llewellyn's restraining hands and with a dignity Rafferty could only admire, she said, 'I am ready to give my statement now, inspector.'

'Sandrine! No!' Now it was Felicity's turn to be the supplicant. 'Don't, I beg you, tell lies just because my behaviour has hurt you.'

'But they won't *be* lies, Felicity, will they? We both know that. And I'll be making a statement and telling the truth because of what you have done to other people, not just me. You are capable of loving no one but yourself. I see that now. I suppose, in my heart, I always knew it, always suspected things between us would come to a swift end once I had served my purpose. And I was right. Wasn't I?' she challenged.

As if recognising that Sandrine's statement would certainly cast plenty of doubt on her claimed innocence, Felicity became hysterical.

'Make your statement, then,' she screamed. 'Maybe I'll make one too, and tell the police how you bullied me into going along with your plans for Raymond. I didn't want to, but you forced me. I was frightened of you. But it's true that I never loved you. How could someone like me have ever loved someone like you? Take a look at yourself, why don't you?'

Sandrine's dignity was punctured by neither Felicity's threat to make a statement of her own nor by her ridicule. Instead, it strengthened her as she responded with the simple truth.

'Oh, I have looked at myself, Felicity, many times. But I wonder have *you* similarly looked at *your*self and seen what is really there? I think not.'

Felicity Raine had done her best to spread the police's suspicions among her family, friends and acquaintances. Quite deliberately, she had planted clues to put doubts about her early, readily confessed guilt into their minds, whilst ensuring their suspicions of those around her grew stronger.

First, she had implicated Stephanie, who

would benefit financially from Ray's death, by using her computer to order the drugs she had needed in order to subdue Raymond so she could murder him in what she had hoped the police would consider an unlikely, unwomanly scenario.

Then she had implicated Nick Miller, the gardener/handyman whose services and 'poste restante' greenhouse both Felicity and Stephanie used, the Miller who was something of a ladies' man to judge from his strictly female – attractive female – client list. No wonder Sandrine Agnew had either removed herself or been removed from it once they'd had the chance to take stock of one another.

She hadn't even scrupled to leave her ex-husband out of the list, though admittedly he had met her more than halfway by watching the house hoping to speak to her – doubtless encouraged in both this act and his hope that they might get back together by Felicity herself, when she had telephoned him and planted the seed.

Sandrine Agnew, the best friend and would-be lover, who had supported her staunchly throughout the investigation, was another one of those callously used and exploited by Felicity. Rafferty suspected she had deliberately encouraged Sandrine's obsession with her, promising they would leave the area and set up home together once

Felicity was free and the case was over. This promise had encouraged Sandrine to promote the lie that Raymond had beaten his wife – though whether she knew it was a lie or had been duped over this by Felicity as she had been over so much else...

But Felicity had never had any intention of setting up home here or anywhere else with the plain and dumpy Sandrine Agnew; it was that deceit which had ultimately been her downfall. Arrogantly, she had dismissed Sandrine and Sandrine's love as of no importance to her.

Rafferty was astonished when he remembered he had been concerned for Felicity Raine's mental, emotional and physical health in prison should he not manage to find sufficient proof of her innocence.

Now, as the echo of the words she had used with callous cruelty to taunt Sandrine Agnew seemed to reverberate in the high-ceilinged hospital room, he thought Felicity would in reality do very well in prison. With her manipulative character, feminine wiles, beauty and acting skills, she would probably end up the governor's pet and would shortly probably be all but running the place – to her advantage, of course.

Two days later, out of hospital and back in prison on remand after Sandrine Agnew had given her damning statement, Felicity Raine seemed at last to face the fact that the game might be up.

'How could you imagine I could possibly have loved such an unprepossessing creature as Sandrine, inspector?' she asked Rafferty when he and Llewellyn paid another visit to her there. 'If only you knew how suffocating and embarrassing I found her love. Michelle was right about that.'

'Why did you encourage it, then?' he asked. But, of course, he already knew the answer to that question, for Felicity had used Sandrine Agnew, much as she had used everyone else in her life.

But it seemed that even though Felicity Raine appeared to have accepted her fate, she still preferred to disguise her true nature behind the air of an ingénue. For now she opened her limpid grey eyes wide and stared at him from their hypnotising depths.

'Encourage it?' she asked softly. 'Is that what you think I did?' She wrinkled her smooth brow as though in thought. 'I suppose it could look that way. I hadn't realised. It's my own fault, I suppose. I was too friendly when we first met. I hadn't realised how lonely and clinging she would be. When I did, it was too late and she was attached to me like a limpet.'

'You always had the option of telling her plainly – of being cruel to be kind.'

'True. But somehow, each time I nerved

myself up to do it, Sandrine was going through some life crisis or other.'

Lightly, she touched her slightly rounded stomach, and commented, 'And now, I have a new life to consider.'

She was still play-acting, Rafferty realised. Only this time she was playing the role of the Madonna. Felicity Raine had missed her way, he thought, and instead of the great dramatic actress she might have been, she had taken on the even more dramatically demanding role of murderer.

Strangely, even now, Felicity seemed to think her dramatic skills might be enough to enable her to achieve a reversal in her currently unattractive fortunes, for she gave a rueful smile. 'I realise now, of course, that she must have sensed my air of tension, guessed what it presaged and set out her little emotional bombs. I fell for it each time. And now...' Artfully her voice faltered and to his horror, Rafferty realised she could still make the doubts about her guilt return. With some difficulty he managed to suppress them as Felicity continued. 'Now, she is getting her revenge by lying about me.'

Sandrine Agnew wasn't a liar, that much was plain, as plain as the woman herself. Ms Agnew was too transparently honest in her words and emotions to lie convincingly – unless it was to come to the aid of an adored lover. But he doubted she would be willing to offer Felicity her support again.

Now, of course, he knew that even if Felicity *had* made a pretence of trying to prise off Sandrine's clinging, love-sick grip, she wouldn't have tried very hard. Indeed, she must have deliberately set out to nurture the love that Sandrine, in her heart, must have known was merely love's masquerade.

She had needed Sandrine to add to the numbers of those required to muddy the waters of her guilt and the case against her sufficiently to ensure the police dropped the charges. Then, gloriously pregnant, she would be home free and all set to take charge of the bulk of the Raine family fortune held in trust for her child. At least that had been the plan. He thought even the self-deluding and devious Felicity must now realise her grand plan lay in ruins.

And as he considered the baby in her womb, he thought, Poor child. What an inheritance this infant would get. Although he hadn't managed completely to disprove Felicity's fabricated pretence that Raymond had been violent towards her, deep in his heart Rafferty knew that this had been yet another deceit.

Hadn't it been enough for her to kill the poor man, he wondered, without also casting him in the role of wife beater?

Maybe the diary entries Elaine Enderby had told him she made each time she saw

Felicity with fresh bruises, together with Raymond's business diary, would go some way to proving that Felicity's 'bruises' had been self-inflicted. Safe in the knowledge that Stephanie would have no reason to visit when she knew Raymond was away, Felicity's deception was kept strictly for those who would be taken in by it.

Rafferty had checked back with Raymond's business diary and discovered that Felicity's bruises and black eyes only appeared in public after Raymond had left for some business event or other. Miraculously, these marks of violence had vanished by the time Raymond returned home, usually several days later. Elaine Enderby had remarked on what good healing skin Felicity had. 'Just as well in the circumstances,' had been her sad comment, he recalled.

But, of course, there had been nothing fortunate about this miraculous healing ability, as he had discovered.

With his interest in history and old buildings and with the prod to initiative provided by Llewellyn's finding of the secret drawer in the desk in Raymond's study, Rafferty had suggested the team might usefully employ themselves in some more judicious measuring and tapping of the Raines' sixteenth-century home.

Sure enough, they had eventually, with the help of the local architectural historian, found the priest's hole. Concealed within this tiny, claustrophobic chamber, they had found Felicity's extensive, professional make-up box. Make-up bruises she had removed before Raymond returned home and questioned her about them.

One thing he *had* apparently questioned, though, was the unreasoning dislike he sensed their near neighbour, Elaine Enderby, had felt for him.

Mrs Enderby had told them Raymond Raine had even had the 'temerity' to ask her why she was always so cool towards him and, mysteriously – to him, at least – she had replied, 'You know why.'

Raymond hadn't pursued his questioning any further. According to his stepmother, he had just put Elaine Enderby's inexplicable and barely contained dislike down to a mix of jealousy and hormonal upheaval brought by the menopause and had metaphorically shrugged his shoulders and left it at that.

Seemingly, Felicity Raine's whole life had been a lie. A life of duplicity in which she had married her deluded first husband for his money, as her own father had suggested. She certainly hadn't scrupled to leave Dunbar when he lost it. She had killed her second, wealthy husband, once she had become bored with him and his obsession with business and his neglect, as she saw it, of *her*.

The final straw, as Felicity had clearly seen it, was when, digging through Stephanie's financial documents – which were as carelessly safeguarded as was her computer password – she had learned, pretty much together, Rafferty believed, that she was pregnant and that she would inherit nothing from Raymond but through their mutual child. The rage of the adult child spoiled and indulged by the mother and ignored and neglected by the father had, he believed, engulfed her and she had decided that, this time, her wealthy husband had to die. That way, he imagined, she had felt she would need to make no more marriages that required her to give her actress skills a good work-out.

Now, Rafferty found himself wondering if the car accident Peter Dunbar had mentioned he had been involved in several years before, while still married to Felicity and before his business fell apart, might not also be down to Felicity Raine. Perhaps, if that *had* been attempted murder, it was fortunate for Dunbar that he *had* lost his business – maybe it had saved him from any further attempts on his life.

Raymond Raine, of course, hadn't been so lucky.

Epilogue

Finally, when Rafferty had began to despair that such a thing would ever come to pass, there came some good news from Wales. Abra rang to tell him that the charges against Gloria had been dropped.

'Really?' Rafferty exclaimed. 'But that's great news. How did it come about? Because when I spoke to him that Welsh DI seemed determined on pursuing the case.'

'Ah, but he didn't count on someone going above his head. At least, that's what I understand must have happened. When he rang Gloria to tell her she wasn't to be charged, he was practically spitting feathers. He muttered darkly about plots and evidence being "got at".'

'Well, I can't imagine who can have gone above his head. It certainly wasn't me. And it can't have been Dai Jones either, as I never did manage to contact him.'

'Oh. I forgot,' said Abra. 'That's what I meant to tell you, but Gloria and I have been celebrating so much it slipped my mind.

'Dai Jones turned up at Gloria's home. Seems he's just moved house, but, apart from friends and family, he hadn't got around to notifying any official bodies, which explains why you couldn't contact him. Anyway, it turns out that *he* was the one who managed to get everything sorted, via a superintendent friend of his.'

'Mm. Someone must have told him all about it, I suppose,' Rafferty concluded. And as he thought about it, he suspected he knew just who that someone was likely to be.

Abra's next words confirmed it.

'As I said, this Dai Jones came to see me and Gloria. He took me aside and told me that *Dafyd* of all people had contacted him and asked him to intervene, though he told me to keep this information from Gloria.'

'Wonder how Dafyd found out about it? Anyway,' he said, 'who cares how it was sorted or who by? Let's just be thankful that it has been. So,' Rafferty asked eagerly, 'when are you coming home?'

Abra laughed and repeated the phrase that Michelle Ginôt had all but made her own. 'Will the day after yesterday be soon enough?'

'No. Not at all. But I suppose it will have to do.'

'Well, of course it was me,' Llewellyn said. 'Don't you think I'm aware that my mother's been going through a difficult stage in her life?' he asked Rafferty when the latter questioned him and asked him to confirm that he *had* been the one to contact Dai Jones and ask him to intervene to prevent his mother's prosecution.

'She had a similar memory lapse earlier in the year. Fortunately my friend, ex-DI Dai Jones, was still working then and he dealt with it in an appropriately sensitive manner. He called me and when he realised that my mother was unwell, he simply told her to see her GP and didn't go ahead with the charge against her. It wasn't even necessary for me to go up to Gwynedd to help resolve the problem, although obviously I did go to check that my mother was all right. But to this day, she doesn't know that between us Dai and I smoothed things over on both occasions. It was the only thing, the humane thing, to do in the circumstances. Just don't let my mother know I intervened,' he warned Rafferty.

'Mum's the word,' Rafferty agreed.

'Anyway, after that last occasion, I asked one of my mother's neighbours to keep an eye on her for me. I don't like doing it,' Llewellyn admitted. 'It felt too much like spying. But, I thought if I was to nip any similar problems in the bud I had no choice. So when her neighbour – who's got a cousin working as a constable in the local police station – learned about this latest charge, she rang me and I immediately rang Dai Jones.

So you see, your mission of mercy wasn't really necessary.'

Rafferty's mouth fell open. 'You mean you knew about that?'

Llewellyn nodded. 'But not till you had arrived in Wales, when my mother's neighbour rang me.'

'So why didn't you say something when I returned?'

'Why didn't *you*?' Llewellyn countered.

'Because I'd promised Gloria and Abra that I wouldn't. I didn't want to keep something like that from you, Daff, I hope you realise that. But I suppose Gloria didn't want you thinking the worst of her.' He grinned. 'Maybe now, if she manages to figure out just who was instrumental in getting the charges against her dropped, she'll realise that she doesn't need to keep things from you – not now we've discovered you can be every bit as devious as yours truly.'

'Not at all,' Llewellyn immediately countered. He bridled at what he clearly considered an unwarranted slur. 'I believe I have some way to go before you can make that particular claim stick. But,' Llewellyn unbridled himself sufficiently to admit, 'that apart, I wanted to thank you, Joseph, for your efforts on my mother's behalf. She appreciates it and so do I.'

Llewellyn stuck out a hand. Rafferty was more than glad to take it.

JAN 0 8